Bewitched by the Headless Horseman

CANDACE ROBINSON

To those who would willingly take a ride with the Headless Horseman

I

One ghost. Two ghosts. Three ghosts... No, wait, there's a fourth ghost. Oh, and now she's removing the guy's shirt. The guy ghost looked to be from somewhere in the early two-thousands with his emo band T-shirt and tight jeans, his hair shaggy and plastered over one eye, while the woman seemed to have possibly died during the 1800s. Which decade? That was anyone's guess. Her frilly black dress brushed her ankles, the collar high against her neck with a long strip of buttons.

And there goes her pristine bun. Oh, he's really going at it.

Stevie laughed under her breath—this was the ultimate opposites attract. She sat outside the seafood restaurant on the second floor at a table for two, waiting on a supplier for the comic book store where she worked as her semi-sometimes job. Not only that though, the guy arriving just so happened to run one of the largest comic conventions in New York City each year. Her brother, Gideon, should've been at the restaurant for the meeting since the store was his after taking it over last year, but the torch had been passed to Stevie two months ago when he'd offered to give her two hundred dollars worth of vintage stamps along with regular pay. A deal she couldn't refuse, and

1

after tonight, she would get those stamps to finish one of her bird collections. Owning antique things was a hobby she'd been clutching onto dearly for years.

She continued to observe the four translucent white ghosts around her. A loud bang struck the window in front of her, and her gaze locked onto the two ghosts who were getting mighty frisky on the opposite side of the glass. The woman's dress was now off somewhere on the floor, her body pressed to the window while a table of four steadily ate their meal, not noticing the action that was taking place before them. Their moans and groans were loud enough that Stevie was sure even ghosts lingering in the parking lot could hear them.

And there goes her corset. Stevie smirked to herself and flicked her stare away, not wanting to be too much of a peeper. But they were literally right there, her chair facing them!

She glanced at her phone, seeing Reese was already ten minutes late. Little monsters clawed at her stomach in nervousness—she'd made a grave mistake a few weeks ago when she'd snooped on the convention's website to reveal what he looked like after liking his witty back-and-forth emails. He was pretty much the spitting image of Evan Peters in *American Horror Story* —the *Coven* season. Hard to find a con there. She prayed it was one of those cases where the picture was better than the person so her fingers wouldn't fidget when he arrived.

Stevie set down her phone on the table and peered at one of the other two ghosts not getting freaky—a woman from possibly the 1950s with a tight polka-dotted bodice and a flowing black skirt, her hair in pinned curls. She weaved around the six outside tables in figure-eight movements, the click of her heels echoing, all while chattering to herself about the items she needed to buy at the grocery store. How humdrum. If the ghosts could see the living world, Stevie would've already coaxed the woman into the nearest grocery store and told her to have at it so her unfinished business could be checked off her list.

As she focused on her phone once again, Stevie's leg bounced up and down. *If he stands me up and Gideon doesn't give me those stamps, I swear I'll kidnap my brother's precious pet plant for a day or two.* She brought a piece of the complimentary bread to her mouth and chewed slowly while studying the one remaining ghost near the stone balcony. The one missing his head. *Poor sap.*

But it wasn't as if this was the first headless ghost she'd ever seen. When night gobbled up the day, a vengeful spirit, the Headless Horseman, rode his mighty steed through Sleepy Hollow and collected ghosts' heads. How often did he confiscate them? That was a really good question. And what he did with the heads? That was an even better question since every time she'd spotted him on horseback he was still headless. He probably added them to his secret stash or smugly fiddled around with them during the day when he wasn't out and about. If he ever found his original head, then maybe he would finally pass on and quit pestering the other ghosts. But with centuries having slipped by, his missing prize had to be long gone by now.

"After I finish this bite of bread, I'm leaving," she muttered, trying to ignore the woman's moans of ecstasy from inside the restaurant. Stevie had been seeing ghosts for as long as she could remember, most likely ever since she left the womb. No psychic abilities for her though—*too bad.* However, a seer's blood held magical properties such as necromancy and healing to name a couple. So at least she had that going for her.

"Stevie Rourke?" a melodious voice asked from behind her. She hurried and chewed the large piece of bread as her eyes locked onto dark brown irises, a pretty smile, and dirty blond curly hair brushing his brow. Reese wore a button-up shirt, the sleeves neatly at his wrists. Her stomach dipped at the sight of him. After the meeting she would throttle her sister-in-law, Lucia, for telling her he *so* didn't look like Evan Peters in person because he *so* did.

Stevie choked on her bread, looking like an idiot. She chugged half her glass of milk once she got the food down. "Sorry about that." She sobered and smiled, getting into non-seer mode by blocking out the surrounding ghosts since it would be an awkward first meeting otherwise. "Reese Braun?"

"That's me. Sorry I'm late. The traffic leaving the city was terrible." He raked a hand through his disheveled hair, his chest heaving and his cheeks flushed, while he sat across from her.

"No, it's fine," Stevie said just as a tall waitress came out to take their orders.

Lucia had given the green light that the meeting would be as easy as pie since Reese was a breeze for Gideon to deal with. Stevie's top priority job that she'd had for the past four years was working as a witch's assistant to Lucia. Running local deliveries for her around town and mailing out packages from the online side of Lucia's apothecary, other times assisting in mixing brews for her sister-in-law to spell. Pet plants and small skeletal animals for Sleepy Hollow locals were Lucia's specialty and best sellers, compliments of Stevie's seer blood added to help bring them to life of course.

When Stevie noticed she was staring at Reese's face like an owl, she chipped through the expanding iceberg. "So, about the booth and the auction—"

"The entrance booth is yours and you guys will have front row at the auction." The edges of Reese's lips curled up as he took a piece of bread and met her gaze.

"Oh." It was the only word Stevie could get out—she'd expected more of a challenge. But score.

The waitress returned with a green bottle and poured Reese a glass of red wine.

"You sure you don't want a glass?" he asked after she waved off the waitress from pouring her some.

"I'm a big milk drinker." Stevie winked, raising her glass like she was giving a toast and cursing herself once again for being an idiot.

"I like milk." Reese smiled, his teeth brilliantly white and perfectly straight. Her dentist father would be proud. "The meeting wasn't the only reason I came tonight though."

Stevie blinked, straightening in her seat. "It isn't? Then why?"

He leaned forward, his elbows resting on the table, appearing as if he were ready to spill a dark secret. "Don't take me for a stalker, but I looked up your picture on the store website and found you ... cute."

Cute? No one had said anything like that to her since her ex-boyfriend. "I have a confession too. I tried looking up your picture on your website and you have an *anime* drawing."

Reese chuckled. "Kept you guessing, I hope."

"Terribly so." She bit her lip. "But then I went to the convention website and found your picture there."

His smile grew wide. "Should we call this a date then?"

Stevie cocked her head and grinned. "Guess my favorite color and we'll see if it is." She hadn't been on a date for nine months—ever since her one and only boyfriend dumped her just before her twenty-first birthday. Mister Piss-Baby, who shall not be named. They'd been together since high school, and one would *think* he'd have been used to the fact that Stevie could see the dead, but no. Every time he noticed her gaze drift from him to something he couldn't see, he'd gone pale as a corpse and she'd worried he would faint. Until finally he couldn't take it anymore. A reason she generally stayed hush-hush about her ability at first, especially if a boy claiming to love her couldn't handle it. Not that she'd broadcasted it before.

Reese tapped his hand against the table. "I'm debating between black like your dress or the same bright orange of your hair."

The headless ghost stumbled beside her table, then spun in circles. She didn't even break her act to look at him.

"Only one choice," Stevie finally said. To be fair, her favorite color was closer to a mood ring, and she enjoyed a good gothic dress, regardless of the color. But if she had to choose, it would be the orange he'd suspected which was why her hair had been the same color for the past six years.

"Maybe black," Reese said, taking a sip of his wine. "I've heard things about girls who wear lots of black."

She arched a brow. "What kind of things?"

"Oh shit, scratch that. Apparently, I can't be suave." He cringed.

Stevie placed her elbows on the table and steepled her fingers together. "No, do go on. You have my interest piqued."

"You know"—he cleared his throat—"that they are more adventurous."

She held back laughter, hoping he wasn't about to say what she was thinking. "Adventurous with what, Reese?"

He rolled his eyes, his cheeks reddening. "You know ... in bed."

The laughter did come then and she couldn't stop it, even when it reached hyena levels. "I believe you're being prejudiced to the other colors."

"No, no, I didn't mean *you*. Your favorite color is orange." The red staining Reese's cheeks grew brighter and she covered her mouth to stop from laughing.

Still smiling, she said, "And what has he won for guessing the answer correctly, Mr. Gameshow Host? This is officially a date."

"You are—" Reese's phone dinged, and he fished it out from his pocket. "Fuck. That's my business partner. I need to meet with him about the convention before he royally screws up something else since he decided to get wasted. Again." He paused and kept his eyes trained on hers. "Maybe we can finish this official date soon?"

"If you want a part two, then there'll be a part two." At least she hoped he wanted to actually meet up again because she definitely did.

"We'll plan for a part two then. Oh, and Stevie, next time *you'll* have to guess my favorite color." Reese smiled brightly and drew out several bills to place on the table.

Stevie watched as he walked away, inwardly sighing that someone put together like him was interested in her. When the waitress brought Stevie the food, she stayed to polish off her meal—the untouched one she would drop off to Lucia.

Once the waitress gave her a to-go box, Stevie gathered her things, then walked by the headless ghost who now sat in one of the chairs at a table beside her. "You got this," she encouraged.

Stevie's cell beeped and Lucia was already messaging her.

Wishing you luck that the meeting goes well. You need to get some non-work-action after.

Stevie pinched the bridge of her nose and texted her back with a smile. *The only "some" I'll be getting tonight is some sleep. Reese got called into work, but tell Gideon he got the deal on both things. And by the way, he looks better than his picture by a long shot!*

I lied to you. He totally does.

You little witch! Lol.

Cauldron and all.

Anyway, I have food I'm going to drop off soon.

Stevie had known her sister-in-law for most of her life due to her mom's monthly visits to see Lucia's aunt Ginger for witchy remedies. Stevie had never been close with Lucia since they'd been six years apart, rarely even said hi to one another. All of that changed when Lucia started dating Gideon and asked Stevie to become a witch's assistant.

Stevie entered the restaurant and old twangy country music filled the crowded space. The two lovebird ghosts seemed to have taken their peepshow somewhere else.

She descended the wooden staircase, and at the bottom of the steps sat another ghost—a young girl maybe around eleven or twelve with thick white hair covering her face and knees. The girl's head lay in her hands as she cried. Some establishments didn't have any dead lingering while others were like a beacon to them. Even her brother's store had a resident ghost who'd been there for quite some time.

"I wish I could help you," Stevie murmured, knowing the ghost wouldn't hear her.

"No one can help me," the girl sobbed and stood, then ran

through the wall like she was being chased by a wendigo wielding an axe.

Stevie's eyes widened, and she stumbled forward. Had the ghost heard her? No. Impossible. It had to have been a coincidence—it always was.

"Miss," the hostess called, drawing Stevie away from her thoughts. Bright cherry gloss stained the older woman's lips and her gray hair hung in a straight bob just past her chin. "The gentleman told me to give you this and to apologize again for his sudden departure." She then handed Stevie a pie box.

"Thank you." Stevie glanced down at the clear square top while heading toward the exit. An orange creamsicle pie rested inside and she pressed her lips together, fighting a smile when she read the words written in black ink on the edge of the box.

Sorry it's not your favorite shade of orange.

Stevie bit her lip—she loved orange creamsicle and would gladly eat the whole beautiful thing like a ravenous ogre.

As the crisp fall breeze hit her, Stevie stared up at the night sky, the stars flickering like tiny watchful eyes. The new moon was somewhere up there, its silvery hue hidden, unable to cast its eerie glow down amongst the town of Sleepy Hollow.

Stevie took the path beside the woods, the restaurant not far from her home. The bushes beside her rustled, and she stopped in her tracks just as something that hadn't been alive in quite some time darted out from the tree line.

And ran straight toward her.

2

Stevie knelt against the cool pavement, a wide grin spreading her cheeks as she watched the white-furred animal barrel toward her. The fox barked in excitement while circling her, then leaped through her body. It was true that ghosts couldn't see Stevie, but it wasn't a fact that *all* ghosts couldn't. At some point in a seer's life, they were meant to have a ghost animal sidekick, AKA a familiar, who also held the ability to see both the living and the dead. A bouncy little fox she'd named Roxy had staked claim to her when a seven-year-old Stevie had been at the park with Gideon. Since then, the ghost was akin to a guardian.

"Did you really have to trail me here, Foxy Roxy?" Stevie's hand followed the curve of the ghost's form in an attempt to pet her sidekick. Her fingertips felt nothing but air, not even coldness or warmth surrounding the animal's essence.

Roxy sat on her haunches, her mouth pulled back into a smile, exposing her sharp teeth. The fox purred, swatting the air with her paw.

"Look, we're on what? Year fourteen here of knowing one another? In the next five years, I will make it a point for Lucia to figure out a spell so you'll feel me." Stevie laughed, passing her hand through the fox once more.

Roxy perked up, nudging her nose toward the pie box in Stevie's grasp.

"Oh, this?" She brought the box closer to the fox. "It's from my new friend. He knows how much I like orange."

The fox cocked her head, her ears perking straight up, wanting to hear more.

Even though there'd been a few friends by Stevie's side back in school, Roxy had always been the one she'd revealed her secrets to. "Right, so you know how I told you about Reese? It seems baby sparks might've flown. *Maybe.* But with my luck, he'll end up most likely becoming an acquaintance or someone I used to know. You know my history of keeping people around outside of family."

Roxy released a shrill bark, then took off into the woods, disappearing behind the bushes and trees toward their neighborhood.

"I can't race you with this food in my hands or these stupid boots!" she shouted while smiling. "I'll see you soon!"

A young couple with their arms linked stared at Stevie curiously as they stepped around her. Stevie shrugged at them and gave her go-to response when someone caught what looked to be her talking to herself. "I'm just chatting to my other personality."

They nodded like it was no big deal and cuddled each other closer before crossing the street. The people of Sleepy Hollow were used to a good number of residents holding some sort of supernatural ability, usually witchy. Some outsiders would consider them cursed, while others would shout from the rooftops that they were blessed. Stevie's mom once believed herself to be cursed, but after coming to Sleepy Hollow well before popping out Gideon and Stevie, her ability proved to be, while not quite a blessing, at least an unfortunate ailment that could be maintained. Anyone who lived in the town, regardless if they were paranormal-less, knew to keep Sleepy Hollow's secrets sealed behind tightened lips to outsiders or face the council's wrath.

Stevie resumed her walk home down the pavement since going through the darkened woods would be nothing but a hazard—she didn't have Roxy's superhero eyesight. As a gust of chilly air ruffled her orange locks and tickled her skin, she cursed herself for not bringing a sweater.

Up ahead, in the middle of the street, a white translucent form shook his fist in the air. "Where is my fucking car?" the young guy screamed, his short hair stuck up around his head like a mad scientist. His suit looked like it was straight out of an old seventies catalog with bell-bottom pants and a button-up shirt tucked into the waist.

"It's long gone now, buddy," she hollered.

The ghost glanced her way, his lips twisted into a snarl as he yelled, "It isn't. It's coming this way, missy."

Stevie stilled, sucking in a sharp breath, her lungs tight while her gaze glued to the back of his head. This was *not* a coincidence. He'd *heard* her, *seen* her. She'd chalked up the girl at the restaurant as nothing, but it had been *something*. Unless ... he'd been a seer before he'd died and the other ghost at the restaurant really hadn't seen her.

Stevie peered up toward the star-filled sky, where the new moon should've been. A cloud drifted toward the west, revealing a flash of red and she gasped. *No way.* It couldn't finally be ... but it was! Giddiness seeped further toward her bones with each pound of her heart. The *Eye* of Sleepy Hollow had opened!

A story had been passed down from generation to generation that one day—no one knew when—two magical new moons would fall a cycle apart. During the first new moon, one Eye of the Hollow would open, and the dead would see the living. It was said that for an entire month the veil over the departed would remain lifted, until the following new moon when the second Eye opened and all the living would see the dead for a single night before the Eyes sealed once again, separating the two worlds.

Stevie cupped her hands around her mouth like a megaphone. "So you can see me?"

The ghost scowled at her. "Of course I can. We knew this day would eventually come. It's a fucking curse I can't return to not seeing you, though," he grumbled just as a car came around the curve and passed through him.

Well, then... "I was going to see if you needed help with any unfinished business, but since you have the most *wonderful* attitude I've ever come across, you can figure it out yourself."

"I don't give a fuck about that," he grunted and flipped her the bird, then chose to ignore her.

"Good luck to you then," Stevie sang.

"He's a fool. Ignore him," a female voice said from behind Stevie, her small form hidden behind a tree a few feet away. The ghost was maybe in her forties, her hair in a long braid down one of her shoulders, and an ill-fitted dress dwarfed her body.

Stevie stepped toward the woman. "Not that I can for sure complete your unfinished business, but do you need anything?"

"No thank you." The woman shrugged. "I'm waiting until after the second Eye opens. I want to tell my daughter I'm sorry. That's my unfinished business. It's a shame that a lot of the ghosts are trapped inside their own minds, believing they are still alive or already in Heaven or the Hollow. With the Eye open now, some will continue to not see what's right in front of them."

The Hollow was really what Hell was to outsiders, only the fiendish things that were down there were far worse than any book or movie had ever described. Demons in the Hollow could shift into any horrific creature they wished.

"That's good she's still here for you to find." For others who'd died longer ago, they wouldn't be so lucky. But on the bright side, they could possibly meet up with another blood relative.

Stevie studied the Eye of the Hollow, the night surrounding

the town, knowing the Headless Horseman would slither out sometime soon since darkness was here. As though her thoughts had summoned the psychopath, a horse's hooves pounded in the distance, the ominous sound filling the air. Since everyone drove cars these days, she couldn't chalk it up to just any rando horse, not in this tech-driven century. The bridge was just across the street, and the hoofbeats of the horse picked up, thumping across the earth.

"Go!" the woman slipped from behind the tree, shouting at the ghost still standing in the middle of the road.

"Yeah, you don't want to be caught up in that maniac's head-stealing game," Stevie added half-heartedly since he'd been a dick.

She stepped back into the foliage, listening to the hoofbeats slowing against wooden planks, becoming measured when the vengeful spirit broke out from the enclosure of the bridge, appearing in all his narcissistic glory as his cape billowed behind him. The Headless Horseman and his stallion were both the same translucent shade of white as every other ghost, not swathed in black as memorabilia liked to show. The only colorful thing about him was the glowing orange jack-o'-lantern in his gloved right hand. A sword hung at his hip, and Stevie couldn't pinpoint exactly how he could see or hear without a head. It had to be the vibrations which was why the jerkwad in the road needed to remain still. Even then, without a brain, how could the Horseman think? Or did the stallion just guide him to pluck a toy of his choice? Unless the pumpkin's cut-out eyes were like his own? Stevie was leaning toward the second option.

But before she could think on it more, the ghost in the road seethed at the Horseman, "Ah, fuck you, asshole."

The Horseman sat taller, his shoulders squaring as the stallion turned to face the idiot. Puffs of air escaped the horse's nostrils, and brilliant white eyes glowed bright while it focused on the Horseman's prey.

Stevie gazed at the scene, unable to turn away. "This point

now goes to the Headless Horseman," she whispered to the woman.

"You should leave," the woman stuttered, her body trembling while creeping toward the darkness of the woods.

Stevie didn't need to be as wary as this woman. First, Stevie wasn't a ghost, so he couldn't just choose her head for the picking. And second, that was it. She'd never seen firsthand a head taken by the Horseman before. Only caught sight of him galloping through the streets when she'd been driving to or from somewhere at night.

The horse whinnied, and Stevie craned her neck to get a better view as the psychopath hopped down from his stallion, the sound of his boots against gravel crunching. Her gaze raked down his muscular form, and she set the thought on fire that his body looked *good*.

As he edged toward the ghost, it was like a scene from a movie, the anticipation, the wondering which direction this would play out even though she had a pretty decent hunch. If there was a bowl of popcorn beside her, she would've been reaching for it as she watched on.

The Horseman lifted his pumpkin, his bicep flexing beneath his tight shirt, while the other ghost flipped him the middle finger the way he had at Stevie. Taking a cocky step forward, the Horseman hurled the flaming jack-o'-lantern at the ghost's chest. The guy stilled, his body frozen, his coloring changing from ivory to orange like flickering embers.

The Horseman effortlessly freed his sword from the sheath at his hip. With one fatal swing, he sliced it clean through the ghost's neck. No scream. No blood. Nothing. *Not gruesome at all, to be honest*. The Horseman reached into the ghost's chest and ripped out his pumpkin. He then picked up his prized head from the ground before placing it on his own neck.

"Real tough guy," Stevie muttered under her breath as she stepped back onto the pavement to get to her house.

The Horseman whirled around, the head he'd just placed on his neck no longer there, seeming to have vanished. *What in all the witchy magic?* He faced her, and she blinked, realizing that even though he was without a head again, he could sense her, possibly somehow hear and see her, since the Eye was open.

"He's such a tough guy that he stood me up for our date," Stevie rambled while fishing out her phone from her purse and walking at a normal pace, pretending as though she was like the general public, unable to see ghosts. "This world sucks sometimes. Sucks the life right out of people." *Unless they're taking heads instead of sucking.* The Horseman's boots didn't crunch across the gravel, nor did his stallion's hooves. Yet she could feel them both watching her.

Trying to appear casual, she whistled to herself as if she didn't notice he was somewhere behind her being his head-stealing self.

And so what if he could notice her? It wasn't like he could touch her and rip her head off for himself. Her head would remain happily in place.

Yet she still didn't want him to follow her home and get stuck with a demonic spirit who was akin to something that would come straight from the Hollow. As she turned the corner, she lost her cool and took off running in case he decided to tag along. Her boots weighed her down, and she stumbled, but it didn't stop her from hurrying to the duplex on the next street.

Roxy stood outside Stevie's door on all fours, wagging her fluffy tail.

Stevie drank in deep breath after deep breath, her chest heaving, perspiration dripping down the back of her neck. "Looks like you beat me again. Sorry it took me so long. I got caught up with Sleepy Hollow's nightly *guest.*"

Stevie's phone dinged, and she glanced at the screen. Reese. The edges of her lips curled up.

Just wanted to say you're even cuter in person, and I can't wait to see you again.

Likewise. And thank you for the pie. I'm not sharing it with anyone.

On part two of our date we can share something else then.

Stevie arched a brow. A tap came at the window of the other half of the duplex, startling her. She rolled her eyes when she found Lucia waving from her and Gideon's bedroom. Her sister-in-law lived on one side of the duplex and Stevie on the other. With the rent being cheaper this way, she'd been able to move out of her parents' house a couple of weeks ago. Finally.

"Delivery." Stevie shook the bag in front of Lucia. "And apparently the Eye of the Hollow is *alive*."

Lucia's gaze widened and Stevie waited a few seconds for her to open the door. She stood in nothing but an oversized Wolverine T-shirt that fell just above her knees. Her jet-black hair was thrown up into a messy bun on top of her head.

"The Eye opened?" Lucia gasped, taking the bag from Stevie while staring up at the red glowing spot above them. "Witch's tits! I wasn't expecting it to happen in our lifetime."

"That's not all. I left the restaurant and crossed paths with Mr. No Good, and—" Hoofbeats piercing the neighborhood reverberated around them, and Stevie clutched the pie box tighter.

"Seriously? He's like a vulture you can't get rid of." Stevie grasped her sister-in-law by the arm and pulled Lucia inside the duplex. She slammed the door shut and locked it. Roxy was already behind them, silent, looking toward the window.

"What is it?" Lucia asked.

"Shh!" She put her finger over her lips. "The Headless Horseman is coming."

Lucia arched a brow. "I didn't need the quiet signal."

Stevie held her breath until the hoofbeats picked up and faded before releasing a sigh. It wasn't abnormal to hear the stallion as she'd heard him over the years riding up and down the streets. But just in case, it was better they weren't in the same proximity again.

Lucia set the bag of food on the floor and placed her hands

on her hips. "Can we talk now?" she whispered. "I only feel Roxy's presence." Besides being one of the most powerful witches in Sleepy Hollow, a little psychic ability pulsed within Lucia's blood. But she couldn't see the ghosts the way Stevie could.

"His Headlessness is gone." Stevie angled her neck to peek inside the empty bedroom. "Where's Gideon?"

Lucia batted her hand behind her. "In the living room playing his new video game with his headphones on."

"We could be getting our souls sucked out by a band of demons and he wouldn't hear a thing." Stevie rolled her eyes. "As I was saying before we were rudely interrupted, the Eye is open and I can talk to the dead now."

Lucia rubbed her chin. "Hmm. Not much different than in the movies for a seer then."

"I'm waiting for you, Lucia," Gideon purred, his annoying voice drifting down the hallway. "The game's done, I put Maxine in the kitchen, and I'm undressed." Maxine was Gideon's plant that resembled a cross between a Venus flytrap, the one in *Little Shop of Horrors*, and the snapping flowers from the Super Mario video games. Lucia had given the plant to Gideon as an anniversary gift one year, and he'd babied it ever since.

"Be there in a minute. Just telling your sister goodnight," Lucia yelled over her shoulder as Stevie wrinkled her nose.

"And you owe me stamps!" Stevie added.

A couple of grumbled curses came from the living room.

"I'll let you get to *that*," Stevie said to Lucia, "and we can discuss more tomorrow."

"That we will do. The owner did bless the house recently, but I'll put up some stronger wards tomorrow."

"I'm glad to have my own personal witch next door." Stevie smiled, cracking open her exit, then bolting inside her half of the house. The pie rattled again, most likely crumbs by now, but still devourable.

As she locked up for the night, a thought struck her. *If the heads vanish when the Headless Horseman puts them on, then where do they go?*

Stevie shrugged and looked down at her pie—somewhat intact. "Time for a much-needed dessert after this night." She held up the box in a toast. "To the next thirty days and helping any ghost who asks for my assistance."

3

A loud *thump* sounded and Stevie jerked up in bed. She frantically looked around, her eyes practically glued shut from sleep, until her gaze landed on Roxy. The fox stood beside the bed, hopping up and down as her tail wagged, her nails clicking against the floor.

"You don't even eat." Stevie yawned, stretching her arms over her head before shoving the covers off her legs. "So why are you waking me up this early?" She glanced at the time on her phone where a reminder had popped up about breakfast at her parents. Kneeling on the floor, she ran her hand over the outline of her pet's back, and in a posh British accent, she said, "Oh, right, I forgot about that. Apologies, Foxy Roxy."

Stevie rummaged through her closet until she located a pair of black jeans and a white and blue polka dot button-up shirt with capped sleeves.

Her phone dinged, and she checked it after fastening the last button of her shirt. Lucia.

Are you sure you don't want a lift to your parents?

Stevie would normally take the offer, but she needed to catch up on a few things. She messaged Lucia back as she went into the bathroom. *No, I'll be jetting early. I promised Gideon I'd research a few hard-to-find comics for him, and then I'm going to finish up the orders for the apothecary.*

Ugh, fine. Sometimes I wish you would take a day off and relax. Orders can always be fulfilled tomorrow.

One day I'll take a daredevil of a vacation. See you soon.

There was a missed email on her phone from the council, a generic one that she was sure they'd sent to the whole town. *For the next month the council will be on watch, and anyone who isn't a resident of Sleepy Hollow will not be permitted to enter the town until after the next new moon sets.*

The council was run by a trio of older witches who didn't want to pass the torch of authority to others just yet even though their magic had dwindled the past few years.

Her brother's engine rumbled to life, and she rolled her eyes. The thing was ridiculous. Big truck, huge wheels. Like three times taller than her. But the lime green color was nice, so she would give him bonus points for that.

Stevie looked in the mirror and quickly ran a hand through her short curly bob, even though her hair would get tangled from the ride. She fluffed her bangs, wishing they were thicker, but they would have to do.

As she finished getting ready, she thought about the night before, the Eye of the Hollow opening. It wouldn't make a difference to Roxy since she could already see the living, but on the next new moon, for one night, Sleepy Hollow would be a full-blown party where the living and the dead could mingle. In the meantime, the witches would spell Sleepy Hollow to make sure it remained under the radar and no visitors stepped foot past the town's barrier. The paranormal activities needed to be kept a secret—ghosts wouldn't create chaos, but outsiders could.

Stevie grabbed her backpack purse from the kitchen counter, and Roxy stayed on her heels as she went to slip on her Converse.

"I take it you're coming?" She smiled.

The fox trotted past her through the front door which meant a thumbs-up she was tagging along.

Outside, the breeze rustled the trees, their red fall leaves floating to the ground in a ghoulish sort of dance. Roxy sat on the seat of Stevie's sparkly black moped, anxious for the ride. Stevie laughed while taking out her pumpkin orange helmet from the storage seat. "I do always appreciate your timely manner." As she fastened the strap beneath her chin, she added, "You still don't find it odd that the dead can touch objects, but they can't feel the living?"

The fox brought her paw to the handle and released a high-pitched bark.

"Touché, my little fox friend." She sank down on the moped, and Roxy's body rested through Stevie as her pet attempted to lean against her.

Stevie grinned while leaving the driveway, but it fell slightly when she recalled the Headless Horseman riding down her street just after they'd spotted one another. She expected him not to change his hermit during-the-day life just because the Eye had opened, but she searched for his tall, broad form anyway. No horse or headless caped man in sight. He most likely just wanted to be a cliché murderer of the night and not break that mold.

Speaking of cliché things, Stevie thought as she passed the abandoned house at the end of the neighborhood where she had yet to get an up-close look. Nearly all the yellow paint was gone, revealing white and gray undertones. Shingles were missing from a sagging roof, the foundation making the house crooked. Boards covered the windows, some broken, others with planks nailed across for extra security. Deep cracks ran up the driveway that appeared as if it had been hit by an earthquake. Overgrown weeds, accompanied by dead bushes, decorated the front garden in front of a wide porch. Ever since moving into the duplex, she'd wanted to see what rested inside but hadn't gotten an opportunity to check it out. Anything worth value was probably long gone. Or maybe something could be hidden... Stamps?

Coins? Ghosts could also be trapped there that required her assistance before the living was separated from the dead once more. It was an opportunity she couldn't refuse.

"How about we finally sneak a peek inside this place when we get back, Roxy?" Stevie glanced down at the fox to find her swatting at a fly in front of her. "I'm going to give the yes box a checkmark then."

A car drove in front of her, cutting her off. "Watch where you're going, dirtbag!" Stevie shouted. Not that the idiot could hear her, but it made her feel better.

She curved around two headless—non-Horseman—ghosts stumbling through the streets. Another translucent white form, a young girl in a frilly dress, waved at the cars when they drove by, her other hand holding a few balloons.

Stevie waved, and the girl's smile grew wide as she bounced on her feet in glee. Even though she wanted to stop and talk to every ghost on the street, she second-guessed that choice since there was a group of maybe twenty. She didn't need a mob of the dead showing up on her doorstep, demanding she help them, which could lead to the Headless Horseman knowing where she lived.

She drove past another scene, a woman walking down the street while a ghost strolled beside her, attempting to get her attention. *Soon.*

Her parents' pristine one-story home slipped into view. A black roof, gray brick, and a long porch wrapped around to the side of the house. The neon orange rocking chairs on the porch, that Stevie had painted to give them some pizzazz last year, shifted back and forth with the wind. As expected, Gideon's truck was parked in the middle of the driveway and she skirted around it, then stopped in front of the garage beside the Saint Francis statue.

While Stevie put away her helmet, the front door swung open and Roxy darted inside with a loud bark, her way of shouting hello even though the family couldn't hear her.

"Stevie, baby sister, you finally decided to grace us with your presence. And, unsurprisingly, late," Gideon called, his teeth flashing. He was a foot taller than her, four years older, and he wore his usual Batman shirt, his beard reaching his collarbones. The only thing that mirrored the siblings were their brown irises and hair color, which her natural one hadn't been seen in years.

She rolled her eyes and met him on the front porch. "By like two minutes. I was prepping my research for *you*."

"On a cell phone. From home. That's the dream right there."

"You mostly work in the back of the comic book store doing accounting things."

Gideon chuckled. "Bet you didn't know accounting has a high suicide rate. But I'm *fine*."

"Whatever, I at least look presentable." She poked a finger at the Batman graphic on his chest. "You've been wearing the same shirt for like three days in a row."

"Dude, it's not the same shirt. I just have five of them!" He leaned against the door frame. "Besides the Eye of the Hollow opening, I hear other news happened last night. With Reese. He's not your type, and I'm placing a wager now. You'll get tired of him in the next two weeks."

"Thank you, oh holy brother, for letting me know this most magnanimous opinion. But you're wrong a lot." She playfully shoved his arm.

"Never." He smirked, reaching inside his pocket and fishing out a few coins. "I got these at a garage sale for your collection. The stamps are on their way. I ordered them this morning."

Stevie's eyes saucered as she looked at the two half dollars. 1912 and 1917. "Sometimes you make me not regret having a brother. Thank you!"

He chuckled. "Aww, such wonderful words spoken by my baby sister."

"Quit dicking around with the door wide open," Stevie's mom, Morgan, shouted.

"If Gideon wasn't blocking my entrance I would've been inside like five minutes ago," Stevie called with a grin.

"Five minutes minus two," he pointed out.

"Cauldron's teeth, you're a nuisance." She laughed and walked past him. Pumpkin spice clung to the air like it always did inside her parents' house during the fall.

Their mom lingered at the end of the hallway, her arms folded against her chest. Her hair was pulled back into a high sleek ponytail and gray streaked the strands. Silver eyeshadow painted her lids, black liner winging out at the edges. A pink and white striped dress hugged her curvy form, and a sleeve of tattoos covered her left arm.

"About time you showed up, my precious girl." Her mom wrapped Stevie into a fierce hug as though she hadn't seen her in a year. "Let's catch up. Lucia is giving your father a special seasoning she made for the sausage."

"Please don't tell me she brought that spicy kind," Gideon groaned, scurrying toward the back of the house to go outside where their dad was barbecuing.

"Nothing she brings is that spicy," her mom barked to his back, then turned to Stevie. "He's twenty-five and still acts like he's fourteen."

"To be fair, I can do that sometimes too."

"We all can." Her mom smiled and led Stevie to the leather couch, patting the spot beside her. Roxy lay on her back against the fur rug, staring up at the rotating fan—her own personal entertainment.

As her mom reclined into the cushions, Stevie studied her, remembering when her parents first discovered she could see ghosts. Then finding out her mom held an ability too, one she hadn't confessed to Stevie until that moment.

Once a month, her mom's heart would begin to die, and she'd have to replace it if she wanted to continue living. Before coming to Sleepy Hollow, her mom hadn't known what she was exactly, only that she needed a fresh, healthy heart from someone so she didn't keel over and die. She'd tried both dying human and animal hearts, neither of which worked properly. At least not until Stevie's dad had located a witch in Sleepy Hollow who could put a specific spell on a pig's heart each month to do the job. Lucia's aunt—Ginger. Her mom still didn't know what she was, but regardless, Stevie loved her.

"Dad's been cooking a lot lately," Stevie said, staring out the window as her dad tossed the spatula in the air and caught it as if he were auditioning to be a juggler at the circus. The sound of his punk rock music drifted through the walls from outside, something Stevie had grown up on.

"He's now found a new dream profession once he retires from the dentist office." She laughed. "Did you bring Roxy with you?"

Hearing her name, the fox rolled onto her side and pawed through her mom's ankle. "She's near your feet."

"We miss you, Roxy, and you know you're welcome here any time." Her shoulders sagged as she sighed. "First Gideon, who by the way I never expected to leave, then you. I miss you both."

"If it wasn't for Lucia, I think Gideon would've died here." Stevie grinned.

Her mom straightened and clasped her hands. "More importantly, the Eye of the Hollow opened last night. I always sort of believed it was a story, but I guess not."

"Definitely not." Stevie turned to face her mom, propping her elbow against the couch cushions. "For the first time, I had a couple of ghosts return my one-way conversation, I watched the Headless Horseman take a head, and not much else yet."

"The *Headless Horseman*? That asshole?" her mom gasped. "I've told you since you were younger to steer clear of that demon ghost. I have no room to talk because of my past, but Ginger confirmed that none of the souls lingered who I took hearts from." When her mom discovered ghosts were real, she'd been terrified that some of the souls might not have passed on.

But that self-loathing case had been closed when she repented with one of the priests.

Her mom had done it for survival though, not just eating hearts to eat hearts like a vicious beast. And technically, it wasn't eating—only swallowing them. "I will. It was just something I had to see. Kind of like those people who want to go into places that are supposedly haunted." Except for seers, no one had seen the Horseman, but psychics, mediums, witches, and priests had all attempted to rid Sleepy Hollow of him in the past. Yet like a virus, he wasn't easy to get rid of.

"Just be careful with the ghosts. Even if they can't touch you, that doesn't mean a pervert can't waltz into your bathroom."

Stevie wrinkled her nose. "Gross, Mom!"

"Well, it's true." She pursed her lips. "Moving on, Gideon said you went on a date last night. It wasn't Alex, was it?"

Alex didn't have a job and played video games all day at his parents' house. "I would never go out with any of Gideon's friends. Ever. And it was a meeting that I guess turned into a date. Or a five-second date. We're supposed to finish it."

"Does he know you're a seer?" her mom asked, worry lacing her tone.

"No, we haven't gotten that far yet. But he did buy me a pie that almost matched my favorite color."

Her mom tilted her head and studied her with concern. "I'm just thinking about your ex-boyfriend's reaction who we shall not name."

Stevie had dated Mr. Piss-Baby for a few months before telling him, hoping his reaction would be thrilled—it wasn't. "Don't worry about me confessing all my sins to Reese right off the bat." Just because Sleepy Hollow held a good number of paranormal residents didn't mean one went around spilling what they were to strangers. Reese could be a werewolf for all she knew.

"Oh," Stevie continued. "Back to the Headless Horseman. I forgot to mention that something strange happened. Once he put the victim's head on, it vanished into thin air! So maybe he doesn't have a collection after all?"

"Unless they appear in a collection somewhere else..." Her mom pursed her lips again, mulling something over. "When I get a new heart, it pushes out the old withering one. It could be that his body needs the head, but that doesn't explain why it would disappear." She took a deep ragged breath, her eyes closing briefly.

"Are you all right, Mom?" Stevie asked, grasping her arm.

"I'm fine. I've just been tired today is all."

The door opened and Stevie's dad came in carrying two trays filled with smoked sausage. "Jack, let me get one of those." Her mom hopped off the couch and grabbed one of the trays.

"Looks great, Dad." Stevie took the other tray to the granite kitchen counter.

The music outside turned louder, only it was deep and slow beats pulsing through the walls. Her dad shook his head while raking a hand through his gray hair. "Your brother comes by here every day and still puts on shitty music."

"It's as if he never left," Stevie sang.

Lucia came inside, clutching a few glass jars of purple seasoning. Her gaze found Stevie's and she drew an invisible line across her throat. "No more Horse Man?"

"Makes me think of a legitimate horse that is a man." Stevie lifted a finger. "But! I'll officially be off the hook once the next new moon is finished and I'm invisible to him again."

4

Stevie took off her helmet and ran her fingers through her mussed hair as she peered toward the abandoned house near the end of the street. *To wait for Roxy, or to not wait for Roxy—that is the question.*

She was never a Shakespeare fan, so she wouldn't endlessly debate between the two—she would check the house out. Especially as she thought more on it—ghosts could touch Roxy, not Stevie. But for her own safety, in case there was some morally gray person, of the living persuasion, who leaned more toward the dark side slinking about ... well, she took out the special brew from her purse that Lucia had made which would work better than any pepper spray. It would turn the person into a toad for twenty-four hours.

As a backup, she sent her witchy sister-in-law a text after bringing her purse inside the duplex.

So, I decided to go look at the abandoned house down the street. If you don't hear from me by tonight, that means to come save me. I could've been sucked inside the walls and trapped or something.

Stevie smiled just as Lucia messaged her back. *Charms and hexes, you're going without me? You better have the spray I made and your lucky ring still on.*

Special attack toad brew already in my hand and ring on my thumb —check.

Stevie then headed toward the abandoned house, the neighborhood quiet. She rotated the lucky thumb ring, made of glass and embedded with spelled tiny clovers and white petals, round and round, until she reached the driveway that appeared more shattered than cracked when she stood this close. She stared up at the house, its boarded-up windows, the bars in front of a small basement window behind the dead garden. On the wood of the entrance door, a question mark was spray painted in faded red. She had plenty of questions herself—like were there ghosts inside, was it cleared out or had things been left behind, and what was the spray painter wanting to know?

Nothing supernatural wandered the yard. No ghost slipped out from around the house to ask for help with their unfinished business. Vampires wouldn't be caught dead in a place like this, and instead they lived the highlife in their extravagant gothic mansions.

Skating her finger over the spray-painted question mark, Stevie studied the door—she might need to go back and see if she could find a crowbar. If Lucia was there, she could've easily unlocked the door with a spell. But when Stevie tried to turn the locked knob, the door pushed open, a soft creak echoing. The door frame was splintered, most likely kicked in. And if it was recent, squatters could potentially be there now.

Stevie gripped Lucia's toad brew as she stepped over the dirt-smeared threshold. A musky smell mingled with dust tickled her nose, not wholly unpleasant but not a scent she would want to be made into a candle either. A thin line of light spilled into what had to be a sitting room, due to the old fabric chairs and a torn leather couch, the cushions and pillows missing.

She removed one board from the window that rested on the sill and wasn't even nailed into place. The other two boards were in the same boat as the first one when she set them on the floor. Full light illuminated the room, casting a charming glow into the other areas of the beautifully dreary home. Tangled silken spiderwebs decorated almost every corner, and graffiti covered the walls and wooden floor. Most of the wallpaper was peeled in places, some with chunks missing.

Mysterious black splotches rested on the couch's leather and before she started shouting for ghosts, she would search the home to make sure it was empty of any living souls.

Stevie took out her phone and turned on the flashlight. The kitchen appliances were gone, leaving yellow stains in the empty spots. Most of the doors were missing from the cabinets, and the drawers were all empty. "Oh no wait, there the cockroaches are," she sang softly to herself as she shut a drawer that wouldn't close all the way. The door beside the pantry led down to what had to be the basement.

The living room came next, and it was as if Stevie had just traveled back in time. Cracked and worn recliners awaited her in the middle of the room on top of a filthy teal carpet. Photos of geese wearing bonnets and cross-stitching designs of mushrooms hung across the walls, the glass frames fractured and destroyed. Two large wooden shelves were empty of figurines or books that might've once been there. But....

"Whoa! Look at this badass TV!" Stevie grinned, crouching in front of the busted-out screen. Aside from that dismal part, it was perfect—no graffiti or scratches marred its surface. She messed with the knobs, rotating them in different directions, pretending she'd gone through a time warp. It was a shame the TV wouldn't work, or she would've lugged the heavy thing all the way home. *Might take one of those geese pictures for my living room though*. It would only need a new frame.

Brushing lint from her dark jeans, she stood and finished up on the first floor, passing by a bathroom with broken mirror shards scattered across the white ceramic tile flooring. Dark and questionable puddles sat stagnating inside the bathtub and seashell-shaped sink, the toilet reeking of how she imagined a zombie corpse would smell. She then went by an empty master bedroom, dusty beer cans cluttering most of it, half the carpet ripped up.

Stevie reached the end of the loop that circled the first floor entirely. She stared up at the wooden staircase and started up the steps, where only a tiny bit of sunlight trickled into the area above. Rectangular yellow spots stained the white walls in place of picture frames that once hung there.

Another large board blocked a window at the top of the stairs, and she used all her strength to tear it off the wall. The space was empty as were most of the rooms except for the beds, dressers, shelves, and damaged desks. An ashy odor clung to the cooler air of the second floor. It might not be her lucky day since there'd been no sign of anything of value or a single hint of a ghost.

She opened one of the doors in the last bedroom, and a narrow staircase led to an attic that looked as if it hadn't been dusted in decades. A frayed mattress leaned against a wooden-paneled wall beside a few cardboard boxes containing cheap holiday décor coated in mouse droppings. Another couple of boxes held moldy hats and ruined fabrics. In the shadowy corner rested a hoard of more cans accompanied by a pile of ... bones? Lips parted, eyes squinting, heart anticipating something unusual to hopefully happen, she brought the flashlight closer and let out a heavy sigh. Just a pile of chicken bones that someone had eaten the meat off of and tossed aside, or from a witch who'd come in to perform a little séance.

As she came back to the bedroom, the house appeared to be crystal clear of the living. "Hello," she called. "Are there any ghosts here?"

She waited a full sixty seconds. No answer came, and she shrugged. It was worth a shot anyway.

Stevie took the board from the window, then inspected the remainder of the bedroom. Dolls stood in a neat line along one corner, a few of their heads severed and nestled beside them, others cracked and burned. Broken plates and teacups gathered around them, and in spray paint, beside the grim collection, it read, *Our sacrifice for the Headless Horseman.*

Stevie snorted before lifting the bed skirt to peer under it. Near the center, a small rectangular paper grabbed her attention.

Stretching through the dust, she grasped the mystery object and yanked it out. "Jackpot," she said. It was an old Garbage Pail Kids card folded in half and most likely not of value to anyone else. *Nasty Nick.* The picture showcased a vampire holding what looked to be a Barbie. Stevie would add it to her stash at home.

She tucked the card into her backpack and stood, just as a shrill squeaking sound vibrated within the house, and the creaky stairs protested beneath heavy footsteps. It could be one of two things. Living or dead. Fifty-fifty chance since she could hear and see them both. Raising her toad brew, shoulders tense, she hovered beside the doorframe and peeked out. She relaxed when a cloud of white struck her vision. Just a ghost.

Stevie was literally one second from shouting a "Hey, fancy meeting you here," until her gaze swept across the ghost's whole form and she froze. No head and a cocky cape. *Son of a thousand hexes!* What in all the Holy Spirit was the Headless Horseman doing here? Was this where he hung out all day until night fell? She'd bet her entire life he had a collection of prized heads down in the basement that she'd yet to explore. It didn't matter now since she would avoid this house like the plague once she left. Today her lucky ring wasn't so lucky after all.

Pulling herself from her statuesque state, Stevie plastered herself against the wall and attempted to become one with it. When she'd come in hopes of helping a ghost, she didn't mean for his psycho self to answer her call. But here the demon ghost was in all his headless glory.

Unless he'd just shown up.

The sound of his heavy boots faded, and she slowly released her breath. She needed to get ahead of him so he wouldn't catch up and follow her home. It wasn't her she was worried about, but Roxy's head staying right where it was.

As Stevie took a hesitant step forward to get ready to fling herself out of the room and down the steps, her phone dinged. She clenched her teeth so hard she believed they might shatter while inwardly cursing the texter. Reese... Any other time would've been perfectly A-okay.

I wanted to see what you were doing later this evening.

Stevie ignored the message. Maybe the Horseman hadn't heard her phone ... maybe he would go back to the depths from which he'd come. But the sound of boots pivoting against the hardwood floor reverberated through the walls, thudding in her direction like a serial killer slowly coming for its prey.

New plan. Pretend once again that I don't see him and casually leave the house. Simple.

Stevie looked around the room, figuring out where to start to busy herself, to seem as if she was on a whole different mission than to help a ghost.

Whistling to herself, she opened a drawer and inspected it. "No curious or peculiar discovery here," she chirped. Behind her, the steps of the Horseman's boots grew louder as he entered the room. She didn't whirl around to face him, just moved on to the next drawer where an empty pack of cigarettes lingered. "No need for that."

Stevie turned to the cracked oval mirror hanging on the wall, angels embedded into the gold of the frame. She combed her fingers through her hair, catching a glimpse of the Horseman in the glass' reflection. Standing only a few feet from her, his translucent ivory form glowed like a beacon inside the room. Even without a head, he was much taller, broader, and more muscular than her. She remembered the full view of his body the night before, not wholly unpleasant ... if he wasn't a psychopath ... and had an actual head that belonged to him. The Horseman's sleeves were rolled to his elbows, his pants hugging his thighs. The only difference now was his mighty steed and jack-o'-lantern were missing in action.

Could he actually see her or just feel her vibrations? A part of her didn't want to go, wanted instead to find out what else this so-called legend of a ghost would do, if he would indeed hide inside the basement after leaving this room since she'd never seen him out during daylight, or would he venture somewhere else?

Stevie knelt in front of the pile of dolls and lifted one with half its face melted and burned, then set it back down. "I'll come back for you pretty ladies soon."

The Horseman inched closer, hovering in her personal space. Not a single scent wafted from him which was no surprise. But if she were a ghost and could smell him, she had an inkling his scent would be of leather and pumpkins.

Stevie stood and brushed through him, then headed down the stairs at a leisurely pace.

"Hmm, aren't you brave breaking into a house that doesn't belong to you. And foolish," a deep, hypnotic voice rumbled from the Horseman and her eyes widened. She didn't still, nor did she turn around. But how had the voice come from him? He had no mouth!

The stairs creaked behind her as she reached the last step, and he continued, "Don't deny it, Pumpkin, you can see me. And I can clearly see you." So that answered her question—he could easily pick her out of a crowd now that it was verified he knew what she looked like.

He saw straight through her game, but it didn't matter. She wouldn't have a demon ghost lurking around her or her family.

Once she hit the fresh air, footfalls didn't follow her. She wasn't idiotic enough to lure the demon to her porch either, so she looped around the neighborhood to the park where she would enter through her back gate.

Stevie waited at the park for a few minutes, surveying the area as her fingers twitched. Only one ghost lingered—a little boy wearing a baseball hat sitting on a swing. His gaze met hers and she held his stare.

Her conscience got the best of her, knowing she needed to at least offer the ghost kid some assistance. "Hey! Do you need help finding anything? Figuring out your unfinished business?"

"Stranger danger!" he shouted and fled away from the park with his arms flapping around like a bird, the creak of the empty swing filling the air.

"No more going out of my way to search for ghosts in abandoned places. I've learned my lesson," she whispered to herself as she opened the gate.

Chest heaving, heartbeat relaxing, Stevie took out her phone and messaged Reese back to pretend the incident with the Headless Horseman had never happened. *I can't tonight, but how about tomorrow?*

Sounds perfect. I'll bring dinner to your place.

I won't shoot that down.

With a smile, she entered her home.

Ghostless.

5

"Goodbye, Headless Horseman," Stevie chanted as she shut the door behind her. No matter how tempting it might be to go back to the abandoned house to check out the basement and see what could be down there—*ghost heads?*—that was a definite no crossed off her list of things to do.

She fished out the bent collector card from her back pocket, satisfied she'd at least found Nasty Nick. Still, she'd put Roxy in harm's way, but to be fair, she hadn't suspected that the Horseman would've made a grand swaggery entrance. She always assumed he was either hovering at a cemetery or hidden deep in the woods somewhere. He'd said that he knew she could see him, and yet he hadn't followed her. Maybe he just wasn't impressed by her which would brighten her day.

"Roxy, are you here?" Stevie called, heading to her room to slip the card into her collection binder.

No bark in reply.

She set the binder back on the desk and checked the time on her phone. Still early. That meant her sidekick might not come home for a few more hours. At least Roxy had been in a safe zone while Stevie was traipsing around the Headless Horseman's abode.

She sent Lucia a quick text as she padded toward the kitchen. *I'm back. And guess what?*

Stevie swallowed, her throat parched. She knew exactly what she needed. Opening the fridge, she grabbed a carton of milk and chugged the remainder of it down. She shook the carton, finding a couple sips that would have to hold her over until she went grocery shopping tomorrow. There was normally enough, but Gideon had come over the previous morning and hogged most of it.

As she went into the living room, she was a few words into her message to Lucia about what had happened at the abandoned house when rustling, the shuffle of fabrics, stirred from the couch.

"Are you trying to get yourself stuck in the blankets again?" She laughed, then froze when her gaze didn't meet Roxy's furry form but instead an ethereal white muscular build of a man—absent of a head.

Stevie screamed, inwardly cursing herself for pretending like she couldn't see the devil of a ghost. Lucia's wards hadn't prevented this entity from entering.

If the Headless Horseman had a face she could see, Stevie knew he'd be smirking. His cape lay on the back of the couch, taking up half its length, as if this were his home. He leaned back, his legs spread wide, the buttons of his shirt fastened pristinely to the top collar like a proper gentleman. A gentleman who reaped heads for funsies.

How did he know she was here? She thought she'd been sly by going the back route and making sure no ghosts were in sight. There hadn't been a sign of him at the park at all, but maybe the little boy ghost was a narc? No, he'd run off in the opposite direction like a chicken with its head cut off. Unless ... the Horseman had found him and...

Stevie stood still, staring at the blank space above his partial neck while they played some sort of game of who would speak first since she now knew he could *talk*.

"We meet again," the Horseman drawled, his voice just as deep and hypnotic as before. "You can see me. Don't deny it."

Well, she wouldn't deny it since at this point the jig was up. "You have two minutes to leave my house before I spell you to the darkness, deep into the Hollow, demon!" Stevie whirled around and bolted to her room, hoping he wouldn't catch her bluff. She had a few witchy brews near the bed that she needed to deliver, but they were for healing sicknesses, bringing dead plants back to life, getting over a loved one, looking younger, and none of those would do a thing. Even after priests had blessed the lands of Sleepy Hollow, here the Headless Horseman still was, ruining her life. Overdramatic? Maybe. But not if it was protecting Roxy who could come home at any moment.

Ah-ha! The crucifix inside the head vase!

Stevie opened her china cabinet stuffed with antiques, selecting the ceramic head vase that was crafted in a bust of Lucille Ball, showcasing all her giant eyelash glory. Pulse thrumming, she glanced toward her open door while plucking a solid silver crucifix from inside, followed by the toad brew that was still in her pocket. When she discovered that the Horseman hadn't followed her, she frowned instead of rejoiced. Was he waiting for her to skip back into the living room? Or maybe he'd listened and fled.

As she moved to place the vase back on its shelf, a glimpse of white caught her attention in front of the window. She flinched, tripping over her own two feet. The ceramic slipped from her grasp and crashed to the floor. The pieces sliding *everywhere*. That was it. The last straw.

Gritting her teeth, Stevie looked up at the Headless Horseman, and even though he had no face, her gaze latched onto where she assumed his demonic eyes should be. And glowing red at that. "Look what you made me do!" Stevie growled, holding up the crucifix. She then sprayed him with the toad brew, but of course he didn't turn into an amphibian since he wasn't a living man.

"What *I* made *you* do?" he asked, incredulous. "I was merely standing here watching you fiddle around with a ghastly ceramic head. That you keep a collection of inside that cabinet of yours, I might add."

"If they were real heads, you would take them all to add to your secret *collection*," Stevie bit back, lifting the crucifix higher. "Get out of my house, demon."

"That would all depend on the head. Never assume things," he answered, his voice matter of fact. "And put that thing away. I'm not a demon."

"Close enough," Stevie grumbled, not lowering the cross. He hadn't slinked from his position, and he kept his shoulders relaxed as if he were having a fun day in the park. "I told you to leave, or I would banish you from this world."

"If you had the ability to do that, I'm certain you would've already, *seer*. The Eye of the Hollow is open, and I know that you can see me. You made that quite obvious on all three of our encounters now."

Stevie narrowed her gaze at him. "The Eye might be open, but it will close soon enough with its twin, so you might as well tiptoe your way out straight through the wall. My sister-in-law is a witch, and she'll be home any second."

He ignored her words, slowly having a turn around her room, seeming to take in the details. The frames of collector cards, stamps, and coins, covering every inch of the walls. The stacks of shoeboxes and binders resting on her desk filled with even more, the antique figurines on the shelves. "You have too many nonsensical things."

Stevie blinked, her brows lifting up her forehead. "Excuse me?" She lowered the crucifix but didn't slacken her grip on it. When he didn't speak, she continued, "Listen, um, Headless Horseman, I—"

He held up a gloved hand, cutting her off. "Kit."

"What?" she asked, wrinkling her nose. "What kind of kit? Do you need a first aid one? Because I think your neck wound healed a long time ago."

"No." He stepped forward, his broad shoulders squared. "My name is Kit. *Not* 'Headless Horseman.'"

Kit... She wouldn't dare admit it aloud, but it was a charming name for a not-so-charming man. Without seeing his true face, she wasn't sure if he even looked like a Kit because right now he only looked like the Headless Horseman.

He inched toward her, his body like a tower in front of her. "And you, Pumpkin, what do you go by?"

"Not *Pumpkin*." She scowled. "If I tell you my name will you leave?"

"Perhaps," he said the word ever so slowly which only made her scowl deepen.

"First, tell me how you knew where I lived." All she could think about was him removing that sword at his hip from its sheath and slicing it through the little ghost boy's neck.

"Easy enough. I went through each of the houses in this neighborhood until I found you."

She should've guessed he would do something as stalkeriffic as that, but a sense of relief washed through her that no ghost had been harmed in the process. "My name's Stevie," she relented.

"Stevie." Kit drew out her name in that deep baritone of his, making it sound more like Ste-vieeeeeeeeeee. "It doesn't resemble a seer name."

"Kit doesn't sound like it would be the Headless Horseman's name either, but here we are," Stevie started. "And anyway, my dad named me after one of the greatest singers ever to walk this earth. Stevie Nicks. Who I guess you wouldn't know—unless you've talked to other ghosts somewhere after like 1975?"

"No," he said simply, his boots remaining planted in place.

"I told you my name, so will you go?" She folded her arms.

"Not yet."

Stevie thrust her hand forward with the crucifix, and it pierced through his chest. Nothing. He couldn't touch her, and she couldn't touch him. But the sigh of relief didn't come, not as she remembered Roxy and swallowed deeply.

"Why would you do something so ridiculous?" Kit asked, wiping the front of his chest as if she'd sullied him.

"To make sure my head was protected," Stevie said. As he grunted, she added, "What will make you leave me alone? Helping you with unfinished business? It's no secret around here that you ride through the ghost world at night in search of your head. And I have news for you, I wouldn't know where to find it unless you want to spend years digging up every inch of Sleepy Hollow. If it's somewhere else outside of this town, I might be dead before we even finish that."

Kit remained silent, his gloved fingers flexing at his sides. "I'm not confessing what I need from you just yet. That will come soon enough."

Stevie pursed her lips at the thought of what he could ask for. What if he wanted her to lure innocent ghosts to him? "Last night I saw you take that guy's head. Given, he was a jackass, but still. The point is, you put on his head and it vanished. So the question is, how are you still talking and seeing things without one?"

"You're quite inquisitive," he said, amusement in his voice. "At first you pretended as though you didn't see me, then you pretended to be a witch, and now you think I'll so easily provide you answers to quell your curiosity?"

"Well, yes." She glowered. "It's only courteous since you made yourself a guest in my home, isn't it?"

"To make what is to come simpler between us, I will answer you. The head I took is still here. Only no one can see it. At the start of each new moon, it begins to fade, requiring me to collect a new one unless I don't want to see or hear. So I do what I must."

Stevie bit her lip, thinking about her mom and the hearts

she'd eaten to live. Human hearts she'd taken in the past before she discovered the witch who would save her. It was something he thought he had to do, a choice he made.

"And do you ever ... take heads from animals?" At that precise moment, Roxy burst through the door, barking up a storm at him. "Roxy! Stop. Get back and go to Lucia!" The fox didn't listen, and Stevie stepped between them even though it would do no good.

Kit made a tsking sound. "If you think I would wear the head of an animal when there are plenty of ghosts wandering about, then you are madder than you seem."

Stevie rolled her eyes. "I'll give you one positive point for that."

Roxy's barking halted and she hesitantly padded forward to sniff Kit's boot. His shoulders hunched forward as he must've been peering down at her sidekick. "You have a ghost fox for a ... pet?"

"Yes, she's my ghost sidekick. Seers have them, and if you touch one little ghost hair on her head, I'll make sure you never gallop through the streets again," Stevie promised.

Kit chuckled, deep and mocking. "Your tiny fox is all yours, Pumpkin. I prefer to claim stallions as mine."

"Speaking of, where's your horse? Does he stay with you at that house? Is that even where you actually stay during the day?" If so, maybe the horse had been in the backyard or only appeared to him at night.

"He comes when I desire it." Kit shrugged. "Now I must go, but I'll be calling on you very soon."

"I didn't really agree to anything just so you know."

"You will," he said, his voice assertive of what he believed to be true. "Good evening."

Stevie balled her hands into tight fists, her nails digging cres-cent moons into her palms. "Listen, you—" Before Stevie finished her sentence, Kit turned his back on her and sauntered through the wall leading to her backyard. She shoved the curtain to the side, but his white form was already gone. "Good riddance," she grumbled under her breath.

Roxy observed the shards of ceramic scattered on the floor. If there weren't so many little pieces, Stevie would've had Lucia spell the vase back together. At least it wasn't one of her favorites. Still, they were hard to find in excellent condition at a decent price.

"His fault for barging into my house," Stevie said to Roxy, "but I *guess* it started with me going into his. He stays at the abandoned house."

The fox's eyes widened and she cocked her head.

"Yes, I went alone. I thought it was safer you didn't go. Although, I guess it wouldn't have mattered now."

Taking out her phone, she sent Lucia a text.

I know you're still at my parents', but apparently the Headless Horseman resides at the abandoned house. Oh, he also knows where I live and we had a little chat.

What? I'm coming home now!

No, it's fine. He's gone. Maybe you can put up a stronger ward or something.

I can try, but it's probably a situation like Roxy. Where you've seen him and he's seen you which would cancel out the spell. The Crowned Witch would maybe know a secret about the living and the dead seeing one another, but she's still away from Sleepy Hollow. Once the Eyes close, this pesky issue will be solved.

From one new moon to the next, it took about twenty-nine days, which meant she had a measly twenty-eight now. She could handle that.

Stevie cleaned up the vase's broken pieces before sinking down on the living room couch where Kit's cape still lingered. She tried to knock it to the floor with her hand, but her fingers passed through the fabric.

"Can you take that thing outside?" Stevie asked Roxy.

The fox grasped the cape between her teeth and dragged it through the door.

"Ah, that's better." Stevie turned on the TV as Roxy bounded back inside and hopped up next to her. A fantastic musical score cut through the room, one she instantly recognized from the movie playing.

Sleepy Hollow.

The edges of Stevie's lips curled up at the corners as she watched the man being chased. The Headless Horseman closing in, lifting his arm, sword in hand. And ... swipe.

"It's a sign, Roxy." Stevie drew the blanket over her legs. "But what the sign is for? Only the Headless Horseman can reveal that."

6

"What in the Hollow?" Stevie groaned as Roxy pawed at the kitchen window. She stared at the line of ants snacking at the salt she'd sprinkled around the sill, courtesy of Lucia bringing over a *Keep Out Spirit* remedy to try.

Stevie looked up on her phone if ants usually ate salt, and apparently, some were more attracted to it than sugar. She cleared out the salt with a wet rag and the ants scattered before slipping back into a small hairline crack at the bottom of the backsplash. Later she would ask Lucia about a stronger remedy when she stopped by the apothecary.

The day before trickled into her skull like a pesky gnat swarming about. The Headless Horseman in her house, the crucifix not burning him to a crisp, and then him vowing he would be back with a request—a request she could deny. He wasn't her puppeteer and didn't seem to have dark magic that could control her into doing his bidding.

Stevie headed next door to Lucia's basement to collect a few additional items that had been ordered. Most vials and jars were already ready to go and spelled except for Stevie needing to add a drop of her blood to enhance the properties. Twelve empty canisters sat on a table beside the cauldron, ready for the next batch. She sprinkled a few powders into the liquid and stirred it before pouring some into each jar for Lucia to spell when she returned.

Once she opened the jars and vials that needed her blood, Stevie took a needle and pricked her finger, pinching a bead of scarlet into each jar. One was to keep a bouquet of flowers alive for two months, another was special delicacies for pet plants, followed by hair grower, a brew to help with vision, and several room sprays that would last longer than the standard air fresh-ener. After grabbing a couple more items from the shelves, she located the last thing on the list. A sack of healing crystals. The new owner—her mom.

Stevie boxed everything up and brought the packages to her car instead of the moped since gray streaked the sky. It was times like these when she was glad she'd kept her much older high school car.

Kit's cape was no longer near the tree where Roxy had thrown it out the previous night. *Maybe he wouldn't come back then.* She shrugged, then checked a few emails on her phone from her brother about a list of comic books he wanted to find for the store before leaving.

As she passed the abandoned house, she pretended it didn't exist. A few droplets pelted the window shield, then a couple of seconds later switched to full-blown rain and she turned the wipers up.

On the porch of a large two-story house, an old ghost woman, with long braids, shifted back and forth in a rocking chair while a small living boy played beside her on the ground, watching it rain.

Stevie caught wind of a headless form in the distance, and her heart accelerated. But as she drew closer ... it was only one of the Horseman's victims. "Can't get rid of him even when he's not here," she said to herself while curving down her parents' street.

"Can't get rid of who?" a deep, familiar voice silkily asked from behind her.

Stevie inhaled sharply and slammed on the brakes, throwing the car into park. She whirled around in her seat, coming face to no face with the Headless Horseman.

"What are you doing here?" she shrieked, her voice a higher octave than she'd ever heard it. "And when did you sneak into my car, you stalker?"

Kit relaxed back, stretching his arm along the top of the seat. "Just after you got inside. It's not my fault you didn't notice I was behind you. Seems a bit *dangerous* that you don't pay attention to your surroundings."

Stevie cursed herself for being distracted by her phone, and then him for not being in the line of sight of her rearview mirror. Which was also due to the fact that he had *no* head.

"When you acted like you'd come back at some point, I didn't think you meant you would spontaneously show up two seconds later." She waved her hand frantically in the air.

"Your judgment of time is lacking," he said, unenthused.

She rolled her eyes and pinched the bridge of her nose. "Whatever. Less than twenty-four hours, then."

"So, where are you taking us, Pumpkin?" Kit adjusted the collar of his shirt like he was getting ready to meet a hot date.

"Nowhere with you. Bye." She unlocked the doors, signaling him to leave even though he could just walk through whatever he wanted.

"Tonight you will not turn me away. We have much to discuss." Before she could tell him to go suck a bloody bat wing, he stepped through the car.

Stevie eyed him in the rearview mirror, the way he sauntered away, adjusting the cape in his grasp. He must've gotten it just before he'd slinked into her car. Her gaze dipped downward to the way his pants hugged his backside, and she couldn't pull her eyes away from it. As he brought the cape over his shoulders, she flicked her gaze up, pretending like she hadn't been ogling that part of him. What was wrong with her? She continued watching his *upper body* until he vanished from her sight. She searched the backseat one more time to make sure he hadn't somehow snuck inside again. But he was officially gone.

"And no, I have other plans tonight, Your Headlessness," Stevie muttered to herself, resuming driving.

She parked in front of her parents' garage, and their cars were inside of it like always. The rain had let up, the sun peeking out from the clouds.

Stevie grabbed the small sack of crystals for her mom, then rang the doorbell. A moment later the door opened wide, her mom wearing a bright smile and a flowing black dress decorated in ruby red cherries. Her silver hair was in pin curls, and deep red heels covered her feet.

"Well, aren't you dolled up." Stevie grinned.

"Your dad's taking me out for an early anniversary dinner," she said, brushing her hands down the skirt of her dress. The edges of her red lipstick-stained lips pulled into a frown when Stevie glanced over her shoulder to make sure Kit hadn't wandered back to eavesdrop. "Why do you look like you've seen a ghost? Pun intended."

Stevie's fingers tightened around the sack. "It's nothing. Just this ghost I came across after I left your place yesterday. He's shown up a couple of times, but he's gone now."

Her mom furrowed her brow, her expression becoming serious. "Is this some sort of pervert ghost? I swear on all of Sleepy Hollow if this man thinks because you two can see each other, he can—"

Stevie laughed and grasped her mom by the shoulders. "No, it's definitely not that. He wants help with a little unfinished business is all." He just seemed to have a hard time spilling the beans on what it was.

Her mom pressed her lips into a tight line. "There's something you're not telling me. I used to be the queen of lies, remember? What else is it?"

Stevie battled with herself on what to say, but she didn't want to weaken her mom's heart further since she'd been more tired than usual. If lie detector was a paranormal ability, her mom held that benefit. "It's nothing," Stevie said slowly. "The ghost was just in my car on the way here."

"*What?* So the ghost is stalking you now?" Her eyes widened and she ran a hand down the side of her face.

"Not exactly. He's only a nuisance and not dangerous to me. One positive aspect to note is it isn't like he's a demon or anything." Stevie told her pretty much the entire situation that had happened, about going into the abandoned house, and him following her home, only leaving out the detail about the ghost being the Headless Horseman.

"Well," her mom huffed. "Even if he's not a demon that doesn't mean anything. A ghost can still be an asshole. If this man or any other ghost fucks with you, I'll round up every witch I know and they won't like what's coming."

"Don't worry, I have it in check." She handed her mom the sack of crystals. "Oh, and here's your order. Lucia could've just given them to you for free."

"Nope, I'm not doing that. I'm helping my babies' shop make money." Stevie always liked how her mom considered Lucia to be one of her own.

"Fine. Have it your way." Stevie grinned.

Her mom winced and placed a hand over her chest.

"Is your heart all right?" Stevie grasped her mom's arm. "I knew I shouldn't have told you about the ghost."

"My heart is strong as a bull. You don't have to worry about me every month. When it's my time, it's my time. But it won't be any time soon. And always be honest with me—you know I won't ever judge you." She wrapped her arms around Stevie. "Now, I gotta finish getting ready for my date. I love you."

STEVIE PULLED into a parking spot in the back of the strip center where both the apothecary and comic book shop were located. She went inside her brother's store, finding Georgie—a woman in her mid-forties with a scarf covering her hair as usual since her gorgon ability could be a bit risky—at the front desk.

"Is Gideon in the back?" Stevie asked.

"He's at the antique shop next door, but he should be back any minute now." Georgie slapped her hands on the counter and pushed forward. "Did you hear about the Eye opening?"

Stevie nodded. "I did!" Amongst other things.

"I guess I'll find out if anyone I know is still lingering about at the next new moon."

"Definitely." A glimpse of white in the corner drew Stevie's attention, and she left Georgie to go and officially meet the store's resident ghost who was there more often than not. And when he was, he always had a comic book in his hand. The dead could touch and pick up things, but once they held them, they vanished from the living's sight—besides a seer's. So it wasn't like the movies where things mysteriously floated around.

She crept closer to the ghost who wore jeans and a T-shirt, his backpack beside him, and his fingers flipping through a comic. He was maybe close to thirty, his hair drawn back into a knot at his nape. Roxy always visited and let him pet her when she was with Stevie.

"Hey, you," Stevie said. "At last we can finally meet!"

The guy looked up from his comic and pointed at himself as he blinked. "You can already see me before the second Eye opens?" His face was all sharp angles, and a small bump rested along the bridge of his nose.

"Mm-hmm." Stevie stepped closer and skimmed her fingers across the top of the comics beside her.

"That means you're a—"

"Seer." She knelt next to him. "I wanted to thank you for being nice to my fox."

"She's yours?" he asked, a crooked canine showing. "She's a sweet little thing."

"Her name's Roxy in case you ever wondered." She peeked at the comic book in his hand. "What are you reading anyway?"

He held the withering comic up—*X-Men*. "I've read every issue multiple times."

"So has my brother," she said, then paused. "Any unfinished business you need help solving?"

"No, I like it here and have a few more comics to get through." He chuckled. "But a lot of the other ghosts are also waiting until after the new moon passes."

She stood and adjusted her purse. "That makes sense, and I'm sure I'd do the same thing. I'm Stevie, by the way."

"Erik."

"I'll see you later, Erik."

"If we could officially shake hands I would." He held up his translucent palms. "However, ghost and all."

She laughed just as a bell chimed throughout the store. Gideon came in, carrying two large boxes, and his gaze met Stevie's. "I know I needed you for something, but I can't even remember."

"Cauldron's teeth, Gideon!"

He set the boxes on the counter and ruffled her hair. "Nah, I remember, baby sister." Stepping behind the counter beside Georgie, he pulled out an envelope from the drawer. "Your stamps are here, so it looks like we're even-steven."

"You're the best. By the way, I found out your resident ghost's name. It's Erik." Stevie grinned. She opened the envelope to take a sneak peek as she headed toward the apothecary. Perfect condition.

As she entered Lucia's shop, a mixture of spicy scents

enveloped her. Lucia was organizing herbs on a back shelf, no other customers around at the moment.

"The town is seriously gearing up for the next Eye opening. You missed the crowd that was just here. Off subject though, look what Don next door got for us." Her sister-in-law pointed to an object wrapped in bubble wrap sitting beside a large cardboard box. "He cleaned out his mother's things. *Antiques.* Including that *head vase*." She drew out the last two words.

"Oh! One to cut my losses from yesterday." Stevie unraveled the bubble wrap from the ceramic. No chips. Perfect blonde hair. Yellow lacy hat. "How much?"

"Free. Of course."

"Before I get sucked in to what else is inside that box," Stevie started. "The salt is a no-go. Ants were eating it up like it was the greatest delicacy in existence, and the Horseman was in my car earlier."

One of Lucia's dark eyebrows rose. "He wanted you to drive him somewhere?"

"No, he was just being vague. No threats or anything though."

Her sister-in-law shrugged. "I say, just see what he wants, and then I can go from there. What's the harm in that? I think Sleepy Hollow has been wrong about him all along. It wouldn't be the first time in history an accused was a victim."

His vagueness didn't make Stevie want to sympathize with him just yet. "Kit said tonight we'll meet, but he'll have to wait until my date is gone." She set the vase on the counter. "I better deliver the rest of the orders so I can get ready for Reese. There is one ghost I need to help on the way though."

STEVIE HAD FINISHED DELIVERING the packages around town and the rest she mailed out. Before coming home, she'd stopped by the seafood restaurant and lured the ghost she'd seen a few nights ago to the grocery store. Unfinished business complete—the woman had officially moved on.

As Stevie wiped away the last speck of dust around the TV, the doorbell rang. There wasn't time to vacuum, so a couple of crumbs here and there would have to do. On the thumbs-up side, Roxy never left behind any ghost fur.

She opened the door to find Reese standing on the porch with a bottle of red wine in one hand and a sack of food in the other. He wore a blue button-up, short-sleeved shirt and loose jeans that didn't hug his thighs as well as Kit's. *Cauldron's teeth*. She wasn't going to that oddity of a place and shoved that thought into the furnace inside her mind where it could incinerate.

"Your favorite color is blue," Stevie said.

"It is. I shouldn't have made it so obvious."

With a smile, Stevie took the sack from Reese and motioned him inside. "Are you going to drink that whole bottle of wine yourself?"

Reese furrowed his brow, then sighed, seeming to remember her drink of choice. "Damn, I forgot you don't do wine."

"No, it's fine. That night was a bit hectic. We can eat in the kitchen." She led him to the table that was big enough to seat six people. The owner had left almost all of the kitchen things when Stevie moved in, which saved her from buying a rinky-dink table that would barely fit two people.

Reese sank into one of the chairs at the end, and she set down the bag in front of him before grabbing two glasses.

"Looks like the town is seriously getting ready for the second Eye to open, huh?" he said, taking out the two plastic containers from the bag.

"The cemetery will be the hot place to venture to that night. Are you going?" she asked, filling her glass with milk.

"Nah, I don't have the desire to. I don't see the point, you know?"

Oh... Something about his words took her back to her ex, remembering how he'd once said something similar. They both ate their burgers quietly, and she wasn't sure what to really talk about. Finally she chopped through the quiet with an invisible blade. "So, do you prefer Marvel or DC?"

"Marvel. You?" Reese leaned forward.

"I have a secret," Stevie whispered. "I don't really read comics or watch many of the movies."

"But you work with comics." He chuckled, taking a sip of wine from his glass.

"Only sometimes. Gideon's given me the CliffsNotes version on so many characters though." She grinned. "My main job is actually being a witch's assistant for Lucia."

"What does a witch's assistant do exactly?" Reese lifted a brow, his interest seeming piqued.

"I help her make brews and run deliveries around town. Much easier than brushing up on all the comic characters."

"No nightly séances then?" Reese cocked his head, studying her as if he were trying to read something.

"Not unless it was necessary but can't say we've done one of those yet. I'm not a witch if that's what you're thinking..." She waited for his curiosity to slip out further and nudge her about what other paranormal ability she might hold so she could just get it out of the way, but instead he only nodded and went in the opposite direction *entirely*.

"So, circling back to comics, how about I catch you up on one of the movies you haven't seen?"

Stevie inwardly cursed herself for bringing up the superhero subject earlier. "Sure. You can pick one for us to stream." She cleared the table while Reese headed into the living room.

As she sat next to him on the couch, she was close enough to finally take in his scent. It was a bit too beachy, but it wasn't unpleasant enough for her to send him packing.

Stevie handed him the remote to choose something. He then settled on one she hadn't seen, so she crossed her fingers that it wouldn't be completely awful.

Once the movie started, Stevie bit her lip, not knowing whether to inch closer to Reese, reach for his hand, or what. The only other first date she'd ever had was with her ex. When she was sixteen.

As the movie went on and on, dear witches, she wanted to fall asleep. She probably should've picked one she knew she liked, at least for these beginning stages. But Reese stayed captivated, not once pulling her to lean into him. It wasn't as if she was scooting closer either though.

"Is this fool truly your lover?" Kit said behind her, his tone bored. "He seems more aroused by this play in a box than the woman beside him."

"Cauldron's teeth!" Stevie startled but didn't turn around. She held back from correcting Kit that it was a *movie*. "That part got me good," she said to Reese, and he nodded, not really looking at her. At that moment she was relieved she hadn't told him about her ability yet, because on her life as a seer, she wouldn't dare want to tell him that the Headless Horseman was in her house, hovering right behind him. The date was already not going as planned. But thank this awful movie that they weren't tearing off each other's clothes before the Horseman had made his deathly silent entrance.

"Are you going to speak or pretend as though you don't see me again?" Kit said, his voice amused as he sat on her other side. Roxy barreled into the room and lowered herself near Kit's feet, not seeming to mind Stevie's scowl.

Traitor.

The credits of the movie rolled and Reese looked down at his watch. "I better go. I have an early start in the morning, but how about we get together next Tuesday night?"

"Sure, and I can bring you a meal this time," Stevie said as they stood from the couch.

"And I'll have milk for you."

"Is he feeding you like a damn infant?" Kit chuckled, low and deep.

While walking Reese to the door, she glared over her shoulder at Kit who'd followed them.

Reese stepped onto the porch and remained there for a beat too long before finally saying, "Tonight was nice."

She hesitated to give him a kiss but decided against it, not with the ghost snooping at her back.

"Well, have a good night," Stevie rushed the words out and shut the door. She narrowed her eyes at Kit as he now leaned against the wall, his arms folded. "Seriously, you could've at least waited for him to leave before interrupting my night."

"You were falling asleep already." Kit shrugged. "Besides, I told you I was coming tonight, didn't I?"

"And I told you I can't find your head to help you pass on." Stevie tapped at his broad chest, not caring that her finger went straight through him.

He pushed off the wall and lingered a hair's breadth from her. "Who said anything about passing on, Pumpkin? You will help me return to the living."

7

Stevie wasn't sure that she'd heard the Headless Horseman correctly. "You need *me* to help *you* return to the living?" she asked, incredulous. "I think it's a little too late for that, buddy. Do whatever unfinished business you have, forgive yourself for a misdeed, or *misdeeds*, you did in your past. You should then be able to move on to the ... wherever you'll be going."

"It isn't too late. You will help me." He said it in a way that meant the answer "no" would not be an option.

She pinched her lips together, forming a tight line. "I don't like your tone, Horseman. Besides, why would I bring you back to life or whatever when you could easily start taking heads from the living? Did you even think about that?"

"You're not making a lick of sense. Why would I go about slicing off people's heads if I have mine back? Did you even think about *that*?" Kit sat on the couch and reclined against the cushions, getting just as comfortable as he had the previous night.

He did have a point, but having everything they needed in life didn't stop psychopaths from committing horrific acts they'd grown used to doing. "Just make yourself at home, why don't you?"

The phone rang, and her brother's name showed up on the ID. She snapped it up as Kit leaned over to read the screen.

"Stop being nosey." Stevie shooed him away, then answered the call, keeping her voice even. "Yes? What does my big brother, who never rings me, need?" It was always texts or emails, usually only a couple of words unless it was about work.

"I was just checking if Mom seemed tired today when you saw her," Gideon said, his tone concerned. "She went to dinner then dancing with Dad, but when I stopped by to bring them the cookies Lucia made, she seemed more exhausted than ever around this time of the month."

Stevie thought about her mom earlier and how she'd grasped her chest. "A little, yeah. But I mean, she also did go dancing and she does have to get a new heart soon. She'll be all right. The heart this month might've not been as strong as the last." Ginger generally made sure not to pick one that had been the runt of the litter, but it was still anyone's guess how strong a heart could be.

"Yeah, I think that's it." He sounded more upbeat and like his normally positive self.

"Just let me know if anything changes with Mom though, and I'll be there in a nanosecond," Stevie promised.

"I will. Later, baby sister."

"What's wrong with your mother?" Kit asked from behind her, his deep voice rumbling in her ear.

"Seriously?" Stevie startled and whirled around to face him. "When did you get up from the couch? And why are you listening to my phone calls?"

"It's not my fault you don't pay attention to your surroundings and that you talk louder than anyone I've ever met." Kit shrugged. "But what is this about getting new *hearts*?"

"That's none of your business," she snapped.

"Mmm," Kit purred. "It sounds to me as if your mother takes

hearts once a month, yet you're offended about me reaping heads that are necessary. Seems a bit hypocritical on your part, Pumpkin."

Stevie scoffed and placed her hands on her hips. "Fine. My mom takes hearts. You take heads. You're two peas in a once-a-month pod. But my mom stopped eating human hearts before I was born. Now they are *pig* hearts. She was taught from an early age by her parents to feed to keep herself alive, so it was all she'd ever known. Also, she's repented, prays a lot."

Kit folded his arms over his chest, not saying a word, but she could feel his watchful, invisible gaze like a thick blanket of fog in the room.

Stevie held up a finger, her blood growing warm in her veins. "If you're rolling your eyes and cocking your head at me, I'll find a way to remove that invisible head from you. My sister-in-law is a witch, remember?"

He chuckled. "Not a good one if I can walk right in here."

Stevie was having enough of this conversation. He'd ruined her date, not that it had been going anywhere tonight, but that was beside the point. "You're a jackass," she ground out.

"Donkeys have a great ability to learn as well as an exceptional memory," Kit pointed out, the cockiness oozing from his alluring voice.

"Oh my God! Just stop talking."

"Tut, tut. It's not good to use the Lord's name in vain," he reprimanded, laughter still in his voice.

Stevie bit her tongue before she said anything else that would continue to lead in this never-ending, back-and-forth, nonsensical conversation where more asinine words would pour out from his invisible mouth. "Anyway, we're wasting time. Tell me what you need me to do, oh wondrous Horseman, to bring you back to the land of the living. And this isn't me agreeing to anything yet."

He sank down on her couch, then patted the spot beside him. She arched a brow at Kit, her feet planted where they were.

"Just sit down. It isn't as though I can touch you," he cooed.

His words were true... Stevie remembered how her hand had easily punched through his ghost form and not even a lick of coolness or warmth had brushed her skin. Regardless, she hesitantly sat down, ever so slowly, until she was two feet away from him. And yet, he'd been much closer to her a few seconds ago. "Here I am. So do continue, Your Headlessness."

Kit adjusted the sword at his waist before settling back into the cushions. "You're accurate that I can't find my head, but the story about that matter will come another time. Tonight, I need you to retrieve the rest of my bones. As I'm certain you know the dead are unable to touch remains." Just as they couldn't touch the living.

Stevie pinched the bridge of her nose and sighed. "Let me get this straight, you want me to go to the cemetery, dig up your grave, and become a felon in the process? Even though Sleepy Hollow is different than other towns in the world, the council won't allow it."

"Didn't you go into an abandoned house that doesn't belong to you?" Kit drawled.

Stevie really didn't have a problem going to a cemetery and doing something the council was against if a ghost needed it to fulfill an important task—it was because *he* was asking her. But... If the Headless Horseman returned to the living, he'd be less dangerous since he wouldn't be an immortal ghost. He'd be mortal, could bleed, could die, which might turn him right back into a ghost... For now, it was a way to help the dead, not just Kit.

Kit tapped his fingers against his knee, and she couldn't remove her gaze from his digits, wondering what they looked like beneath his gloves. Why did he wear them anyway? It wasn't like he had fingerprints to leave behind. But she couldn't help but notice how his digits were long, graceful, and ... what was wrong with her? They were *fingers* for witches' sake.

"Fine," she relented, "we'll go to the cemetery."

Kit's fingers stopped drumming and he scooted nearer. "Who

said anything about us going to the cemetery? You're rather presumptuous."

"Then where are they?" she asked. "If they're at the Sleepy Hollow museum, then fat chance you're going to get me to break in there. Even if we get past the witches' spells, they have cameras *everywhere*. We would be spotted in no time."

"You said your sister-in-law is a witch? I'm certain she could easily make it so you're unseen, but we don't need her for this task." Kit paused, leaning closer, his voice softer as if telling her a secret. "My bones aren't there—they are hidden at the abandoned house."

Stevie wrinkled her nose, recalling how the only bones she'd come across were the chicken ones in the attic. "Where? And why are they there instead of the cemetery?"

Kit sighed. "If I could've seen the living before the Eye opened, I could tell you the precise story, but I can only assume someone dug up my remains and hid them there. During the day I used to linger wherever I wished. Then it altered when my bones were disturbed and I was trapped during the day at the house on this road, drawn to my remains. But at night I would ride, searching for my head. That all changed when the Eye of the Hollow opened and I could again leave whenever I wish."

That made sense somewhat... "So where are the bones buried? In the back or the front yard?"

"Neither." He stretched his back and adjusted his cape. "They're in the basement, Pumpkin."

The way he said it nonchalantly rubbed her the wrong way, and she knew he still wasn't telling her something. "I swear on every ghost in Sleepy Hollow if you're lying to me about any of this, I will find a way to rip that invisible head of yours off and make sure you can't get another one."

"So violent." He chuckled before continuing, "I don't have a reason to lie to you about any of this. A living person, *you*, is what I need. The only one I've come across who can see me."

"Really, you could've waited until the second Eye opened to

talk to someone else. But whatever, let's get this over with," Stevie said, pushing up from the cushions to help the dead. "I'll grab flashlights, then you can lead the way."

The part of Kit's neck that was there bobbed, signaling a nod of agreement. He then stood from the couch before slipping through the wall.

Roxy, who'd remained silent the entire time, perked up from her place on the floor to follow Kit.

"No, stay here, girl," Stevie instructed. "The house seemed safe enough when I was there, but keep here just in case. Lucia can feel your presence if she needs to follow you to me."

Roxy let out a low whine.

"If I'm not back in a few hours, then you can come check on me. Deal?"

The fox barked her agreement and rolled to her back. Stevie left the room to collect two flashlights from the kitchen drawer. One for now, and another for backup in case the batteries went dead.

Kit lingered out front, his back against a tree, his body rigid with what might've been impatience. "Took you long enough."

Stevie rolled her eyes, the cool wind tousling her curls. "Sorry, I don't easily float through walls and can't see well in the dark."

"Come." Kit started walking ahead, his cape billowing from the breeze, his ethereal white hue aglow. Above, in the night sky, the ruby of the open Eye shone down on Sleepy Hollow. A light fog, maybe an inch tall, swayed against the ground.

"So," Stevie called, catching up to Kit's side. "Since you've said you take heads for a purpose, do you feel any remorse?" Her mom had once told her that she used to not have shame over what she'd done—it was about survival. But after she met Stevie's dad, things started to change, and once they'd moved to Sleepy Hollow, her conscience weighed more on her.

"Hmm." Kit rubbed his invisible jaw. "I don't think we're fond enough of one another to have deep conversations just yet."

"Only having me dig up your bones. Got it." Stevie gave him a false smile and a sarcastic thumbs-up.

"That's the first step, yes," he said, edging ahead of her to cross through the front of the abandoned house before she could argue.

Stevie pushed open the door, a repeat of last time. Flipping the flashlight switch on, she swept the yellow glow around the room to make sure they were alone.

"No one's here. Dead or living." A smile was in Kit's voice as he added, "Unless you consider me."

"That's the only good news of this night, it seems." Stevie's shoulders relaxed, and he led her toward the basement. She descended the wooden steps, each one creaking louder than the last. Dust pluming around her tickled her nose, the air damp against her skin. A musty odor permeated the basement, much stronger than anything upstairs. She sneezed as her gaze drifted toward the window.

A board covered the small rectangle and she tore it off to let the moonlight filter into the large room from the iron bars guarding the glass.

Stevie roamed her flashlight around the basement, catching on nothing of importance as she searched. Only a rusted water heater near the AC. All that was left of the washer and dryer were frayed cords, the appliances most likely hauled away ages ago. Cement walls lined the room except for one that was fully bricked, its color a reddish hue.

"I don't see a single bone anywhere," Stevie muttered, guiding her flashlight across the space one more time. "If they're buried under the foundation we'll need a jackhammer. Even then, my weak little arms couldn't operate one to retrieve them any time soon." She focused her light on the AC and water heater—unless they were hidden in there. That could easily be doable.

"No, they aren't buried down there," Kit said, patting his hand against the wall. "The bones are just behind these bricks."

Stevie lifted her light to where his hand rested, looking for any sign of an opening. The wall might've been added at some point to specifically hide the Headless Horseman's bones. But why?

She traced her fingers over the wall, along the mortar between the bricks, trying to find something like a door that would budge as she pushed. Nothing gave way. Not until she reached the portion near the bottom where a sliver of mortar was missing. She wrapped the tips of her fingers around the brick and tugged. It didn't budge. And she had a pretty big hunch it was *spelled*.

"I have an idea!" Stevie stood and brushed the dust from her hands. "Give me a couple minutes, and I'll be right back."

Hurrying home, Stevie snatched a vial and needle from the kitchen pantry before hauling butt back down to the basement of the abandoned house. Uncorking the vial, she spread Lucia's spelled liquid around the seal of the bricks, then pricked her finger.

"Your sister-in-law taught you this, I'm assuming," Kit stated when she pressed the droplet of blood to the seal. A spicy scent filled the air and tiny smoky hands dug at the previous spell, appearing like zombie arms battling away at dirt to come out of their graves.

"I can't create or make spells, but from being her assistant, I do know my blood can break a good number of them with this brew. Lucia made it for me when I purchased a sealed box at an estate sale, where I'd been hoping to find some unusual antiques. The contents were old love letters, so the reward had been a lost cause." Stevie brought a finger to her lips. "Don't tell anyone I have this since it's something she would never sell in her apothecary."

"You have my word."

With a small smile, she tugged on the bricks, and it wasn't one brick that shifted but several rows of them. Like a hidden door, except that the stuck-together bricks pulled all the way out from the wall in one large rectangle.

A cloud of dust stormed out and Stevie covered her mouth while hacking up a lung. She swiped her hand through the air, then held up the flashlight.

Stevie's stare landed on something black—a metal trunk. "Score!"

Kit attempted to haul it out, but his hands passed through the box since his bones were inside. Stevie gripped the side handle and pulled the trunk from the hidden space. It was like a pirate's wet dream of a chest, jewels embedded along the top.

A small golden plaque was displayed on the front. Wiping away the thick layer of dust, she read the quote aloud: *The Headless Horseman darkens the sky!*

"If people believe that, I can see why you believed me to be a demon," Kit said sarcastically.

Stevie rolled her eyes and brushed her fingers against the lock, rattling it. Of course it didn't break... "Come on, Horseman, looks like we'll have to bring the loot home to get your bones out of this beast."

8

Stevie lugged the trunk down the sidewalk toward her home, the fog now creeping around her ankles. The trunk was heavier than she'd expected and definitely more than the twenty pounds a skeleton normally weighed—one of the facts she'd learned in an anatomy class that she never thought she would need to know. If her science teacher could only see her now, she might've changed that B to an A.

She studied Kit's tall frame, his broad shoulders, his narrow hips, his strong thighs. He wasn't a giant, only a healthy male ghost with a pleasant body that she needed to stop staring at. She flicked her gaze away when he turned in her direction and she began whistling "Fifteen Men On A Dead Man's Chest."

"Yo-ho-ho, just getting into pirate mode here." Stevie rolled her eyes to herself, her cheeks heating.

"Do continue. I won't stop you," Kit said.

"I was only offering the teaser version." She hefted the trunk higher, concluding that either the metal was super-duper heavy or something else was packed inside with his bones.

Roxy bolted toward them from the yard, her mouth pulled back into a smile, happy for their return. Stevie struggled to fish out the key from her pocket. "You might not be able to carry the trunk, but can't you be a proper gentleman and get the door?" she grunted, the trunk tilting sideways while she waited on the porch.

"All you had to do was ask, Pumpkin. Don't put yourself in these conundrums." Kit shrugged and slipped into the house.

"Conundrums, he says," she mumbled between gritted teeth as the lock turned, the door opening wide.

"My lady." He motioned her inside with what she assumed was a mock bow. She really, *really* wished she could see his expressions.

"Thank you, good sir," Stevie drawled and brought the trunk into the living room, sweat slicking her palms as she placed the metal beast on top of the coffee table. She knelt on the floor while fiddling with the gold metal lock dangling on the front. "Do you know how to pick this?" she asked, glancing back at Kit.

"No." He took a seat on the couch and leaned toward the lock, his hand passing through it.

"Of course you don't." She sighed. "I'm the one doing all the work here for a man who has only thrown a couple of bread-crumbs of secrets at me."

"I can't reveal everything to a woman who so easily would've cursed me to the Hollow with a crucifix, now can I? You'll have to *gain* my trust." His voice came out sultry, deeper than usual.

She scoffed. "Were you this annoying when you were alive?"

He chuckled, ignoring her comment. "And what about you, Pumpkin? Do *you* know how to pick a lock?"

"Well, no. That's why I asked you." Stevie frowned, shaking the lock one more time, hoping it would just break off.

"Seems we're even, so get rid of that line between your brows." His gloved finger ran up the spot, and her response was more delayed to duck back than she'd expected. For whatever stupid reason, she'd wanted to find out if he would be warm or cool to the touch.

"Put that dirty finger of yours away," Stevie grumbled. She

surveyed the room, thinking of something she could use. There wasn't a crowbar simply lying around, not that she knew if she could even use one properly on this. She grabbed a knife from the kitchen and as she slid it into the slit of the trunk, then put her weight onto it, the blade broke from the handle.

Stevie was about to look up how to break a padlock on her phone but decided to just go next door to wake Lucia to spell it to open. As she walked to the door, Kit said silkily, "I do believe you can just unscrew the backing of the padlock."

Her eyes bulged and she spun around, her gaze falling to the four screws that her idiot self hadn't noticed. "How long have you known *that?*"

"I assumed a tool was what you were getting from the kitchen and when you returned with a pitiful knife, I figured I'd wait and see how this played out. It didn't go very well," he replied, amusement in his voice.

Stevie shot him a glare. "You're seriously driving me crazy. Hold on." She riffled through the kitchen drawer, past junk and the tool kit her dad had given her, until she found a screwdriver. "Ah ha!"

Sinking back to the floor in the living room, Stevie worked on the first screw. She fumbled a few times, seeing as the little pest was in there tightly.

"So, where do you keep your jack-o'-lantern?" she asked as she finally got the first one out, the screw clinking against the wooden table.

"Hmm." He tsked. "I call on him when it's time to replace my head."

"That's weird. Sounds like witchy magic was involved in this. I don't think you're a warlock though, so someone helped you before." Stevie blew out a breath as she removed the second screw. He still hadn't uttered a word. "Your silence means I'm right. I'll get your secrets out soon enough." She would pester him about them until he told her or he was so annoyed he'd never come back.

"You think so?" A smile lingered in his voice.

"Oh, I know so." She grinned, setting the third screw on the table. "How did you come across your horse?"

"Why?" he cooed.

"Because I don't see any other ghosts riding horses." Her hand slipped on the last screw while turning it. "Okay, these screws are getting on my nerves. I should've just woken Lucia."

"You could've asked for my assistance," Kit said.

Stevie arched a brow at him. "You could've mentioned that five minutes ago, and anyway, it wouldn't have worked," she grunted, pulling the last screw out.

The padlock easily came off, the scraping sound echoing off the walls. Holding her breath in anticipation, her heart thundering, she pressed her hands on either side of the metal lid and drew it open.

Stevie blinked as she gazed into the box's depths, her breath slowly coming out, her eyes widening.

"Your head is in the way. Do you see my bones?" Kit asked.

A loud snort escaped her while she sifted through the trunk's contents. "Not yet, but you've got to see this, Kit! Get over here." She scooted to the side and made room for him to sink down beside her.

Stevie lifted a straw doll swathed in black clothing and a long cape, its head missing. She shoved the doll into Kit's invisible face and grinned. "It resembles you perfectly."

"That's just appalling," Kit muttered, taking the doll from her and rolling it over in his gloves as he inspected it.

Stevie reached in and fished out four bulky books and set them in front of him. All different versions of the *Legend of Sleepy Hollow*. A stack of pictures with a disintegrated rubber band around them came next. They were of someone dressed as the Headless Horseman years ago. Below that, a heavy snow globe showcased the Horseman on his mighty black steed inside the glass.

Adding to the collection was a film reel with a yellowed,

peeling sticker on the front of the 1949 movie, a dinner set consisting of plates and teacups—the Horseman painted on them—and a sack full of handmade items.

"It looks like you had a hardcore fan," Stevie snickered, then sobered as her fingers brushed a large wooden box at the bottom.

Beside her, Kit's body stilled when she pulled out the box and attempted to open it. But it wouldn't budge. "I can't get it open." There wasn't a lock or anything on it, and she knew at once a spell had been cast on this too. "Give me a second." Stevie repeated her motions as she did with the basement wall by using Lucia's brew and a drop of her blood. A spicy aroma brushed her nose and smoke swirled through the air.

When she pressed on the lid again, this time it lifted, an earthy scent striking her senses, not reeking of death as she'd expected. "Yep, these are definitely bones. And if you say they're yours, then I'm going to take the risk and trust you on that." She scanned over the pale remains and her eyes glued onto what had to be a femur. Most she couldn't remember the names of. "I don't know if they're all here though. If you need me to count I can. Off the top of my head, I remember a skeleton has 206 bones, but I'm not sure how many should be here since a skull isn't one bone."

"178," he said, his tone assured, and so she would go with his answer and maybe verify it on her phone later. "Take them out and I'll count to confirm they're all here."

Stevie rolled her eyes. "Yes, Your Headlessness."

"You are *amusing*."

The edges of her lips curled up as she moved the trunk onto the floor to give them room at the table. She slowly took out one bone after the other while Kit counted aloud and she mirrored his numbers inside her head. While she knew only a few of the names of the bones, he spouted off every single one. She wondered if in his living days he'd been a doctor or something close.

Plucking the last one from the sack—another rib—she asked when curiosity finally got the best of her, "How do you know all these names?"

"My father was a physician," he said. "178."

"My dad's a dentist, and I don't even know all the names of the teeth. But guess what? All the bones are here!" she sang the last sentence, running her finger against the rib. Kit shivered beside her and her lips parted. "Can you *feel it* when I touch them?"

"Mm-hmm," he drawled.

"Oh, sorry about that." Stevie dropped his bone onto the pile, cursing herself for unintentionally caressing it. Thank the witches it wasn't a hip or thigh bone.

"No complaints from me." Kit's voice came out gruffer than she'd expected, and he cleared his throat as he handed her the wooden box. "I need you to hide them here in your home until it's time to use them."

"And how long do you expect me to keep them under wraps from prying eyes?" Stevie lifted an eyebrow while using a velvet cloth from the trunk's contents to pick up each bone and place them gently into the box.

"My head needs to be found before the next full moon."

"I'm not a detective, and I'm pretty sure that almost every witch has attempted to locate it at one time or another. I mean, even Lucia played a game with her friends when she was younger to see who could win by finding it first. And you know what happened? Nothing. No one uncovered it." She tilted her head, mulling something over. "What happened to your head anyway? Was it like in the story? You do know the story, right?"

He drummed his fingers against the table. "I know there is one. I would be a fool not to know when there's a statue of me near the old church."

If he didn't know accurately, then he needed to. So she broke down the story and movies for him to see what matched and what didn't. "You and your horse are both translucent white instead of swathed in black. That's one difference I know. Oh, and I guess you can only play with ghosts, not the living. So two things."

"Everything you've heard is preposterous," Kit scoffed. "A cannonball taking my head with it? Pitiful."

She would loop around to that another time since it wasn't important right now. "Then if you can feel me touching your bones, why couldn't you at some point feel someone holding your head? You did know the bones were at the abandoned house without touching them as well."

"For someone who is a witch's assistant, you should've uncovered that by now."

"Witchy vibes," she whispered. "That makes more sense. So someone hid your head with magic. But why?"

"That is a good question, isn't it?" he said. "Now, where are you going to hide my bones?"

Stevie knew the best place to store them for the time being —the back of her closet in a safe that was spelled to keep her most valued collections extra protected.

"You owe me." Stevie shut the box and carried it into her room with Kit hot on her heels. She pushed the clothes in her closet aside to get to the large safe. After she spun the combination lock to the correct numbers, she removed her special boxes of coins, stamps, and collector cards, then placed the bones into the empty space. Shutting the door, she draped a blanket over it to make the safe a little more hidden before moving her clothes to cover it. "There."

"Thank you. I'll find a way to return the favor," Kit promised.

She blinked. "Oh, I don't need a favor. I'm just doing my Sleepy Hollow duty and helping ghosts' heads remain intact."

"Good night." He brought two fingers up to his invisible mouth and released a high-pitched whistle.

Stevie covered her ears. "I think you just blew out my eardrums. How about you warn me in advance next time?"

"If it's necessary." He chuckled.

Before she answered him with a snarky reply, his horse whinnied outside her bedroom window. Eyes widening, she shoved the curtains aside. The white glow of the ghost illuminated her backyard. "It's your stallion!" she gasped, lifting the window. Up close, the horse was like a sculpted art piece, beautiful, its eyes shining brighter than candle flames. She'd never paid attention to its striking details before, not even the other night when she'd been too busy watching Kit reap a head.

When Kit didn't respond, she turned around to find him gone from her room. She glanced back out the window, and he stood only a couple of millimeters from her, startling her.

"Please don't do that again," she groaned.

"I'll call on you soon," he said. "Time is of the essence, and I must continue my search. Keep my bones safe, Pumpkin."

"I thought you needed my help?" Stevie should just want to get rid of him, but after tonight, she'd only grown more curious. Itching to find out more. And she bet that was exactly what he'd wanted. Either way, she wasn't a ghost that could stay awake for twenty-four hours and endlessly search for his head. Needing sleep was a downside of being a part of the living.

"In due time. Tonight I have Inferno to guide me." Kit backed away from her and stroked his horse's mane. He easily mounted the stallion, his powerful thighs pressing against the animal's body. Without another word, the horse bolted forward, Kit's cape flapping in the air. They slipped straight through the fence—the specks of white light vanished from sight.

Stevie shut the window and drew the curtains closed. Roxy's feet padding against the wooden floor sounded behind her.

"What a night, huh, Foxy Roxy?" Stevie plopped down on the mattress and patted the spot beside her.

As Roxy curled up next to her, a strange feeling formed in the pit of Stevie's stomach. She sucked in a sharp breath when she realized something. Kit had whistled for his stallion, and the horse had answered his call... She remembered his words from the other night, *Your tiny fox is all yours, Pumpkin. I prefer to claim stallions as mine.* And then... *He comes when I desire it.*

If she ever needed Roxy, Stevie knew she would come to her if she whistled, hearing the call from anywhere she was. It wasn't just any horse ... it was a *ghost sidekick*.

And only seers had those.

9

Roxy rolled on the floor, playing with a ball of yarn like a baby kitten as Stevie looked at the list of items that were sold overnight from the apothecary. Stevie stood over the cauldron in Lucia's basement and tossed a few wilted petals into the spelled lavender liquid, then pricked her finger to add one drop of blood. Once she stirred the contents, a sweet scent wafted through the air and the color changed from lavender to a light shade of blue.

With this particular spell, the magical brew could be used for several things. Hair color that lasted a year without roots ever showing—the one Stevie hands down would continue to always choose—a lie detector test for up to three questions, and one broom levitation.

Stevie poured the brew into containers before packaging them up, then worked on the other requests for crystals, candles, bat wings, chicken eyes, and wolf hair. She took the last clove candle and would start on a fresh batch when she returned. But she needed to swing by the apothecary since one of the jars was out of black crystals to complete the order. She already needed to go in that area for her brother anyway.

The cauldron continued to bubble, its fire not hot to the

touch even though it easily heated what was inside the iron. Eventually, Lucia and Gideon were going to get a bigger place like Ginger's since there wasn't room to keep livestock that were necessary for certain spells. Lucia wouldn't want to spend forever running to her aunt's house to fetch a fresh ingredient that she didn't have lying around.

Roxy hopped in the passenger seat of the car beside Stevie, and they headed to her brother's store first.

Gideon popped his head out from the back room. "Give me a few minutes. I didn't know you were coming this early," he grunted.

"You said the packages were literally ready."

"I thought they would be, but you know how that is." He shrugged, his hand skating down his beard.

Stevie rolled her eyes and found Roxy in the corner of the store beside Erik, her head resting on his leg. He pored over a comic and ran his fingers through the fox's fur. Her chest tight-ened—she'd give anything if she could pet her sidekick.

"Have you still not spotted the Horseman anywhere?" Stevie had dropped by the store more frequently for Gideon and had asked Erik each time. He at least didn't freak out from such a simple question as most of the other ghosts had. Besides the kid ghosts—they didn't seem to care.

"No, he still hasn't made his presence known from what I can tell. It's odd, isn't it?" It really was.

It had been two weeks since she'd seen or even heard Kit riding his horse down any streets. She'd assumed he would've slipped back into her life the day after he left, but he hadn't. The *soon* he'd given her wasn't very specific. Although he'd said he needed his head before the next new moon...

Ever since the idea of him being a seer had popped into her mind, she'd been anxious to confirm it. And if he was a seer, then she wanted to know why he'd hidden it, why he'd told her he hadn't seen anyone until after the Eye opened. If there was a chance he really hadn't seen the living before that, then why could the stallion still hear his whistle? Too many questions and a lack of answers.

"What are you reading this time?" she asked, kneeling on the other side of Erik.

"Your brother just got a couple of these in," he said with a smile and held up a *Sleepy Hollow* graphic novel.

Stevie squinted at the pumpkins surrounding the Headless Horseman on the front. "How is it?"

"Dreadful." He chuckled, setting aside the graphic novel on top of his backpack. "I'm about to sift through the rest of the new stash."

"Let me give you one to try." Stevie grinned and stood. She scanned the letters until she got to the "S" category and fished out a 1990s issue. "See if you like this. I used to read the Sabrina comics all the time when I was younger."

Erik took the comic and opened it to the first page. "This is taking me out of my comfort zone, you know."

"That can be a good thing." She laughed. "Just put it back when you're finished or Gideon will flip out."

He saluted her. "Yes, ma'am."

"All right, the boxes are officially packed and ready," Gideon called.

"I gotta go, but I'll see you next time." She gestured to Roxy. "Come on, girl."

Stevie took the boxes and went out the back to load them into her trunk. Gideon had told her it would only be a couple when he should've said ten, but she stuffed them in.

As she entered the apothecary, the familiar scents of herbs surrounding her, Lucia looked up from the counter. "Still no word from the…" Her sister-in-law pretended to remove her head from her shoulders.

"Still zero word from him." Each night, Stevie had wasted time and gas driving through Sleepy Hollow to search for Kit. When she wasn't doing that, she'd open her closet to see if he was there during the day since before the Eye opened he'd linger near his bones. No sign of him had been there either. And then she was frustrated with herself for questioning that something might've happened to him. She'd wondered if he'd found his head and passed on—she'd even tried one of Lucia's contact the dead spells that only worked for Heaven. There'd been no answer from up above. So it was either he was still a ghost or he'd ended up in the Hollow...

"Hmm. Well, if he found his head, you would know." Lucia shrugged. "I don't think he passed on."

Stevie shrugged in return. "Maybe... But I need to talk to him. I've never met another seer before, and if he is one..."

"Then what? You share seer ghost stories? Just because I see another witch doesn't really mean much. But I get it. You want to know more about his story. And hexed flames, I'm nosy enough to want to know too. I don't have anything of his to perform a spell where he would feel you calling him or I'd do it."

"I do."

Lucia arched a brow. "What do you have of his?"

Stevie lifted a crystal from the counter and turned it over in her hand. "I have his bones. Some witch or warlock had them spelled at the abandoned house."

"What?" Lucia hissed. "And you kept this from me?"

"I didn't want you to tell Gideon." She sighed. "We know what a big mouth he has and he'd blab it to my parents. I don't want Mom stressed." Her energy seemed fine after she'd gotten the new heart, but Stevie didn't want her to worry.

"I don't tell him *everything*." She placed a hand on her hip. "Okay, well maybe a lot of things, but my lips are zipped on this. I'll come by your place after work and see what I can do."

"All right. I'll see you then." If it didn't work, and Kit never slinked back into her life, what would she even do with his bones? Just take them back to the basement of the abandoned house?

Roxy had decided to stay at the shop with Lucia to watch her cast scheduled protection spells.

After Stevie added the black crystal to the customer's package and shut the trunk, she noticed she'd missed a text from Reese.

I'm back in town and was checking to see if you wanted to come over tonight? Sorry the past few weeks have been insane.

Stevie smiled. *What time?*

Does 7 sound good?

Yep. See you then!

She'd been too busy with both her jobs and wondering where Kit had burrowed himself to think too much about Reese. He'd had to cancel their previous planned date because of a meeting in New York City.

Before Stevie opened her car door to leave, she caught a flutter of flowing white from her periphery. "Where in all of Sleepy Hollow have you been?" She paused when it wasn't a cape billowing but a long bridal veil trailing across the pavement. "Oh, sorry, I thought you were someone else."

The ghost halted and spun to face Stevie, tears streaming down her pale cheeks. She was young, maybe nineteen, her hair long and curled to her waist, her gown silky with a lacy hem and matching sleeves. It was the bride Stevie had seen pacing up and down the sidewalk for years now, usually lingering in front of the church near the end of the street. Always crying and occasionally screeching like a banshee.

"Can you help me?" the ghost pleaded. "A little girl with balloons told me you might be able to."

Stevie had passed the little girl each day she drove this way, once stopping to ask her about the Headless Horseman. "Possibly," she said slowly, hesitant that she would need Stevie to dig up her bones too. There were only so many bones she could store at her house. "How can I help you?"

"I was supposed to meet my fiancé for our wedding, but I was running late," she sobbed. "An envious old bittie murdered me. Cara was supposed to be my friend. I just need to tell him why I was late. My name is Joanie Wilcher."

Stevie hadn't heard of her before. "What's his name?" she asked, lifting her phone to search.

"Don Worthington."

Stevie's brows shot up her forehead. "Don who runs the antique place right here?"

Joanie straightened, wiping the tears from her cheeks as her face brightened. "Maybe? He was a teacher when we were to be married. First year."

"You know what, we'll find out right now. Come on." Stevie motioned a finger for Joanie to follow her toward the antique store nestled between Lucia and Gideon's shops. As she opened the door, the scent of mothballs and peppermint clung to the air.

She weaved through the aisles and shelves filled with glass figurines, old cameras, tin cans, and other treasures. Behind a small glass cabinet, near one of the side walls, sat Don in his leather recliner. His glasses were perched on the edge of his nose while he read a car magazine. Most of his gray hair was gone except for a smidge dipping down from the tops of his ears and around the back of his head.

"Hey, Don," Stevie said, stopping in front of the counter. She hadn't been there in a few weeks, but she usually came in often to see what new finds he'd come across.

He pushed up from the chair, a few of his bones popping as he approached the counter. "I've got a batch of stamps coming in next week."

Stevie wouldn't pass that opportunity up. "You know I'll be back for that. But I have something else to tell you. I'm a seer."

"Tell him it's Joanie," the ghost said hurriedly, shifting from one foot to the other.

"And I'm a werewolf. I normally keep that the full moon's secret." Don smiled, showing yellowing teeth while adjusting his glasses up the bridge of his nose.

Stevie wouldn't have ever guessed that tidbit about him since he always seemed so calm. "I came across someone who knows you. She's with me. A bride. Her name is Joanie Wilcher. She wants you to know she didn't leave you at the alter—she was murdered by her friend Cara."

His eyes widened. "Joanie is here?"

Stevie nodded.

"Cara died fifteen years ago," Don ground out. "No one knew Joanie was murdered. We all thought she didn't want to marry me and ran away because of my werewolf situation." He paused, his throat bobbing. "Will you ask her if she'll stay with me until the second Eye opens? I'll help her with anything she needs on that night. I just want to talk to her, to see her." Tears gathered on his lashes.

Joanie clasped her hands in front of her. "I will. Of course I will."

"She will, and I won't say anything else so she doesn't pass on sooner than expected. I'll talk to you soon." Stevie glanced over her shoulder while walking away. "And definitely hold onto those stamps for me."

Joanie now stood behind the counter beside Don, her hand pressing through his. It was like one of those magical Hallmark movie moments.

Stevie drove from the shopping strip and parked the car when she approached the bridge where she'd seen Kit during the last new moon, thinking that maybe he might be hanging around there for whatever reason.

But he wasn't.

As she neared the creek, only a single ghost hovered over the flowing water. She was maybe five and clapping at a boat sailing on top of the water.

"Do you know if the Headless Horseman's come through here? He's usually on a stallion. No head." Stevie motioned at her own and the little girl blinked. "No stranger danger here."

"He hasn't been here, but can you help me with my boat?" she begged, pointing toward it.

"Sure." Stevie knew it wasn't the little girl's actual boat from when she'd died. It must've belonged to someone who'd recently left it, but maybe this would help her pass on. The cool water brushed Stevie's ankles when she stepped into the creek and she plucked up the boat, then placed it into the girl's awaiting palms. "Here you go."

A second later, the girl's translucent color faded until she was no longer there. Stevie smiled at a job well done.

STEVIE SAT on the edge of her bed, wearing dark jeans and a black and white striped button-up blouse for her date with Reese. Roxy lay beside her, glued to her side as she'd been since coming home from the apothecary.

Once Lucia had got there, Stevie took one of Kit's small finger bones from the safe for her sister-in-law to spell.

Kit had been a no-show.

Stevie's fist remained tight around the bone even after Lucia left, and she tried Kit's name again to get his headless self to return to her home. But he didn't come.

Heaving a sigh, she tucked his finger bone into her pocket before heading to Reese's. After the date was over, she would take the bone out and try searching the night one more time for him. And if she couldn't find him, then game over, and he could stay lost to the ghost world if that was his choice. She shouldn't be this worried about wanting to ask about his seeing ability anyway. Was that even the only reason? *Yes, yes it was*, she told herself.

"Come get me if Kit shows up here while I'm gone," Stevie said to Roxy and grabbed her purse.

She took the moped and drove toward Reese's house. The fog was thicker than it had been over the last few weeks, swirling around the tops of her wheels like a cauldron of bats. Never before had the town of Sleepy Hollow had straight days of fog like this where it hadn't let up. The council had said it was due to the Eye being open and once it closed, the fog would dissipate.

This was the first time Stevie had seen Reese's home as she turned into his driveway. His two-story house appeared neat and tidy. Everything about it was pristine and proper, not a leaf or a trimmed bush out of place. Even the trees' branches were perfect. No statues rested in the garden as if even one would make it too cluttered.

Stevie rang the doorbell and he answered a couple of seconds later wearing a T-shirt and jeans. He appeared more relaxed than she'd seen him before, yet her heart didn't accelerate as it should've to see him.

"I'm glad you could make it," Reese said and gestured her inside. "The pizza's already here. You look cute by the way."

"Thanks! You look cute yourself." She smiled awkwardly.

Modern metal decorations covered the walls, much different than her antique things. The kitchen was the first room they came across—more metal pieces hung beside cherry-stained cabinets.

He led her into the living room, and she removed her jacket before laying it on the leather arm of the couch. She sank down on the cushions in front of the pizza box awaiting her on top of the coffee table. Reese returned with two glasses of soda, and he stilled once he handed one to her. "Oh shit. Milk, right?" It wasn't a big deal—it was only *milk*—but she already knew the type of wine he drank. So was he even really that into her? Was she interested in him anymore? Whatever spark had possibly been there the first night had rapidly fizzled.

"It's fine." She shrugged.

"All right, but let me know otherwise," he said, giving her the remote. "Your movie choice tonight."

"*Oh*. Seems I have all the control in the world," Stevie teased. She scrolled through the movies until she came across one she could watch over and over. "Let's go with *Scott Pilgrim vs. the World*."

As the comedy played, she noticed Reese was the one nodding off this time. She contemplated kissing him to determine if there should even be another date, or if they should just remain in the friend zone. She scooted closer, the leather couch practically screeching beneath her, and she winced at her attempt to be smooth.

Reese straightened, his arm slipping around her, and no supernatural beings threw a party in her stomach at his touch. She grasped his face and turned it toward her, his eyes hooded.

Here we go... Any minute... Do something, Stevie, instead of looking at him like an idiot!

A horse's hooves pounded in the distance, and she jerked up, her hands leaving his face like she'd been burned. "I-I'm sorry, I need to go." Stevie scrambled off the couch and grabbed her purse.

"Already?" He furrowed his brow.

"It's just this thing I forgot about. I'm so sorry. Can you text me later?" Without a decent goodbye, Stevie flew out the door and started her moped. She sped to the end of the street, the fog slipping up to her shins. Near the end of the neighborhood, she slowed to a stop and turned off the engine to listen. The sound of hooves against pavement had died, leaving only silence.

"Where did he go?" she whispered.

A horse whinnied behind her and she whirled around to find Kit and Inferno, their ethereal white glow shining brightly.

"Seriously," Stevie hissed and got off the moped to walk toward him. "I told you not to just creep up on me like that!" She wouldn't admit it aloud, but she was relieved he had.

"I felt your call. Lucia helped you, I presume?" he said, sliding down from his horse.

"Where have you been? None of the ghosts I've asked have even seen you."

"Time got away from me, I suppose." He shrugged. "I've been in the woods, searching and thinking, attempting to recall things. It's where I was murdered. But I take it you missed me,

Pumpkin?" Behind his invisible mask, he was smirking and she knew it.

"Murdered?" she gasped. "You could've told me that before!"

"And would your nobleness have kicked in that first night, leaving you wanting to help me out of the kindness of your pretty heart?" he drawled.

"Well, yes!" she whisper-shouted. "You also didn't tell me you were a *seer*!"

"About that..." Kit's voice drifted out soft as silk. "I suppose it's time for some of the story then, isn't it?"

10

Kit sauntered away from Stevie toward his horse, and she called out, "I thought we were going to start a campfire and have story time?"

"You're an impatient little thing, aren't you?" He chuckled as he mounted his stallion. "I'll meet you at your home."

Stevie frowned but started her moped and rode beside Kit to her house. Up above in the sky, the stars appeared dimmer than usual as if their lights could flicker out at any moment. However, the red Eye continued to hold its glow.

Stevie wondered how Kit was murdered—his head had to have been cut off somehow. But why? Or was his murder random? She ran a hand across her throat, hoping to never uncover the secret of what a blade through her neck felt like.

Once she turned into her driveway, Kit was already off Inferno, brushing his hand down the stallion's back. The horse then took off like lightning, and his hooves pounded down the street.

Kit tugged at the top of his glove. "Inferno has always preferred the woods. But more so now after seeing what the town has become. He finds it too chaotic here."

It was much quieter back then for sure. No loud car engines, no pollution. "Sometimes the world is pandemonium for me too, and I was born in a chaotic time." She laughed softly.

As Stevie unlocked the front door, Kit slipped through the wall. Roxy barked a shrill greeting and launched herself toward them, her tail wagging when she peered up at Kit. He didn't kneel to pet her, only stood with rigid shoulders.

"You know you can pet her," Stevie drawled, motioning him forward. "That's what she wants. I mean, it's not mandatory, but she would like it if you did. She did search for you too, after all."

"It's not proper etiquette to pet someone's familiar unless the owner allows it. But since you don't mind." Kit knelt in a robotic manner as if he hadn't touched any other undead souls besides Inferno. Which if she were to wager it, she bet he'd only put his hands on the heads of ghosts he'd taken. "Hello ... Roxy. You're a ... fox." He stroked her back, his shoulders relaxing as he petted her. The fox released a satisfied purr and rolled to her back, pawing at the air.

"Roxy appreciates it very much. Now come on, you have a story to tell, *seer*." Stevie sank down on the couch and patted the spot beside her. "Make yourself at home and remove your sword if you want. That thing looks uncomfortable."

"If you insist." Kit placed his sword on the coffee table, then unfastened his cape and rested the fabric on the couch. He leaned back beside her, his legs spreading apart. Her gaze lingered a little too long on his strong thighs before she tore her gaze away.

"So," Stevie started, "first things first. Did you lie about not being able to see the living before the Eye opened? Not that it matters, I guess, if you could've." She'd also been a stranger to him—but still, he'd known she was a seer so he could've spilled the beans instead of held onto them.

The cushions shifted as he turned toward her. "Yes, Pumpkin, I'm a Seer. Yet after I was murdered, my ability died with me. Once I accepted my first head, I still couldn't see the living since the eyes didn't truly belong to me."

"Inferno comes to you though." Stevie bit her lip. "I always assumed a seer and their sidekick are linked through their sight, so wouldn't the link have been broken?" Not that she was an expert on that though since her eyes were still in their sockets.

"No, a fortune-telling witch once told me that even if one's eyes from the living were removed, the link would remain, regardless if they couldn't see the dead," Kit said. "Or in my case, the living."

"What else happened in your past?" Her voice came out gentle, knowing that talking about his own murder wouldn't be something to cheer about.

"All right." Kit heaved a sigh. "The tale began with me venturing to Sleepy Hollow, which as you most likely know wasn't called that in those days. Before that, I crossed paths with a witch and discovered what I was. She told me there was a town that accepted individuals who held special abilities, oddities to outsiders. Back then, it was easy to get hanged, or much worse, if one was discovered to be 'abnormal.'"

"Like the Salem Witch Trials." Stevie nodded. "Got it." The council liked to sometimes remind the town of what could happen if they were discovered, and Salem was usually the go-to since the paranormal had flocked away from there years ago to start the new town in New York, a place where their secret would be embraced.

"The first person I met after discussing my situation with the council was a beautiful witch," Kit continued. "Her name was Clara, and I easily fell for her. Like you to Lucia, I became her assistant and worked at her apothecary. But mostly I took care of the stables where she kept the animals for her spells. I knew the instant I saw her that I loved her. The way she would look at me with her bright doe eyes, how she would brush her fingers across mine, lingering—I thought she returned the sentiment. So I penned her a letter, confessing my love to her. A jealous warlock named Levi discovered the letter, and that was the nail in the coffin. Or at least the ridding me of my head."

"So he murdered you over it?" Stevie exclaimed. "I hope he was caught and burned at the stake."

Kit laughed darkly. "If only. I know, as much as I know the heart I once had, that he hid my head and spelled it so I would never find it. After he had me strung up in the woods with rope, he brought an axe to my throat. But just before that, he told me that once both Eyes were open during a new moon, I would be sent to the flaming pits of the Hollow where I would spend all eternity after the Eyes shut."

Stevie's stomach dropped, becoming hollow itself. "So that's why you said you only had until the next new moon," she murmured.

"Mm-hmm." Kit hunched forward, his elbows on his knees.

"I mean, you could've said that things were on a vicious countdown and *important*," Stevie said, incredulous.

"I did say time was of the essence, Pumpkin." She could hear in his voice that he was rolling his eyes.

"There's a big difference between saying something is of the essence, which could be anything, by the way, and that you'll go to the Hollow and burn for eternity if we fail!" she hissed. "And if you go down there, you know you won't just burn! The demons there will break you apart over and over. It'll be a good ol' torturous party for them."

"Emphasize your view a bit more," Kit said sarcastically. "I've only had centuries now to imagine it."

Stevie furrowed her brow, thinking about how she could flip this around. "I'm going to talk to Lucia." She left Kit on the couch and ran out into the cool night air, banging on her sister-in-law's door.

Lucia drew it open, dressed in pajamas printed with tiny pink cauldrons, a yawn slipping from her mouth. "How was the date? You're back earlier than I thought."

"What date?" Kit asked as he stepped behind Lucia, his ethereal glow lighting up the dim hallway.

"I said stop doing that," Stevie groaned.

"You said to stop coming up behind you. This isn't behind you," he pointed out.

"I take it the Headless Horseman is back." Lucia whirled around and held up a finger, pointing it at his chest. "I feel a presence right here."

"So your sister-in-law is a *special* witch," Kit purred. "She's good."

Stevie ignored him and grabbed Lucia by the shoulders to face her. "Remember when I told you Kit said time was of the essence? He wasn't bluffing."

"Come tell me everything." Lucia shut the door behind them.

On the kitchen counter, Maxine perked up inside her pot, the plant's mouth widening into a smile to show her rows of teeth. As Lucia poured Stevie a glass of milk, she relayed what Kit had told her.

Lucia released a puff of air. "Sounds like a revenge story. Lots of witches and warlocks have done that over the years. Did they have sex?"

Stevie looked toward Kit who sat in the chair opposite her, remaining silent. "Did you? You don't have to answer if you don't want to." She couldn't lie that she was now itching to know.

"No, we didn't pleasure one another," he said, his voice deep. "But she did kiss my cheek on several occasions before leaving the apothecary."

"Just goodbye kisses on the cheek." A sense of relief washed over Stevie that was *completely* unreasonable.

Lucia nodded. "So back then that could be like getting down and dirty in bed."

She had a point... Stevie bit her lip, contemplating something.

"What is it?" Lucia asked, taking a sip of water.

"If this Levi warlock hated Kit enough to murder him, why wait to send him to burn in the Hollow? Especially if no one knew if or when the Eyes would ever open. Is he a ghost too?"

Stevie focused on Kit. "And how did you know you could put on someone's head to replace your old one?"

"Neither Inferno nor I have seen Levi, so I don't know," Kit said. "As for the other question, I was wandering in the cemetery. I didn't know where I was, only that I could feel my bones below the ground. Inferno came to me with the fortune-telling witch. The one spell that she could provide was with the jack-o'-lantern and placing another's head on mine that would remain temporary. She told me the world would darken if I stayed headless, yet if I found my missing head and reattached it, with the blood of a seer, I could live again. After that she passed on. Her unfinished business, I suppose."

"Blood of a seer?" Stevie gasped. "You mean *me*?"

"That's what I'm hoping."

"What is he saying?" Lucia inched closer to Kit, seeming to think that maybe she could hear his words by doing so.

Stevie repeated what Kit had confessed, and Lucia folded her arms before saying, "This is more than a revenge story. I'm going to contact the Crowned Witch. Adelia would have to know something, but the only way to reach her is by letter. Let me think on it more tonight and I'll come by tomorrow. I'll get started on the letter now though."

Stevie and Kit left Lucia's, and she went straight to her room, plopping down on her bed. Kit sat in the desk chair across from her and Roxy hopped into his lap. He easily ran his long fingers through her fur.

"I think you're forgetting whose sidekick you are," Stevie teased. Roxy didn't hesitate to bounce onto the mattress and paw through Stevie.

A second later, Kit sauntered toward Stevie. He stood before her, then bent his knees until they had to be eye to eye.

Stevie took a deep swallow, unable to find any sort of drive to scoot back or push him away, not that she could've done the latter anyhow. "Yes, Your Headlessness?"

"Are you going to take my bone out of your pocket?" he asked, his voice gruff.

Stevie's eyes widened. "Oh! You've felt it in here this whole time?"

"Mm-hmm," Kit purred.

"Even when you were in the woods?"

"Not as strongly, but of course."

"And you didn't come sooner?" Stevie fished the bone from her pocket, her fingers curling around it. He shivered and she wrapped it in the hem of her shirt.

"I could have, yes," he said, his tone serious. "I was ready to give up all hope after another useless search for my head. With what little time I had left, I believed it didn't matter anymore. And then to put your life in an upheaval for it is selfish on my part."

Stevie's heart thumped at how his shoulders hunched forward, at how long he'd been looking for his head and coming up empty. "Ah, Horseman, you now have a teammate, no matter how much we might bug each other. I'm not going to let you suffer." She moved over, making room for him.

"I'll swallow my pride and take your help." He sat on the edge of the bed and she turned on *Scott Pilgrim vs. the World* to finish. She placed the bone back in the safe but left it out of the box in case she needed to call on Kit again.

Stevie collapsed on the bed and lay on her stomach as a chuckle escaped Kit's throat, surprising her. "You don't mind watching this movie?" she asked, blinking.

"It seems entertaining."

"I highly agree." She grinned.

A BELL RANG and Stevie swatted at the air. But when the sound came again, she realized it was the doorbell, then threw back the covers. She found Kit standing near the front door.

"Who is it?" She yawned, rubbing her eye.

"Your suitor," Kit grumbled.

"What's he doing here?" she whisper-shouted before opening the door. "Hey, Reese. Sorry about the turn of events last night."

His hair was disheveled and dark circles rimmed his eyes. "Not an issue at all. But you left your jacket at my house. Figured I'd bring it over to save you a trip."

"Thank you. This is like my favorite ever." She took the black leather jacket from his hands that she'd had for years since she could never find a comfier one to replace it.

"I was thinking we could try again tonight. Third official date's the charm." He smiled and her heart didn't flutter. Instead, it clenched—she had more important things to help Kit take care of.

Kit hadn't made a remark as he usually would've, seeming to let her decide what she wanted to do. She'd made a promise to help him, and that was more important than going out on another date that might not be any better than the last two.

"I actually have a lot going on until after the new moon. My life is sort of chaotic." She bit the inside of her cheek, holding back a wince. "I think the best I can offer at the moment is being a terrible friend. One that is too busy to do anything."

"The stars just aren't lining up for us, are they?" Reese's expression turned worried, his lips pressing into a tight line. "Is it something paranormal you have to take care of? I know the witches have been pretty busy."

"Yes!" she shouted a bit too loudly. "Lucia has me helping with a few spells to make sure the tourists continue to stay out of Sleepy Hollow. So much to do before the second Eye opens and so little time."

"It's right around the corner." He paused, his fists clenching at his sides. "You know, if you need to talk, you can tell me anything. That's what friends are for, right?" His gaze flicked past her as if he was hoping she would invite him inside.

Reese seemed to suspect she had secrets, which she did, but he couldn't help solve them. Besides, she already had the most powerful witch in Sleepy Hollow helping her right next door. "Thank you, but I'm fine. I'll text you later."

"Sure." He shrugged. "See you later."

Stevie closed the door and turned to Kit, who leaned against the counter, his arms folded.

"What?" She held up her hands. "Did I do something wrong?"

"No. But if I were him, I would've fought harder for you is all."

II

"I find it interesting how you write letters on that," Kit said, hovering over Stevie's shoulder as she typed on her phone.

I'll be there this afternoon with your delivery.

"It's called a text." Stevie grinned while pressing send. "Simple and fast and you don't have to wait forever to receive a reply. I guess some people would rather not have that since Lucia will be waiting a bit for the Crowned Witch to get back to her."

Kit lowered himself beside her on the couch. "Seems an easy opportunity for forgery."

Stevie contemplated that thought and supposed he did have a point, but it was a slim chance her mom's phone would be hijacked. Even then a warlock or witch could easily forge a letter with a spell if they wanted to.

A knock pounded on the door and Stevie tossed her phone on the couch to answer it. Lucia stood on the porch with two plastic sacks in one hand and a briefcase in the other. "I saw Reese pull up when I was leaving to mail out Adelia's letter and run errands."

"That pulse has officially flatlined." Stevie shrugged.

Lucia pursed her lips. "I guess Gideon was right about you

two not being twin flames."

As if hearing his name, Gideon opened the door, his shirt missing and his feet bare as he grabbed the mail. His eyes met Stevie's and he tsked, scratching his hairy stomach. "You should've told me you were cozying up with a ghost. And of all the ghosts out here you choose the Headless Horseman. Real winner, baby sister."

"I am *not* cozying up!" Stevie squeezed the bridge of her nose. "If you tell anyone, Gideon, so help me."

"I know. I know." His gaze flicked to his wife and he smirked while taking the grocery bags from her. "Lucia already warned me she'd hold back sex if I opened my pretty little mouth to anyone."

"You're so gross." Stevie wrinkled her nose in disgust. "Go back inside. I'm borrowing your wife for a little bit." She waved Lucia into her house and shut the door behind them. "My brother, really? Of all the guys in Sleepy Hollow you could've married?"

"Are you going to say that thirty years from now?" Lucia batted her eyes innocently.

"Um, forever," she said seriously.

"Just so you know, he doesn't act like that when it's just us."

Stevie couldn't see her brother as a proper gentleman, but he had to have some sort of buried attractive trait if he'd won Lucia over when she'd been highly sought after by every warlock in town.

Lucia stopped in front of the kitchen table and set her briefcase on its wooden surface. As she popped open the locks, Kit's boots thumped across the tile flooring and he watched from the corner near the fridge.

The briefcase displayed rows of corked vials and tiny jars filled with a variety of different colored liquids. Small boxes labeled bones, teeth, crystals, hair, and stones rested on another side.

"Kit," Lucia said, peering up from the briefcase at him in the corner. "You're already in here, so come have a seat so we can start."

"She's got a knack for this," Kit drawled and lowered himself into one of the chairs.

"He said you're the best witch he's ever met, and he'll owe you whatever you want for helping him." Stevie smiled as she sat beside Kit.

"I didn't say that, Pumpkin."

"But you will," Stevie sang.

"I need to do something to confirm that Kit's not a demon, even though we both believe he isn't. There's always the small chance a demon slinked out from the Hollow to pretend they're a ghost. The crucifix may not have worked since he isn't living, but the holy water will. I just have to make sure before we move on to the next step. It's for Stevie's protection. Is this all right, Kit?" Lucia asked as she slipped out a vial labeled *Burn Demons*.

Kit leaned back in his chair. "It's fine."

"The Horseman said it's A-okay to use it on him."

Lucia whispered an old prayer while clutching the vial. "This holy water was blessed directly at the Roman Catholic Church, and I can finally test it out!" She passed the contents to Stevie.

Stevie uncorked the lid and took a whiff of the sour flavor. "Smells a bit like lemon."

"It's infused with it. Demons *hate* it," Lucia said.

Stevie straightened and turned to Kit. "All right. In three. Two. One." She thrust her hand forward, the water splashing against his chest and invisible face.

For a second nothing happened, then an agonizing shout ripped through the room. "I'm on fire!" He thrashed in his seat before collapsing to the floor and writhing. "End the torment!"

"Cauldron's teeth, he's burning! He's a demon!" Stevie screamed, shoving out of her chair and toppling it over.

"Demon!" Lucia screeched, reaching into her briefcase, then halting her movements. A frown formed on her heart-shaped face. "Hey, there's no smoke..."

A loud chuckle erupted in the room, and Kit's shoulders shook with laughter.

"You jackass!" Stevie ground out as he continued to laugh. She rolled her eyes and met Lucia's gaze. "False alarm. It seems the Headless Horseman has a hidden sense of humor."

"What did you expect me to do after I already told you I wasn't a demon?" Kit shrugged and sank back in his chair.

"Not *that*!" Stevie's lips twitched, hating to admit that she did find his stunt somewhat humorous.

"One up for the Headless Horseman," Lucia said, corking the remainder of the holy water and sliding it back into her briefcase. "I have a couple more things I want to try to see if I can get his real head to appear." She glanced back at Stevie. "Do you have his bone on you?"

"No, but let me grab it." Stevie rushed into her room and snatched the bone from the safe.

Stevie returned to the kitchen, holding it out to Lucia. "Where do you want it?"

"On the table is fine." Lucia fished out a wishbone from inside a small box labeled *Special Bones* and handed it to Stevie. "Grasp one side of that and press your other palm on top of Kit's bone."

Stevie arched a brow. "This is sounding a bit provocative." Especially since she knew he could *feel* her touch on his bones.

Lucia ignored Stevie and focused on Kit. "Ghosts generally can't touch remains, but the wishbone is special. It holds its own unique, magical qualities. With my spell already placed on it and at play, your hand is meant to not pass through," she explained. "Now take hold of the wishbone's other side while placing your palm on Stevie's."

Kit leaned forward and wrapped his fingers around the opposite side of the wishbone. *That part worked!* His other gloved hand didn't slip through Stevie's—instead, coolness rested against hers.

Stevie's eyes widened. "I feel him!" she shouted, meeting where she just knew his eyes were. "Do you feel it?"

"I do," he rasped.

"So it *is* working?" Lucia's brows shot up. "I've never tried this spell, but I didn't think it would! Okay, now I need you both to pull the bone toward you until it snaps. Each of you make a wish to see his true head. And go!"

They tugged on the wishbone until a loud snap pierced the air. Stevie clamped onto the larger piece, Kit's gloved hand sinking through hers. "Looks like I'm the winner. But I can't feel him anymore," Stevie said.

"That means it's still working," Lucia confirmed. "All right, Stevie, place your piece on the table in front of Kit and let him slide the two bones back together."

Kit collected the two pieces which only Stevie would now be able to see. He then brought them together, and the seam fused. A ghostly head attached to Kit's neck, making Stevie's heart gallop to see the spell working. It wasn't the head of the jerkwad ghost from the last new moon, but another she'd never seen. Long white hair brushed Kit's shoulders. A strong jaw, chiseled features, and kissable lips accentuated his face. *Of course* he had to be even better looking than Evan Peters. Like her own personal Adonis. And then, just like that, the head vanished.

"His head was there, but it disappeared again," Stevie breathed. However, the image was tattooed in her mind.

Lucia ran a hand down the side of her face. "We need the Crowned Witch ASAP. If his head isn't staying, then that means dark magic is fighting it and I would have to be near it to break the spell. I want you to go to Ginger's tomorrow when she gets back into town. She might know something that I'm missing."

Stevie finished corking a row of brews, then placed them into velvet bags for local deliveries. "Do you want to come?" Stevie asked Kit, gathering the packages in Lucia's basement.

"You're inviting me to go with you?" Kit's voice sounded surprised.

"I'm sure you would pop up in the back of my car again if I didn't."

"You assumed wrong," he drawled. "I would be your visitor in the front seat."

Stevie rolled her eyes, but the edges of her lips curled upward. Both Gideon and Lucia were already at work, so she locked up their front door.

After loading the deliveries into the trunk, the only thing Stevie could focus on was how she'd felt Kit's coolness against her skin, the tiny spark that had ignited, and how perfectly shaped his lips were. *Calm down, Stevie. He's a ghost.* A ghost that could become a living member of society if they found his head...

She'd placed his bone inside her purse so it wouldn't make things uncomfortable between them. Or for him since she apparently couldn't stop thinking of his stupid gloved hand and what it would look like if he peeled off that leather... *It's a* hand!

Heavy beats poured out from the car's speakers and Kit groaned. "This music is terrible."

"Another thing we agree on." She laughed as she drove down her street, the fog covering the car's hood. "Tell me what you like and I'll see what I have on my phone."

"Violins."

"Um, can't say I have anything just instrumental, but I'll download some later. In the meantime, I'll play Stevie Nicks. Both her solo and Fleetwood Mac catalog." She scrolled until she found one that she thought he might like.

As the music played, the instruments doing their part, the voices blending perfectly, she watched Kit out of the corner of her eye who sat unnaturally still.

"So," she nudged, trying to get him out of statue mode. "Do you find this one as terrible as the last?"

"It's pleasant."

"I'll take pleasant." Stevie laughed, continuing to smile as his fingers tapped his thigh.

After delivering the packages around the town, Stevie pulled into her parents' driveway. She took the last sack from the trunk and knocked on the door.

Her mom answered, her arms folded, and her red lips set in a tight line. "This fog's getting out of hand, isn't it?" She was obviously in a damper mood and Stevie knew why. And it had nothing to do with the fog.

"Gideon told you, didn't he?" Stevie frowned, gritting her teeth. "He's four years older than me and gossips like a junior high kid, I swear!"

"He's not telling anyone else that you have a *guest* at your house. Why didn't you tell me that the ghost stalker was the *Headless Horseman*?" her mom hissed.

"Your heart for one."

"My heart is fine. Please don't start treating me like a fragile piece of glass."

"I promise I won't." Stevie's face softened, guilt washing over her. "Besides, I told you everything except his identity."

With a sigh, her mom wrapped her arms around Stevie and gave her a tight hug. "You're forgiven."

"How did Dad take the news?" She wasn't concerned about her dad since he'd never batted an eyelash with any paranormal dramatics that went on in Sleepy Hollow.

Her mom released Stevie and stepped back. "Your father takes things better than I do. Which is still surprising to me."

Stevie nodded and passed her mom the package. "Kit's not the demon rider everyone believes him to be. He's in the car if you want to offer any words."

"And you didn't start off by saying he's *here* with you?"

Stevie waved toward Kit to get out of the car, and the stubborn man just sat there. He finally listened when she frantically waved again, sauntering toward her, the fog caressing his strong thighs. She swallowed deeply at the way his muscles flexed against his shirt, his assured movements, and she whirled back to face her mom before heat crept into her cheeks.

Fawning over Kit in front of her mom was too awkward. But that wasn't what she was doing—she was only admiring the human, or *ghostly*, anatomy.

Stevie's mom cocked her head, her eyes narrowing at where she thought the Headless Horseman now stood, but she was like two feet off. "I swear, if you're fucking with my family, you fuck with me, Horseman."

He let out a low whistle. "I see where you inherited your way of threatening from, Pumpkin."

Stevie rolled her gaze toward the ceiling. "He said he likes you."

"You have to earn my trust before I return the favor," she warned Kit.

"So, Mom, I do have a question before I leave," Stevie started. "I was wondering if you've ever crossed paths with anything that might stick out about the Headless Horseman. Anything that the witches or the residents here might not know."

Stevie's mom tapped her index finger against her chin. "Have you gone to the old cemetery? And I mean the *old* one where it's believed the Horseman was originally buried. Maybe some lingering ghosts have more information."

Both an obvious and good suggestion. "Seems I have a little trip to make."

"Be careful." Her mom pursed her lips.

"Don't worry, I have my handy-dandy, sword-wielding Horseman with me if I need to scare anyone off."

12

Stevie slowed the car as she approached the cemetery, the fog curling around the old headstones, but she didn't pull into the parking lot. A tour was taking place at the moment, which she hadn't thought about. They weren't tourists, but instead three buses of junior high kids. No visitors would be allowed to sneak a peek until after a couple more groups of private tours.

"So I guess we'll come back tonight when the tour sessions are closed?" She watched a teacher snap his fingers in front of a small group of kids, telling them to pay attention.

"That's fine." Kit sat rigid in his seat, his neck partially turned as he stared out the window. Even with three buses of school kids, more dead than living roamed around the cemetery. It normally wasn't this much of a hot spot for ghosts, but they must've already started to gather early, anxious for when the second Eye opened so they could chat with the living when they showed up.

Stevie studied Kit, who hadn't moved from his position. "Are you reminiscing? You said this was where you were buried." It had been rumored the Headless Horseman was buried out there, but no one knew which grave really belonged to him. Someone else had to have known if they'd unburied his bones though.

"No." He sighed. "Someone I know lingers there is all."

Stevie reached out to tug Kit to face her, but of course her hand slipped through him. "You mentioned a fortune-telling witch helped you but passed on. So who else do you know out there?"

"No one," he grumbled.

Stevie cocked her head. "Hey. We're partners here, right? So that means you can tell me who's out there and I won't shout their name." She pretended to sew buttons across her mouth.

"Clara." And for the first time, his voice sounded melancholic. "I've seen her when riding through the cemetery. Most ghosts will scatter as I pass through, believing they're my next victim, yet she never does."

The witch he'd been in love with... A hollowness filled Stevie's stomach. "Have you ... stopped to talk to her? She is a witch after all."

"I attempted once, but she's like some of the others trapped in their own minds, repeating the same words over and over. Hers is about needing to find her true love." Kit paused. "I'm not that man, and she never returned my affections. I was a fool."

Oh... "Do you still have feelings for her?" she asked gently.

"No. My heart withered long ago in its grave."

"That sounded *very* poetic. But I've seen you around Roxy—the ghost of your heart is still there."

Kit scoffed, and Stevie bit her lip, continuing, "You know with the Eye opened, a lot of the ghosts have snapped out of their prior states. Would it be all right if I tried to talk to her tonight? Maybe I could pass a spell of hers on to Lucia or something."

"If you wish to."

"I can't believe you haven't asked more people questions over the years." If Stevie had been in Kit's position she would've approached every single ghost in town.

"After the fortune-telling witch took the head of another ghost and placed it on mine, fear spread like wildfire. No one knew me as Kit, only the Headless Horseman. The fortune teller had told me my horse and I were the only ghost seers. And even then, because of my sight being gone, Inferno couldn't see into the living world either, not until the Eye opened."

"Tonight my goal for us is to at least find a semi-answer that can get us closer."

STEVIE JABBED the butcher knife into the head, the squishing sound echoing. "I hate you."

"Have you never carved a pumpkin before?" Kit chuckled beside her on the porch steps.

The dark had already blanketed the town an hour ago even though it would've normally still been a bit away. It had been doing that the past couple of days too, she realized. Earlier and earlier…

To pass the time, she'd bought a pumpkin from a kid going door to door, dragging a wagon filled with them.

"I *have*, but I'm not very good." The last time she'd done this was with her mom and brother when they were younger. And it was usually her mom doing it since Gideon complained and Stevie preferred to watch.

"Let me show you." Kit's hand pressed to the knife where hers was, and he lifted the blade, dipping it up and down alongside hers. She blinked, unable to feel his coolness but wishing she could. He stilled their movements. "You have to work with me, Pumpkin. Otherwise, I'm carrying all the weight."

"You did say 'let me show you,'" Stevie pointed out.

"Come on, move with me," he said, his deep hypnotic voice wrapping around her like a cozy hug.

As he started again, she mirrored each slice, each dip and curve. Pulling the blade out and pressing it back in. Together they didn't carve a face but a ... *Headless Horseman.*

She arched a brow at him and a smile spread her cheeks. "I didn't realize you were so vain."

"How can I not be? Look at the perfectly missing head, the smoothness of the top of my neck, not a single bump or uneven line." Kit leaned toward her, letting her get a better view of his neck. He wasn't wrong...

"So your sense of humor has crawled out of its cave twice today." Stevie laughed and watched Kit finish a couple of minor details on the pumpkin. As she stared at his gloved hands, she wondered what it would feel like if one were on hers again, only this time his bare skin. Would it be just as cool? Cooler? And how would it feel if he trailed those long fingers of his up her arm, down her neck, between...

"Do you always wear the gloves?" Stevie asked when her curiosity built to a crescendo.

Kit drew the blade out of the pumpkin. "Would you rather me take them off?"

"Yes!" she answered *too* quickly. "I mean, not for *me*, but for the cemetery. You already have the cape, sword, and horse put away, so might as well do those too. It'll help you blend in a bit more with the other headless victims."

Kit peeled his gloves off, and his hands were both masculine and pretty at the same time. An Adonis face to match his Adonis hands. Why couldn't he have looked like a gremlin? But maybe that wouldn't have even mattered since she'd been admiring his body before even seeing his face.

She glanced down at her phone, realizing it was later than when they'd planned to leave. "Oh, we need to get going!"

The fog rolled around the grass, crawling up the trees as she drove them toward the cemetery. It was the perfectly eerie

October sight, but this only meant that the second Eye opening was growing closer. And that thought now made her chest tighten for Kit. She turned up the instrumental movie score she'd downloaded for him, needing to remain focused and not dwell on the new moon being less than two weeks away.

In the distance, white specks of light dotted the cemetery, appearing like a starry sky across the foggy darkness.

The gravel parking lot was empty when she drove into it. Turning on her flashlight, Stevie stepped out of the car and approached the cemetery entrance. A chain hung from one bar of the iron fence to the other. To her right, a placard held the history of Sleepy Hollow along with a no visitors after dusk sign.

Stevie shrugged and simply stepped over the metal chain and crossed onto what the council deemed hallowed grounds, the blood-red Eye in the sky watching her. "Just so you know"—she glanced over her shoulder at Kit—"I'm risking a troop of ghosts following me home. Remember what happened after I entered the abandoned house? I got stuck with you."

He chuckled. "I do believe you like having me around."

Her cheeks heated, and she was grateful for the dark. The stars above had dimmed further, a few seeming to have blinked out of existence completely. She and Kit passed down a row of crooked headstones, most deteriorated and broken. A middle-aged woman with a long braid sat atop one that held crumbling angels on either side of her.

Her gaze shifted toward Stevie, and the woman muttered, "Oh wonderful, another living hussy making a spectacle of the cemetery. Go home."

"I heard that," Stevie sang, unable to help herself.

The woman froze, her ankles uncrossing. "You heard me?" She looked up toward the night sky. "The second Eye hasn't opened yet. That means you're a—"

"Seer," Stevie finished for her. "Yes. I'm with a friend, and—" she trailed off when Kit was no longer behind her. But she found him a second later hovering near a headstone and studying it.

The woman cocked her head, her skirt swishing. "So, why are you here?"

Stevie stepped toward the ghost. "I'm helping a friend. But while you and I are getting acquainted, what do you know about the Headless Horseman? Do you have any clue where his head could be? Have you heard of a warlock named Levi...?" She didn't even know what his last name was, so she left it at that.

The ghost ticked a finger at Stevie. "Why are you asking about that demon? Are you one of those lovesick girls? Fascinated by him? Lusting over his body? There used to be four of them here who would stand at the fence each night, hoping to catch a glimpse of him as he rode down the streets, gossiping about him all throughout the day. When their ghosts passed on, I was more thankful than you could ever imagine."

Stevie arched a brow. Kit once had ghost groupies? She guessed it wasn't different than the tourists who flocked to Sleepy Hollow because of him.

"She's not one of those," Kit ground out as he inched closer to the woman from behind. "She's asking for *me*."

The ghost's eyes widened and she hopped from the headstone, stumbling backward.

"I told you to stop creeping up on people!" Stevie hissed.

"You said to you and Lucia. Besides, I was already here," Kit said.

"Headless Horseman!" the woman screeched. "He's here to collect a head! Run for your lives!"

An uproar of screams pierced the air, the ghosts scurrying through the cemetery like white ants.

"No!" Stevie shouted as a crowd of them fled through the gates and into the woods. "He's good! He just sometimes needs to take a head is all."

"You tried." Kit shrugged.

"You could've at least used a less villainy tone when you talked to her." She frowned, pointing a finger at his chest.

"I didn't like how she was speaking to you."

"She was too focused on your fan girls." She gave him a sly look. "Which by the way you didn't tell me you had."

"Another reason I avoided venturing to the cemetery on occasion," he grunted.

Stevie scanned the cemetery, not finding a single flash of white light near any of the headstones. "Maybe I should've had you wait in the car while I questioned the ghosts."

Kit trailed a finger across the top of a headstone. "You should've stated that proposal beforehand."

Stevie rolled her eyes before finally spotting three ghosts slipping back into the cemetery. *Not too frightened then.* "Do you see Clara anywhere? What does her body look like since hair and eye color are all the same."

"Not yet. And curvy. Tall, large breasts, tiny waist, curly hair spilling down her back."

Already sounds like an Aphrodite to go with his Adonis self. "All right, I don't see her yet. What was your last name?"

"Crawley."

Stevie cupped her hands around her mouth, forming a megaphone and stepping forward. "Does anyone know a Kit Crawley?"

When she thought no one would answer, a gentle voice, meek and small, came behind her. "I know Kit."

Stevie spun around as Kit cursed under his breath. The woman who stood before them was angelic, beautiful. Her white hair hung in tight curls down to her waist, and a lacy gown hugged her curves, her cleavage on display and perfectly pushed up.

"Clara," Kit whispered.

"It's been a long time." Clara's face softened as she peered at him, and thankfully, she was lucid now. "*You're* the Headless Horseman. I remember you visiting me once."

As the silence stretched between them, Stevie needed to get things moving along unless Kit wanted to stand there until the Hollow swallowed him up. "Clara," Stevie said. "I'm a seer and a friend of Kit's. Do you have any idea of what Levi did to Kit's head? Or if you've seen Levi's ghost anywhere? Do you know of any spells that can maybe help?"

Clara shook her head, tears beading her lashes. "No. Levi told the village that Kit attempted to murder him. I always suspected his words to be false, but I had my two children to worry about. He was such a powerful warlock, could do anything. An illness swept through the village a year later, and Levi succumbed to it first and then me shortly after." Her doe-eyed gaze fastened on Kit. "I didn't mean for you to think I reciprocated your feelings, and I'm sorry. I'm sorry for everything. I'm sorry for not speaking up to the village about what I believed. Telling you that I'm sorry is my unfinished business." After the last word left her mouth, Clara's form grew paler, fading in the moonlight.

Kit pressed his hand to Clara's cheek. "It's all right. You have nothing to be sorry about. I know you loved him, the way you've called out to him for centuries." With each passing second, she continued to become lighter until she was no longer there.

"That bastard lied to *everyone*," Kit growled, his hand falling limply to his side.

Stevie's lips parted as she replayed Clara's words inside her skull like a broken record. "She had children? So since this was centuries ago, I'm assuming she had a *husband*?"

Kit's fingers drummed against the headstone where Clara had been standing. "Yes."

"And you just casually left that part out?" Stevie lifted her arms in annoyance.

"You could've asked me to elaborate more. I didn't lie about anything."

"If I could, I would hurl you across the cemetery. What else aren't you telling me?" Her gaze drifted from Kit's thrumming fingers to the words written on the headstone. "Clara Katrina Bonham." Stevie inhaled sharply. "Her middle name was *Katrina*? Like in the *Legend of Sleepy Hollow* story!"

"Mm-hmm." Kit's fingers didn't stop dancing their repetitive rhythm.

Squinting, Stevie read on to the engraved words below Clara's name. *Beloved wife of Levi Brom Bonham.* Stevie's chest tightened. "She was married to Levi! And not just that, his middle name was Brom! You made it seem like some random maniac killed you out of jealousy!"

He stepped toward her, hovering closely. "No, Pumpkin, you *assumed* that."

"You're frustrating," Stevie snapped. "Going forward, you need to be *detailed.*"

Kit sighed. "Before you start asking more questions, go look at my headstone and I'm certain you'll figure it out."

Stevie huffed. "I'm not a psychic. Where is it?"

He motioned her with a finger which, at the moment, she wanted to break off. She followed him farther toward the back of the cemetery to a faded headstone closer to the woods, the words barely legible from years of wear. As she brought the flashlight nearer, she could still read them crystal clear. *Kit Ichabod Crawley.*

"Ichabod? *Ichabod? Another* character from the story." She spun to face him, her eyes widening into full werewolf moons. "So Clara was with Levi, and then he murdered you over the letter? You knew she didn't love you because she was calling his name!"

"That's nearly accurate."

Stevie ran her hand down her face in agitation. "First, you shouldn't have sent a letter to a married woman. Second off, did you know she had children too?"

"Not at first, no," he whispered, guilt lacing his tone.

"Kit!" she shouted. "Whatever. It's in the past now. But to the author of the story, he put a spin on it that's barely accurate. That aside, let's find out if anyone's seen Levi's ghost, and *I'll* question them with you staying farther back."

13

Of the ghosts who returned to the cemetery, only one was around during the same time as Kit. An older woman who'd been in her twenties when Kit was murdered. Like everyone besides Clara, she didn't know the Headless Horseman's true name.

"Kit was a wicked man, tried to drive a wedge between Levi and Clara," the woman huffed. "Clara had been in love with Levi since she could walk, and as soon as Kit came to town, the entire village swooned over him." And Stevie could tell this woman had been one of those villagers by the way she bit her lip even though she'd just called him wicked.

"Thanks," Stevie said before meeting up with Kit a few headstones away. "No answer. Only that you're a *wicked* man."

As they got in the car to head back to the house, they remained quiet. Once she unlocked the door to her home, Kit finally broke the silence. "I won't fault you if you believe I'm lying."

"I don't." Stevie sighed. "I just think a warlock took his wrath way too far and didn't want to look villainy in front of his village. *But* I still can't believe you didn't tell me Levi was her husband to begin with."

"I said a jealous warlock. I assumed you would've known that meant lovers. It's not my fault you didn't question further." Kit shrugged, brushing past her to the kitchen cabinet to pull out a glass.

"You don't eat or drink, so what are you doing in there?" Stevie asked as she watched him sift through a few items in the fridge.

Without a word, he plucked a carton and poured a glass of milk, then placed it on the table in front of her. "There," he said. "Drink and relax."

Stevie arched a brow, taken aback that he remembered what she liked to drink when Reese had so easily forgotten. "This doesn't quite make us even." She took a swig of the cool liquid, letting it glide down her throat. "All right, maybe it does."

"You look less tense now."

Curiosity got the best of her as she studied his broad shoulders, the invisible face that she itched to get a second look at. "What were you like back in your century? How many women did you date or *court*? Or did you only wait for Clara?"

"If you can dig into my past, then can I dig into yours?" he said silkily, stepping closer to her, his chest nearly brushing hers if they could actually touch. Her heart pounded faster, and to the lucky clovers in her thumb ring, she hoped he couldn't hear it.

"Deal!" Stevie held out her arm and shook hands with the air. Her secrets weren't much to write home about—he already knew about her mom's past.

Kit leaned against the counter, propping his elbows on it. "What do you want to know, Pumpkin?"

"Were you celibate while you were in love with Clara?" She inwardly cringed at her meddlesome question, but she wanted to *know*.

"Women these days, or *you*, are rather forward." And she could hear the smile in his voice. "Was I celibate after I met Clara? Yes. Virginal? No. Now my turn. Did you and Reese..." he trailed off.

She thought about the almost-awkward kiss that she would choose having a hex put on her over going through that embarrassing moment again. "No, not even a kiss. And I have only ever had one long-term boyfriend. Yes, hanky panky was involved, and before him, I'd kissed two guys."

"Interesting." By his even tone, she couldn't tell what he meant by that word exactly.

Stevie toyed with the hem of her shirt before asking, "How many women have you ... bedded?"

"Two," he drawled. "But they were only temporary infatuations."

With a face like that? she wanted to say. But a part of her was thrilled he hadn't banged all the women in or outside of Sleepy Hollow. "We're digging deeper now." She grinned. "What were you like?"

"As you know, my father was a physician," Kit started. "He taught me how to use a sword and died when I was twelve. My mother passed just before my twenty-third birthday which was a reason it made it easy to leave for Sleepy Hollow. Only my mother knew I was a seer. She kept it from my father since he wouldn't have understood. However, she was also one. I had two older sisters who I wasn't close with. They married young and left our small village. And you know about my time in Sleepy Hollow. So I take it with this game, it means it's your turn."

Stevie contemplated where to begin. "And as you know, my dad's a dentist. He fell in love with my mom, found out she stole people's hearts to live, and loved her anyway. Luckily that all worked out because my brother and I wouldn't exist. Sometimes I say I can do without my brother, but really I love him. My ex-boyfriend couldn't deal with me being a seer, so he went bye-bye. I never went to college since I decided to remain a witch's assistant. Oh, and I collect antique things. Stamps and coins are at the top of my list."

"Like those ceramic heads, I take it?"

She rolled her eyes and smiled. "They're head vases, but yes."

Her phone dinged, and Reese's name popped up on the screen. A picture of a house decorated with at least a hundred jack-o'-lanterns and a message reading, *Tis the season, friend.* It was sort of a weird text to send after their earlier conversation.

I wish that was my house, but I can't even carve one pumpkin properly. Or no, that was a lie—the one she'd carved with Kit had come out fancy.

"How about you show me this stamp collection of yours," Kit suggested.

"Really?" She laughed softly. "I've never had anyone want to look at my prized possessions without me badgering them."

"There's a first for everything."

"All right, come pop that cherry then." Stevie grinned wider as she led him into her room. She grabbed three boxes from the desk and plopped down onto the two-seater game chair near the TV. Kit's broad form sank down beside her, and she handed him one of the boxes.

"If you want me to show you how to play a video game after, I can," she continued. "I don't play much, but I have it for when Gideon comes over since it's like the only thing he wants to do. He hates all the movies I like. What kind of person only wants to watch superhero movies?"

"I like the one you showed me," Kit said while running his finger over the plastic of her train stamp collection.

"Then there'll be more." She winked before passing him a set of the presidents.

As he sifted through the boxes, Stevie's eyes fluttered while she watched him. It was late, and the day had been jam-packed, so she gave into temptation and closed her eyes. She slipped further away, possibly into dream state mode, when something hard and cool pressed against her shoulder. A few seconds later, two cool hands wrapped around her legs and back, then lifted her. Was she dreaming about a vampire prince this time? A phantom prince?

But when her body jostled, she realized she *wasn't* dreaming.

Stevie flicked open her eyes to a white glow cradling her. She screamed bloody murder and fell, her backside colliding with the hardwood floor, pain radiating from her tailbone up her spine.

The haze cleared from her vision as she stared up at Kit. "You were holding me!" she shrieked. "And then you dropped me!"

He knelt beside her. "You're the one who opened your eyes."

"And that's my fault?" she whisper-shouted. "How did you touch me?"

"I'm not quite certain, to be honest." He shrugged. "It was a peculiar thing. I closed my eyes briefly and felt you, so I thought I would be a gentleman and bring you to bed."

But how? Stevie thought about when Lucia had come over... "Is it possible because of the wishbone?" Biting her lip, she pressed her hand forward and it slipped through Kit's chest— not even a hint of coolness brushed her flesh.

"I believe it's only if our eyes are shut, Pumpkin." He edged closer, his voice gruff.

"How about you do that then?" she murmured, stretching her hand out for him to touch.

"Only if you don't scream again. I don't believe my borrowed eardrums will last through another one of those screeching sounds," he said, his hand passing through hers, giving her that *Casper* moment she'd always dreamed about. But she wanted more than that—she wanted to feel his palm against hers.

"You're *hilarious*." She stared at him and waited, a smile breaking. "Are they shut? Because, you know, I can't see your face."

"They are closed nice and tightly." And by the sound of his voice, he was smiling too.

"All right. Here we go." Stevie inhaled and closed her eyes, stretching her arm forward again. This time, her hand didn't slip through his but pressed to something solid. His velvety soft palm, its coolness spreading across hers. Becoming a bit more daring, she took her other hand and placed it against his *chest.* Stevie's heart accelerated, her pulse erratic. *Stop that*, she chastised herself. She chalked it up to being a bit freaked out that his chest didn't rise or fall, nor did a heart beat against her palm. But underneath that layer, she knew it was because she liked the way his muscles felt, especially as she glided her hand to his shoulder. Unable to fight her eagerness, she skimmed her fingers up his shirt collar, to his cool neck, then to his ... jaw.

Kit's head was there like he'd said, and she ran her palms over the planes of his face. His chin, cheeks, nose, eyelids, forehead. His hair. It wasn't the long locks she'd seen when Lucia performed the spell, but the shorter hair of the guy he'd stolen the head from. Even though these features didn't belong to him, a low sound rumbled from Kit when she trailed her fingers across his lips.

Stevie bit the inside of her cheek as she left his coolness, not wanting to seem too weird and linger longer than she should've. "So, did you feel all that?"

"*Very* much so."

The urge to feel him again pulsed through her veins, but there was something she needed to do. She opened her eyes and grabbed her phone to call Lucia.

"Stevie?" Lucia answered groggily.

"I know it's late, but this is sort of an emergency." Stevie glanced at Kit, and her heart picked up as if bats were flapping around inside it. "Or a me emergency who needs an answer. I can touch Kit. Does this have something to do with the wishbone?"

"You can touch him?" Her voice rose, sounding wide awake now.

"Only if we both close our eyes."

"Hmm..." Rustling stirred on the other end of the phone. "It could have something to do with you being a seer and winning the larger portion of the wishbone, which in this case would be a heck of a spell I performed. Tell him to come here and let me try it with him."

Stevie nodded to Kit and he slipped through the wall. "He's on his way."

A handful of seconds ticked by when Lucia finally said, "Nope, he can't do it with me. Just you. Is he the only one you can do this with?"

"I literally just found out, so I have no idea," Stevie said as Kit came back into her room.

"Try Roxy."

"Roxy! Come here, girl," Stevie called. She thought about how she'd slept beside her sidekick for years, and even though the fox didn't sleep, her eyes were closed the majority of the time. Not once had she ever felt her.

Roxy bounded into the room and hopped onto the bed. Stevie put the call on speakerphone and knelt in front of the fox. "Let me try something," she said, crossing her fingers that this would work. For *years* she'd wanted to pet her sidekick, feel how soft her fur was. "Can you close your eyes? I was able to touch Kit when we both did this, and I want to see if it happens with us."

"Did it work?" Lucia asked, her tone anxious.

Stevie rolled her eyes. "I haven't tried yet. Hang on and I'll let you know."

Roxy sat on her haunches and closed her eyes. Stevie mirrored the movement, then pressed her hand forward until her fingers didn't pass through the fox but brushed soft fur. She gasped, an emotion brewing within her chest, something raw that she hadn't felt in ages. Pure excitement. Tears formed behind her eyelids while running her hands along Roxy's back, petting her as she'd wanted to do for years.

Roxy let out a low purr, and Stevie smiled wider. "I guess we get to properly meet now, don't we?" Stevie finally drew her hand back. "It works on Roxy too."

"This is amazing! But if it got into the wrong hands... If ghosts know you can do this..." Lucia trailed off.

Most would probably mind their own business, but it only

takes one bad egg to ruin things. "If one came in here while I was sleeping, it wouldn't be difficult to tape my eyes shut or something." Stevie shuddered at the thought.

"You forget," Kit said. "I'm here, and I don't sleep. Not many ghosts want to risk going where the Headless Horseman is."

Lucia hadn't heard Kit, but she was on the same page. "You have Roxy and Kit there. Plus I'll work on creating another ward to protect seers—one that hopefully ants don't eat."

"Thanks, Lucia." Stevie ended the call after Lucia told her she would check on her tomorrow.

Kit backed away from the bed. "Get some sleep. I won't leave this room unless you ask me to."

As she tugged back the covers, she patted the spot beside her. "Just get in here, my Headless Knight in ghostly attire. I'm not going to have you sit in the chair the entire night. Besides, we've crossed enough boundaries already, so this is only one more checkmark to add to the list."

Without a word, Kit removed his boots and slipped in beside her.

Stevie closed her eyes, unable to stop herself from wondering what the rest of him would feel like against her palms. What his—

Cauldron's teeth, get your head on straight, Stevie.

14

Something, no, *someone*, was pressed against Stevie's arm. The coolness of Kit's ghostly form, an alluring airy feel, didn't make her shiver—it only made her want to snuggle closer into him. At least she hadn't draped her arm around his stomach and wiggled into the crook of his arm like a needy little creature. But really, she wouldn't have minded it at all. She was tempted to trail her fingers along the planes of his face again, yet she kept her hands to herself, plastered to her sides.

"You don't sleep, so why are your eyes shut?" Stevie asked, smiling.

The coolness of Kit dissipated, like a flip of a switch, there one second and gone the next. She opened her eyes to sunlight spilling through the slit of her curtains.

"Sometimes I lay with my eyes shut, pretending as if my thoughts are dreams," Kit said. "It keeps me from becoming as deranged as most consider me to be. Over two hundred years of searching for one's head will easily snap their sanity. If I didn't have Inferno, I might not have continued looking."

Stevie's heart lodged in her throat when an awful thought slipped into her mind. "Since he's your sidekick, that means he'll go to the Hollow too?"

"It does," he growled. "Because of that bastard Levi."

Stevie should've realized that—after the living passed, the familiar would go wherever their seer partner went, whether stay a ghost here, go to Heaven, or the Hollow. "We'll get some answers." She checked the missed messages on her phone, finding one from Ginger.

I'll be back a little later than anticipated, but I'll text you when I'm closer to home.

The hourglass was losing more and more sand every second that passed. Soon the new moon would be there and the second Eye would open.

"Looks like we have some time before going to Ginger's. You know what that means?" Stevie said, keeping her voice light even though she was freaking out on the inside.

"Your tone speaks of trickery." Kit rolled to face her, his tall frame taking up most of the bed. And she was also tempted to tell him to close his eyes so she could undo the top button of his collar.

"No trickery here." She grinned while sitting up. "You'll be required to do some research while the *Sleepy Hollow* movie is playing. I'm going to get the apothecary deliveries ready, check in with Gideon, and stop by the council."

Stevie handed him the tablet from her nightstand, showing him how to type in letters to look things up. He caught on quicker than she'd expected, more so than a lot of the living.

After taking a quick rinse, Stevie delivered the packages around town. At each stop she became a Chatty Cathy and asked the residents if they had ever heard rumors about where the Horseman's head could be hidden. She said that it was for a council project to maybe get some valuable information to slip from them. One guessed on the other side of the world, another deep in the ocean, the third mused that it had to be the cemetery, and the fourth told her the Horseman never existed.

Stevie then swung by the comic book shop to bring her brother lunch. "I'm annoyed with you for spreading gossip." She poked his arm and set the paper sack and his drink on the counter.

"Dude, it's our parents," Gideon said, taking a long swig of his soda. "It's better for Mom to know in her condition over finding out when it's least expected and making it worse."

"Mom's fine, but maybe you're right. If she found out the truth on a day when her heart was weakening..." she trailed off. "Anyway, you better not have told another living or dead soul what's going on."

"I'm a normie, so how could I have told a dead soul?" Gideon smirked, and when she narrowed her eyes, he went on, "I *promise* I haven't and won't tell anyone else. On your life."

Stevie tilted her head and shoved his arm. "Why not on yours?"

"Because I love you the most, baby sister." He handed her some of his fries, his way of making a peace offering.

"I need to swing by the council, but I'm going to say hi to your resident ghost before I leave," she said as she popped a fry into her mouth.

"Tell Erik to put the comic books back where they belong next time."

Stevie rolled her eyes because most of the time it was Gideon who put them out of place and his workers had to sort them.

Erik glanced up from his comic as she approached him. "No fox today?" He smiled, warm and welcoming.

"No, she's at home with a ... friend." She knelt beside him and peered at the front of the comic. "You must've liked Sabrina if you're reading more of her comics."

"They're decent."

"Oh, those pumpkins on the cover reminded me of something! Do you ever go to the fall pumpkin sacrifice? It's coming up soon." She never once missed it, but with everything going on, she hadn't really thought about it.

"I will this year. I'm meeting a girl I haven't seen in a while."

"Maybe that'll get you out of this store more." She elbowed him through his arm.

"That's my wish." He closed his comic and leaned forward, waggling his brows. "Did you know that when the town first started the sacrifice, the villagers would toss in fingers of the dead too?"

"Lucia told me about that. Not sure what the Headless Horseman would do with all those dead fingers." She grinned. "Speaking of, you wouldn't happen to have heard anything about the Horseman's actual head, would you?"

He furrowed his brow. "A few rumors circulated that if his head was reattached the Hollow would release its demons. Maybe that's why it's hidden? But who really knows."

"Hmm. Something to consider." Stevie pursed her lips, recalling how the fortune teller had told Kit if he didn't find his head that the world would darken...

"By the way, I still haven't seen him come down the street yet."

She shrugged, knowing Kit was safe and sound at her home up until the next Eye. Needing to discuss the rumor with Lucia, Stevie let Erik return to his comic and headed into the apothecary.

"Hey," Lucia said as Stevie strode up to the counter. "I've got good news, my tracking number for the letter to Adelia tells me that it just got delivered, so we'll see what she says."

"Hopefully soon." Stevie bit her lip. "The resident ghost at Gideon's told me a rumor he'd heard. Supposedly by reattaching Kit's head, the Hollow would release its demons. What do you think? The fortune teller told Kit something different."

"Hmm," Lucia said. "To me it sounds like someone started it because they believed he's a demon. Kit isn't an actual demon who escaped from the Hollow, so it would be like saying, if I removed your seer head and reattached it, then demons would flood out from the Hollow. It doesn't make sense."

"I would just become a reanimated corpse is all." Stevie grinned, relieved.

"We'll mention it to Adelia when she responds, but I honestly wouldn't think too much about it. I've heard too many ridiculous stories about the Horseman." Lucia waved her hand in the air.

"Not this one..." Stevie drawled. "How about you come with me by the council, and I'll tell you about the Horseman's groupies that used to hang out at the cemetery."

STEVIE AND LUCIA walked toward the old stone building of the council. A banshee stood outside it, screaming to be listened to as she held up a protest sign in one hand and groomed her hair with a comb in the other. For that sort of ghost, who would unquestionably stalk her for life, Stevie pretended as if she didn't see the woman.

The red-headed secretary waved them on to the meeting room after Lucia asked to speak to the council. If Lucia hadn't been with Stevie, it wouldn't have been so simple.

Two of the three council members sat behind their desks. Both wore dresses with shoulder pads and lacy hats atop their gray curls. Neither Lottie nor Edith hid their wrinkles and sunspots with potions or brews.

"Lucia." Edith smiled and motioned them both to sit at the two chairs in front of her desk. "How may I help you?"

Lucia let Stevie inform them of what she'd come across the past few weeks, of how the Horseman wasn't a demon at all, how a warlock had done something with his head and no one knew if Levi was still around.

Edith set her pen down and folded her hands on the table. "The town's been looking for the Horseman's head for as long as that tale has been around. You say that supposedly a fortune teller told the Horseman the world would darken if he remained headless, then you have another rumor that if he receives his head demons will flood the earth, yet we've never heard either of those theories, nor have any of our fortune tellers mentioned this. As for this revenge story from the warlock? It sounds like something the Horseman must work out with him. There's nothing we can really do since we don't believe it's affecting Sleepy Hollow. And by the sounds of it, it might calm the ghosts down if the Horseman isn't hunting them. Demon or not."

"If you want to continue searching," Lottie added, "then do so, but we have more important matters to handle. Like making sure the tourists continue to turn away from our town so we don't wind up all over the media."

"That was a waste of time," Stevie muttered as she and Lucia walked back out into the fog, the darkness already surrounding them.

"Told you we need a new council." Lucia shrugged. "I think they really don't know what's going on with this fog and darkness either. Just another way for them to attempt to keep the town calm. To me, it's looking more and more like the fortune teller's theory is right about the darkness. I'm going to send another letter to Adelia today, this one more urgent."

Once Stevie got home, she found Kit composed on the living room couch. His body turned toward her and the first words out of his mouth were, "That movie was atrocious. There's also an abundance of information on the Headless Horseman, most of it myth, nothing close to what truly happened. And no mention of Levi."

"We'll have to just continue digging. Anyway, I spoke to the ghost at the comic book store, and Erik mentioned something new to add." She paused. "Lucia and I vetoed the rumor is true, but it's probably another reason why ghosts either A. aren't really helping, or B. they run when they see you, or a combination of A and B. The rumor is that by reattaching your head, it could free the demons in the Hollow."

Kit scoffed. "Foolishness."

"That's what Lucia said pretty much, but she's going to let the Crowned Witch know every detail. I'm starting to feel it's all connected somehow. The council told everyone the fog was part of the Eye opening, but that was never mentioned in the story. Then there is the night coming earlier each day. Your ghostly history. What the fortune teller said about darkness. Whatever spell Levi cast on your head."

"I agree. I only wish I had an answer to give."

Stevie's phone dinged before she could attempt to search more on old Sleepy Hollow. "Finally. Ginger's home, and she wants us to bring the bone Lucia spelled."

As they stepped outside, Stevie shivered from the gusty air. Inferno stood near the tree, seeming to have tired from the woods. "I think your horse wants you to ride him. Let's see if you can keep up with me." She grinned, starting up her moped.

"You mean, you keep up with *me*, Pumpkin." He chuckled.

It didn't take long for them to arrive at Ginger's cozy home, and of course Kit reached her house first. Fall scarecrows decorated the garden, pumpkins settled between each one. Most tourists that came to town believed witches lived in old cottages in the woods—not that they ever found out the truth. The only one with a hidden home buried inside a forest of trees in Sleepy Hollow was the Crowned Witch.

Ginger met them at the door wearing a plaid skirt brushing her ankles, a peasant blouse, and gold sandals covering her feet. Her gray hair was pulled back into a low bun and blue eye shadow painted her lids. Only a few fine lines were etched into her skin, making her appear closer to fifty instead of approaching seventy.

"I take it the town celebrity is with you?" Ginger squinted, looking out the doorway. "I wish I could feel the ghosts like my niece can."

Stevie motioned to her left where Kit stood. "He's right here."

"If he can cross my barrier, I'll see what we can do to help him." Ginger cocked her head, gesturing them inside.

"Please don't pretend like you're burning again," Stevie mumbled to him.

"I wouldn't dare," Kit cooed before stepping over the threshold after Stevie, whole and intact.

"He's inside."

"I know you and Lucia told me he wasn't a demon, but a witch must confirm these things herself." Ginger started down the hallway, waving them to follow her. "We'll go to the basement and begin."

Citrus and spice clung to the air as they always did in Ginger's house. Horseshoes, cowbells, painted chickens, and wooden wagon wheels hung across the walls. The stables were behind the house, holding pigs, chickens, and goats, amongst a variety of animals. Some were her pets, while others were necessary for her spells.

Just past the small kitchen, Ginger opened the basement door, and the citrusy scent pierced the air, growing bolder.

"Come now, lovelies. Let's see what we can do." Ginger grasped her skirt and descended the lime-green carpeted steps. The basement hadn't changed in all the years she'd known Ginger. When she used to come with her mom, Stevie would watch in wonder at the process of one heart being replaced by another.

Wooden shelves lined the walls, filled from top to bottom with jars in a cluttered and unorganized manner. Labels weren't on them like they were with Lucia's. But from being a witch's assistant, Stevie could easily pick out what each one was. Mummified bones, pig hearts, snake venom, vampire blood, goat's teeth, chicken eyes, werewolf fur, baby's breath, and virgin hair to name a few. Three cauldrons rested in the middle of the room, lit by deep purple crackling flames.

"The second Eye will open soon," Ginger started. "I've noticed a shift in Sleepy Hollow, regardless of what our idiotic council believes."

Stevie bit her lip and nodded. "I have a weird inkling too. Then there's this situation with Kit and the warlock. No one's seen him, but I think he has to be somewhere, waiting to make sure Kit does go to the Hollow." She fidgeted with the hem of her shirt. "Lucia hasn't had any luck finding his head. Only his ghost one returning briefly before boomeranging back to where it was because of dark magic."

Ginger nodded, her face softening. "Let me try something since Lucia has opened the gateway a fraction by using the wishbone. Kit, I need you to sit inside the circle once I make it." She took a jar from the shelf and dipped a paintbrush into the blood and drew a perfect circle.

Kit didn't need any nudging as he stepped over the red barrier. At this point taking *any* risk was worth the alternative.

"He's in the circle," Stevie said.

"Take out his bone and keep it in your left hand." Ginger grabbed a wooden ladle hanging on a chain and stirred the iridescent liquid inside the middle cauldron while Stevie slipped the bone from her purse. "Over the years, I've had dozens of clients pay me to locate the Horseman's head. But I've never had his hollow body here to help lead the way, nor a bone of his. You're a seer, so through you, let me attempt something since you two have formed a connection." She poured the liquid into a glass printed with cows wearing bowties.

Stevie inhaled the brew, and sweet strawberries tickled her senses. As she drank it, the liquid tasted just as it smelled. *Heavenly*. Until a second wave of flavor caressed her tongue, becoming bitter, then rotten. She gagged, bringing a hand to cup her mouth before she puked all over the floor.

"Don't lose your stomach, or it won't work," Ginger warned. "Now pass it to Kit."

Kit took the cup from her and drank the remainder down. She couldn't tell he was affected by it until he said, "That tasted of horse shit."

"You know what that tastes like?" Stevie grinned.

"Silence," Ginger reprimanded. "Both of you close your eyes. Stevie, I need you to place your right hand in Kit's."

Stevie reached for Kit, his bare hand brushing hers. He hadn't put his gloves back on, and she couldn't fault herself for liking that he hadn't. Ginger's palm then came down on top of theirs and Lucia's aunt gasped. "Both his heads are here in Sleepy Hollow. His ghost one and the skull from when he was living, but I can't feel their precise locations. Another spell, much stronger, *darker*, is placing them in murky shadows I can't see past." She fell silent, then grunted and released her hand from theirs. "You can open your eyes now. The Crowned Witch is who we need. Adelia might be able to do more." She tapped her chin. "But, until Lucia receives a response, there might be someone else you can try. Let me text you later to see if he'll allow a meeting."

"Who?" Stevie asked, perking up.

"An old vampire flame who I dated years ago."

15

The text from Ginger had come just before dawn. The vampire, Rainier, could meet Stevie at her house after dusk if she agreed to it. He apparently only let lovers come into his home. She gave the go-ahead for Ginger to pass on her address to him.

Stevie then took Kit to Lucia's basement to try a few brews her sister-in-law had made for him. Stevie added a drop of blood to the four of them, and each one provided zero effect. So after that she dug more into Sleepy Hollow's past while Kit did the same on her tablet. Lucia had swiped two books from the council library along with the password for their online archive which could be beneficial. Roxy stayed attached to Kit's side, and Stevie caught him every so often rubbing the back of the fox's neck.

Stevie opened the second book after the first one was a flop. A light scent of vanilla wafted up from the yellowed pages. There were paragraphs and paragraphs of the history of Sleepy Hollow which she glanced over until she came across something that caught her attention. "Look what I found!" she shouted, leaping next to Kit on the floor. "A connection!"

He set the tablet down beside him and leaned against the

baseboard of the bed. "What is it?" Interest and intrigue filled his voice.

She placed the weathered book between them and pointed at the faded drawing of the family tree, followed by pages and pages of ancestry. "These date back from 1700 to 1940 for the relatives of the author of the *Legend of Sleepy Hollow* AKA Washington Irving. I didn't recognize any of the names until I reached a second cousin of his who was married to a Walter Bonham." She tapped at the name rapidly. "Walter was the son of Albert who was one of the two children of Levi and Clara. And Walter was a *seer*." She grinned, satisfied with herself for this discovery.

"What does that mean? That Washington knew something because of Walter?" Kit asked, running a hand along his invisible chin.

"I'm not really sure. But I have a suspicion that Albert could've. I'm sure Albert had heard the rumors of what happened between you and Levi, then maybe because Walter was a seer he was able to put together that you were the Headless Horseman. Walter then might've passed the story on to Washington." She shrugged.

"Not passed it on very well," he muttered.

"This is true. Either Walter or Washington must've spun it to make it more friendly. Also, someone split you into two people for the story like you're doppelgängers or something." Stevie looked at Levi and Clara's children's date of births. "Albert and Oscar weren't that old either when Levi and Clara died. Five and four."

"Hmm, I'm certain neither of them would've known what their father did with my head if Clara didn't."

"Well, for now, at least we have the mystery solved of how the story came about," she sang, bumping her shoulder through his.

"You're..." Kit trailed off, his voice low.

"What?" She smiled. "If you're going to say I'm frustrating, then I'm sure you can think of a better adjective."

"No, it's nothing. Never mind." He cleared his throat.

Stevie closed the book and set it on the bed behind her. "Keep going. You can't leave me hanging like that."

"You're ... adorable, Pumpkin."

"Adorable?" She blinked.

"Mm-hmm." He lifted the tablet and started to scroll down a page.

In what way did he mean it? Adorable as in a kid sister? Unless he just meant it in a nice way which was just as bad. All the while she'd been wanting to feel her fingers on him *again*. She wouldn't pester him for an answer, and instead, with a frown, she picked up the book to distract herself.

Nothing else stood out from the book, only pages of the different abilities in Sleepy Hollow over the years, which her mom needed to be added to them if they ever updated this book. Giving up for now, she finally went to take a shower before Rainier arrived. After toweling her hair and getting dressed, she found Lucia in the living room seated beside Kit on the couch.

"You're here sooner than I thought. Did Kit let you in, or did you use a spell?" Stevie asked, combing her fingers through her wet hair.

"He let me in." Lucia grinned. "We've been playing yes or no questions to keep me occupied. He leans toward me when it's a yes, making his presence stronger, then away when it's a no. I should've been doing this with ghosts as soon as the Eye opened!"

"Her game. Not mine," Kit muttered.

"We're taking your parents out for dinner soon, and before Rainier comes by I want to make sure you're protected. My aunt swears he's trustworthy, but eat this—just as a precaution." Lucia held out a cookie with white sprinkles. "Keep the toad brew in your pocket too."

Stevie arched a brow and took the cookie from her, inhaling garlic and something ... moldy. "I'm assuming it tastes like garbage?"

Lucia nodded. "Indeed it does. But if he wants a snacky-snack, since vampires can still be unpredictable, he won't suck you dry."

Stevie bit into the cookie and gagged, forcing herself to swallow what had to taste like a rotten mushroom. "What else is in this? Can't you and your aunt spell these things to taste better? Her brew last night was just as rough."

"I could, but I was in a hurry. Besides, it's stronger this way." Lucia patted Stevie's arm. "If you need me, I'm only a phone call away. Ginger knows where his vampire ass lives if we need to go over there and shove garlic down his throat though."

"Toad spray should work wonders," Stevie pointed out while walking Lucia to the door.

She then poured herself a glass of milk, chugging it down to get the taste of the awful cookie off her tongue. As she popped a mint into her mouth, the doorbell rang.

Kit made it there before she did, slipping through the front of the house and back inside. "It's the vampire. I remember seeing him at a village celebration when I was alive, pleasuring two women near the stables."

Stevie bet he'd pleasured thousands of women by now. "You could've just peeked through this spot right here," she said, peering out the peephole at mostly shadow inside the fog. The porch light had been left off to make him feel comfortable.

"Ah, but then how would I find out if he was truly alone?"

"Unless he scheduled a visit for backup later," she added, opening the door.

The shadows lifted a little as moonlight caught on Rainier's pale skin, dark hair, purple eyes, and sharp canines.

"Stevie?" His voice came out low, akin to a seductive musical note.

"Yep. I take it you're Ginger's friend Rainier?"

"That's correct. *So*, are you going to invite me in?" he asked, his boots remaining firmly in place.

"Oh right. Sorry. Come on in." She waved him inside. "I would offer you a drink, but I don't think I have what you like."

"That's perfectly fine. I drink mostly blood bags these days, *unless* my lovers want me to feed from them of course," Rainier uttered. He looked like the generic vampire type. All black, long sleeve button-up shirt, leather pants, his boots covered in silver buckles. An alluring face that was more pretty than handsome, and she could see exactly why Ginger had dated him.

Kit exhaled loudly, his shoulders squared in annoyance.

"Did Ginger tell you why I needed you here?" Stevie glanced at Rainier over her shoulder as she led him to the kitchen table.

"She told me you're a seer and that you have someone rather special who you're protecting. And if I speak of it to anyone, she will gladly take a stake to my heart," he said, relaxing into a chair before stroking his index finger seductively over the wood like he was home sweet home.

Stevie smiled at Ginger's use of words. "Do you remember a man named Kit Crawley from centuries ago? He worked for a witch and her husband was a warlock. Clara and Levi Bonham."

Rainier lifted his finger and trailed it across his chin as the corners of his mouth curled up. "I do. Haven't thought about Kit in centuries though. Poor fellow. Succumbed to death from attempting to woo the witch wife of a powerful warlock. He should've known how that would end. Levi spread such vicious lies about how Kit tried to murder him out of pure jealousy, that he'd planned to hurt Clara for not returning his affections, and the village certainly gobbled them right up. After having tasted his blood and seeing how dark his thoughts were, I knew better though. Yet it was really none of my concern."

"That bastard," Kit growled under his breath.

Stevie didn't know if he meant Levi or Rainier, but what the vampire did or didn't do then wasn't what she needed now. "What else do you know about Levi?" Stevie leaned closer toward Rainier, hoping his answer would lead *somewhere* that could help Kit.

"He had me bite him once for a spell, and besides that, he bargained with me for my blood on a few occasions, always made it worth my while." A wide grin spread across his cheeks. "Blood. Women. Things were different back then."

Stevie didn't need to know about his *sexcapades*. "So I take it you don't know that the Headless Horseman is Kit Crawley?"

Rainier swiped his tongue across his lower lip. "Now *that* is an interesting turn of events. I take it he's the *special* guest you have here. Don't worry, I won't tell anyone. I'd do anything for Ginger. Even now."

"Do you know anything about Kit's head? What became of it?" If he didn't know Kit was the Headless Horseman, then she doubted he knew where it was. But maybe…

"No." And as her shoulders fell, he shortened the gap between them. "But I can try to find out. However, I need a tasty treat to make it happen."

"I'll murder him," Kit growled, stepping between them just as Stevie scooted back.

"I'm not going to force you." Rainier smirked. "And it won't *entirely* be for pleasure. You are a seer, so perhaps I will find something through your memories of the dead."

"Tell the bastard no." Kit sounded as if his jaw was clenched.

"It's fine, Kit. Just a nano bit of blood." Or at least she hoped.

Kit cursed under his breath, not stepping from between them, even though it would do no good.

"Come closer then." Rainier slowly drew her chair beside him, the scraping sound echoing through the room. "Where would you like me to taste you?" His purple irises fixed on her neck.

She wrinkled her nose. "Um, my arm. And nothing intimate."

"Perfect," Rainier purred. He took her wrist in his hands, his thumb caressing her vein, and her heart thudded nervously. She should've had Lucia skip dinner with her parents and stay there. "You forgot to ask one important question—if I've seen Levi over the years. I may not know where the Horseman's head is, but three decades ago, after a sensual evening of drinking the blood of special twin sirens, it did a number on my vampire sight, and I could see ghosts for seven days. While driving to seek out the sirens to question them the following night, I briefly saw Levi carrying a large satchel into the woods where Kit was murdered. There is a chance he could've passed on since then, but a powerful warlock like him? No. He wouldn't want to do that." He seemed lost in thought for a few seconds before adding, "As for the sirens, I never saw them again."

Stevie hadn't known that it was possible for a vampire to be affected that way, or at least by sirens who generally veered away from anywhere that wasn't the sea. However, that meant Levi was for sure a ghost, and she knew without a doubt he hadn't passed on and was remaining under the radar for nefarious reasons. "And you didn't find anything in the woods?" she asked Kit.

"I've searched many times. It's where the bonfire is held," Kit said.

"Now we begin." Rainier's slitted eyes met hers, his sharp canines lowering. His fangs pierced her flesh and sharp pain shot through her as he buried them deeper into her wrist. Her chest heaved as she tried to block out the pain. *Why would any woman in their right mind want this?*

"Garlic," he ground out, then resumed drinking, the pain turning to something lighter, freer, a warmth spreading through Stevie, and her eyes fluttered at the sensation. "I can't see any images in your blood. Something isn't right. I need to dig deeper." He continued to feast on her and the room spun, her head dizzy.

"Enough," Kit seethed at the same time Roxy came into the kitchen barking, even though the vampire couldn't hear either of them. "He has to stop, Pumpkin."

Stevie didn't want to at first, but as Kit begged her to take her arm from his grip, she finally ripped it away. "No more," she moaned, the sound of her voice revealing the opposite of what she wanted.

"You should've warned me sooner, but the garlic would've only allowed me a little more." Rainier raked a hand through his silky hair, his face concerned. "Let me get you to the couch." He looped his arm around her waist and placed her on the cushions. "Watch your back. I know the taste of Levi's dark spells, and it's inside of you. He must've cast a spell to make certain no one could find answers in your blood."

Stevie shuddered, unable to clearly focus as Rainier left her side. The lock of the door clicked, and Kit came toward her after telling Roxy to go into the bedroom for now. Her gaze trained on the top button of his shirt, the one she'd been wanting desperately to unfasten. Warmth spread through her, venturing deeper, lower, igniting crackling flames inside her entire being.

"Unbutton your shirt," Stevie breathed. "Or maybe your pants first."

"It's best you stop talking, Pumpkin." Kit sat across from her on the coffee table. "You're not going to like what you've said when the vampire venom runs its course."

"You're no fun." She giggled. Was she giggling? She never *giggled*.

"Close your eyes and sleep. That will be the best thing for us both." Yet the way his voice came out didn't sound like he was speaking the entire truth.

"But I don't want to sleep," she pouted. "Close *your* eyes and sit beside me so we can touch." Her eyes became hooded as she bit her lip and studied the rolled-up sleeves of his shirt, exposing his muscular arms. "So we can *fuck*."

Kit drew in a sharp breath of air. "*Sleep*."

Stevie roamed her gaze down his oh-so-manly form to between his legs where a *very* visible bulge pressed against his pants. "I don't think you *really* want me to sleep. I think you want us to fuck like werewolves." She giggled again, covering her mouth. "Make sure Roxy stays in the bedroom and come closer."

"Insufferable woman." Kit knelt beside her and placed a finger over her lips. Even though she couldn't feel it, she ran her tongue through it. "I'm not going to pleasure you while vampire venom runs in your veins."

"But you would otherwise?" She smiled seductively, arching into him.

"Lie down and sleep," he instructed, his voice serious. "I'll watch over you." It wasn't a no...

"Yes, Your Headlessness." Stevie giggled louder and settled deeper into the cushions. But the flames inside her only blazed, and no matter how tight she squeezed her thighs together, she needed his touch, his tongue, his *cock*.

"I need you," Stevie begged, her body humming with lust. "*Please.*"

"Not now," he said, his voice strained.

"Then I'll take care of myself while you *watch*."

A deep growl escaped Kit as Stevie slid her hand down the waistband of her skirt and slipped her fingertips inside her panties. She gasped as she stroked her center, gentle at first, then circled harder, picking up the pace while she imagined Kit pressing his fingers against her, dipping them *inside* her.

STEVIE'S EYES flicked open and she stretched, her temples throbbing. What was it she needed to do today? She let out a yawn, then stilled—the night before coming back to her like a slap across the face. No, no, *no*! Just a dream—she was in her bed, not on the couch *touching* herself. She hadn't met with Rainier yet... But as she looked down at her wrist where two bite marks lingered, she wanted to bang her head against the wall until the memories disappeared forever. Kit must've carried her to bed after she— "Please tell me I didn't act like an idiot last night," she whispered to herself.

"You didn't act like an idiot last night," Kit echoed from near the window where he sat on the floor beside Roxy. One leg outstretched, the other bent toward him with his arm propped on top of it.

Stevie palmed her forehead. "Cauldron's teeth, pretend as if none of that happened." She'd never acted like such a horny little minx in her life.

"There's nothing to be embarrassed about. A vampire's venom would make even a nun beg for pleasure."

His words relaxed her a fraction. "Thank you, Kit." Her gaze drifted to his pants for a brief moment before she flicked her stare away. She definitely hadn't dreamed or imagined how he'd hardened against his pants. And even though the venom had worn off, she couldn't stop herself from wondering what his fingers would feel like trailing up her thighs.

16

Ametallic scent filled the air as Stevie spilled a bit of blood into three brews. She and Lucia were working in the basement together since an influx of orders had come through after the fog and darkness had only gotten worse —they wanted protection charms as a precaution, and the apothecary was closed on Sundays.

Kit had waited for Stevie to make it into Lucia's house before leaving on horseback to search the woods once again. There was so much she'd been thinking about. How Levi was most likely wandering around in hiding, how he'd somehow spelled her blood from letting anyone see her memories, how she'd touched herself in front of Kit. The last matter should've been the least important thing, but she couldn't stop inwardly groaning about it.

"All right," Lucia started as she stirred a brew for Stevie while she rubbed healing ointment on her finger. "So you said Rainier once saw Levi's ghost go into the woods where Kit was murdered after drinking blood from siren twins, and he couldn't see anything in your blood because he could taste the warlock's magic, right?"

"Yep!" Kit had also described Levi as having hair past his shoulders, his height a little shorter than Kit, a slim build, high cheekbones, and an amulet around his neck. But with the white coloring being so generic, ghosts were much harder to pick out of a line-up.

"Hmm." Lucia pursed her lips together. "From what Rainier found out about your blood, this will be enough for the council to have to dig up Levi's bones and allow me to see if I can locate him."

"That would be ideal." Stevie took the brew from Lucia and drank it down. She clucked her tongue against the roof of her mouth. "This one doesn't taste bad. Like lemonade."

"It won't lift the veil in your blood for two weeks. You have to drink one a day to fully cleanse everything. At least we can get that dark spell out of you though. But now this means your blood might help with another spell I want to try at the bonfire since the warlock's magic is inside you. With all the sacrifices —"

"Pumpkin sacrifices," Stevie clarified.

"*Pumpkin* sacrifices, which are still sacrifices, to add to the spell. With that, Kit's bone, the link between you and him, his ghost there, you there, my spell, the first Eye opened, and Levi's lingering magic, it could potentially work. No, it *will* work!" She squeezed Stevie's shoulder. "I'll make sure of it."

If any witch could make it work, it would be Lucia. And if not, they would come up with a Plan Z if they had to after trying every other letter.

"So what else happened?" Lucia asked. "Rainier drank your blood which means vampire venom was included. My aunt's told me things that I wish I could unhear about her times with Rainier."

Even though Kit was long gone, Stevie scanned the room to make sure he hadn't slinked back in behind her somewhere. But the coast was clear.

She pinched the bridge of her nose as the images flashed in her mind. "Rainier was fine and left. But after ... things got a little R-rated with Kit."

"You two had *sex?*" Lucia gasped. "After you said you two could touch, I knew it was highly probable."

"No!" Stevie hissed. "I mean, I sort of asked him to... And when he didn't, I took care of myself. In front of him. Like an idiot," she mumbled under her breath.

A grin spread across Lucia's face. "You knew the warning label that comes with a vampire's bite. And how sweet that Kit didn't want to take advantage. You're not under the venom influence anymore though..."

"The sex with the ghost part wouldn't be weird per se. At least not to us in Sleepy Hollow, but if he doesn't find his head, he won't be here after the new moon." A pit formed in her stomach at the thought of him in the Hollow, being picked apart by demon vultures.

"That just means I'll work harder on the spell for the bonfire. Give me a moment." Lucia went upstairs and brought back Maxine. She set Maxine on a nearby shelf, the plant looking less lively than usual. Lucia plucked a small vial, the smoke settled, completing Lucia's part of the spell. "Can you add one more droplet in this and place another on Gideon's plant? He was upset last night when he found Maxine wilting. I'm going to have him drink the vial—he was freaking out that he's balding because there were a few extra hairs in the sink."

Stevie shook her head and sighed. "My brother has thicker hair than me! He's such a drama queen."

After squeezing a bead of red into the vial, she approached Maxine. The plant snapped at her hand, her rows of sharp teeth on display.

"Calm down," Stevie soothed when Maxine snapped at her again. "I know you're hurting, but this will help you feel better." As she squeezed one more droplet into the flower's mouth, the doorbell rang.

"Always right after I put the gloves on," Lucia said, peeling the latex from her hands, pieces of hair falling against her face from her messy bun. "I'll be right back."

The flower hissed, and Stevie stroked the plant's blue and white polka-dotted head. "Just another second." Maxine leaned into her touch, a teeny purr escaping her sharp-toothed mouth. The leaves at Maxine's side perked up, the deep green returning to the spots that were browning.

Lucia bounded back down the steps, a cheek-to-cheek smile on her face. "Important news finally showed up on my doorstep!" She waved a golden envelope in the air like she was waving Willy Wonka's golden ticket, which in this case, it sort of was. "Adelia replied in her vague manner in case her letter was intercepted. She'll be here as soon as she can but definitely before the new moon. She's taking care of a rabid vampire problem in Maine first. Adelia said that suspicions and no proof isn't a reason for her not to finish her current task. But this is good news!" She tapped a finger against her chin. "I don't know if she'll receive the letter I sent yesterday before she leaves. But if she does, I know she'll come sooner since the sky darkening earlier has to be some sort of proof. The priests are blessing the land and witches are putting extra protection spells down. Maybe I'll do another one at the bonfire."

"Probably two."

"Before I forget," Lucia said, "when you meet with Adelia, you're going to have to dress up. And by dress up, I don't mean a fancier dress, but a *fancier* dress."

Stevie arched a brow. "You mean like the last time you went and saw her?" She recalled Lucia's tight bodice, the poofy lacy skirt of the dress reaching her ankles, the white wig, the fan, the pearls. Lucia had been Marie Antoinette reincarnate.

"That was a witch coronation, but close. Just think old Sleepy Hollow times. Like Kit." She beamed. "But don't worry since I'll be dressed up and going with you and the Headless Horseman. Only us three are allowed to attend."

Stevie snickered. "Gideon's going to throw a fit."

"We'll probably have to pick him up a suit just to wear for when I come home." Lucia chuckled.

Stevie wrinkled her nose because she knew what that meant. Sexy roleplay.

"Looks like we'll go shopping today so we're prepared for when Adelia arrives," Lucia said as she corked her potions and handed Stevie the Crowned Witch's letter to read over.

STEVIE STARED at the sapphire gown in the mirror. When she'd thought she would just pick up something cheap at a thrift store, Lucia had waved off that idea and taken them to one of the best costume shops Sleepy Hollow had to offer. The strip center wasn't as busy since the tourists weren't flocking toward the stores. They normally visited the costume shops and put on historical suits and dresses to take black and white pictures that would make them look as if they were from that time period.

Studying the bodice of the gown, Stevie ran her palms against the silky material. Black lacy buttons lined the front, and a square neckline accentuated her décolleté. It was the first dress that had caught her eye when she'd entered the store, but Lucia had made them try on dress after dress, needing to make sure Adelia knew they weren't cutting corners while in her presence.

"That's the gown!" Lucia screeched when Stevie stepped out of the dressing room.

Stevie rolled her eyes. "This is the original one I picked out."

"We needed to confirm it was the best." Lucia swished her red skirt, then brushed a finger across the sweetheart neckline. "Do you think this dress is the one?"

"That's the winner!" Stevie looked down at the price tag on her sleeve and her eyes widened. "Actually, how about we go to the thrift shop instead? Or can't you just spell one of my old dresses?"

Lucia's grin grew wide. "I could, but Adelia can tell. Besides, that's the purchase price. We're only renting these. So as long as you don't ruin the dress, you'll be fine. *Or* have sex with a certain ghost who's staying with you while wearing it." She waggled her brows.

Stevie pursed her lips. "It was the *venom*."

"*Sure* it was." She laughed softly and whirled around. "Can you unbutton me? I think I need to retry two on. Just to make sure."

"That dress is literally perfect on you." Stevie unfastened the buttons lining the back of the velvet dress. But really, all the gowns looked good on Lucia, except for maybe a puke green one that wouldn't have worked for anyone.

Stevie returned to the dressing room and hung her gown on the hook. As she slipped her skirt back on, her phone rang and she scurried to answer it.

"Hi, Mom," Stevie grunted while shoving on her boots.

"So, I hear you have a secret meeting coming up."

"Did Gideon call you cry-babying that he couldn't attend?" Before Stevie left with Lucia, her sister-in-law had asked Gideon to deliver the package to her mom since there were pressing matters to attend to. And of course he was going suit shopping after like Lucia had guessed.

"You know Gideon," her mom said. "But don't worry. He's keeping it hush-hush with everyone else. So did you find a dress?"

"I did. It's something straight from centuries past. I'll be a good little girl and have my ankles covered."

"I've never met Adelia, but I hear she's a headstrong woman." She paused. "And don't forget to send me pictures. You chose to attend an antique auction over going to prom, so I want to see you in something lavish."

"I have no regrets about that day. I'll send you a picture though." Stevie smiled, and an instant later it fell from her face. "What about the weird stuff going on around town with the fog and it getting darker earlier? Are you feeling okay? More customers than usual are asking for protection spells, and I just want to make sure you're all right."

"You mean that my *heart* is all right," her mom said gently. "And it is. A little extra fog and darkness isn't going to make it leap out of my chest, sweetie."

She was right of course, but the more of it that came, the closer the second Eye was to opening. Kit only had so much time in the hourglass he was currently standing in before it covered him completely. And the question she had was, when had Levi spelled her? Was it before or after the last new moon? What if the satchel he carried held Kit's ghost head? Could he use a seer's eyes as his own? With magic, *dark* magic, she bet he could.

"Earth to Stevie," her mom chimed.

Stevie blinked, snapping herself out of her thoughts. "Sorry, what?"

"I asked if Kit was being a gentleman, or do I need to kick his ass?"

"He's been a good little Horseman, Mom." It was her who hadn't acted in a very *ladylike* fashion.

17

Stevie found Roxy curled up on the rug beneath the coffee table after she got home from the costume shop. "Has Kit been here at all?" she asked, resting her dress on the back of the couch.

The fox shook her head, then barked.

"Fine. I'll go look for him." She had to know if there was a possible way that Levi could've been a seer all this time by using the Horseman's ghost head. It had to be the reason Kit never felt it, not just the dark spells. As for his actual skull, Levi's magic had to have hidden it extremely well when he was part of the living world.

She stepped out into the fog, and Roxy took off for the woods. Stevie whistled, causing the fox to still, her ears perking up as she trotted back toward their home.

"I know it's not ideal, but I don't want you going into the woods alone right now. You can ride with me though." Stevie patted her seat and the fox hopped up.

As Stevie drove through town, the fog grew thicker, sliding up just past her waist. She went down a quiet street where a ghost walked beside a middle-aged woman, most likely anticipating the Eye opening. Unless he was a pervert as Stevie's mom would've said.

She pulled up near the woods, and before she trekked down the trail to look for Kit, a horse's hooves filled the air, coming in her direction. A second later, a broad white form on horseback broke through the trees.

Stevie waved, and as Kit slowed, her heart pounded like heavy drums in her ears. And it wasn't from nervousness, only the comfortable sight of seeing him.

Kit tugged on Inferno's reins, and the horse's gaze met Stevie's. The stallion let out a low whinny, puffs of smoke escaping his nostrils.

Kit easily slid down from his horse, his feet striking the earth. "I heard your ride. You were planning to traipse in here alone?"

"I wasn't alone," she said. "Roxy's here. Besides, aren't *you* alone?"

"I've been taking care of myself for centuries, Pumpkin."

"So that means we're both stubborn." Stevie smiled. "Anyway, when I was with Lucia earlier, I thought of something." She told him about the brew Lucia had given her, the spell her sister-in-law would soon perform at the bonfire, and then Stevie's theory about Levi. "Do you think that maybe he's been using your eyes to see things over the years, and that's why you can't feel them? Possibly even why your head vanished so quickly when Lucia used the wishbone? Not just because of dark magic? It's possible that your ghost head was in the satchel Rainier saw Levi with."

Kit's fists tightened at his sides, flexing and unflexing his fingers. "That has to be the case. He's planning something, and I know he's been using my eyes all along. But I don't know where he is or why he would do something to you. I will tear his ghost apart before he gets near you again."

Stevie bit her lip, mulling over more. "The council library book mentioned that his grandson was a seer. I think they might've had contact."

"He could've." Kit paused, his shoulders pulling back as he studied something above him. "There's certainly more to it than sending me to the Hollow. Clara once told me that Levi wanted to learn more about the demons' home, and she had me help her make a few spells to make him forget about it."

"So a Hollow obsesser... The council weeds those people out whenever possible. An illness took him a year after your death, but somehow he still had your ghost head hidden during that time. He knows something about the Eye that we don't, and it would have to be from dark magic. Tonight we're coming back here for the bonfire and we'll see if Lucia's spell helps find your head. And if it's not here, then we'll just continue looking for it and Levi. The Crowned Witch got the letter and is coming soon, and I know she'll help us uncover something."

"This bastard is tricky," Kit ground out. "If I've been riding every night for over two hundred years and have never spotted him while sweeping up and down every square inch of Sleepy Hollow, then he must be using a cloaking spell."

"We're getting somewhere. Little by little." Stevie frowned, a chill racing up her spine as she peered around, wondering if Levi was watching them right then. If he did use that spell, he could've been around her at any time, any moment.

"Slowly but surely. Time is truly of the essence now."

Kit was right. A little over a week was left until the second Eye opened, and if nothing happened in Sleepy Hollow besides the living getting to visit the dead, and their theory was wrong, Kit would still spend eternity in the Hollow regardless. Before she met him, she would've sworn on her life that he was a demon and was meant for the Hollow. But one visit to an abandoned house had changed everything.

She let out a long sigh. "Let's go home and get ready for the bonfire. Lucia and Gideon will be meeting us soon."

STEVIE GATHERED a small garden shovel and rake from the back of the dusty shed. The tools were pitiful, but they might be able to perform their duty. She hadn't thought to search the shed before since the owner sent someone every week to take care of the garden and yard.

Stevie drank a glass of milk before finding Kit hovering over her dress in the living room, trailing a finger down the material. "If you like it that much you can cuddle it tonight." She grinned.

He snapped his hand back. "I was only wondering what it was."

She laughed softly, plucking the fabric up and dangling it in front of him. "It's my gown for our meeting with the Crowned Witch. I have to dress fashionably like you for a night, so we'll be twins. Even though you'll be Mr. Invisible to her."

"Mmm, I prefer the clothing you wear."

"And why is that?" she drawled, placing her bare foot on the coffee table. "Do you like seeing my ankles and calves?" She held up her arm. "Or maybe these pretty appendages."

He cleared his throat. "You're very peculiar." But his voice came out deeper than usual.

Stevie's heart pounded faster, her teasing manner fading as tension filled the air.

The doorbell rang and Stevie jolted, tearing her gaze from him. "That's probably Lucia." Without another glance at Kit, she hurried to the door.

"Good news before we go." Lucia smiled, wearing a deep purple cloak for the bonfire. "Levi's remains are being dug up tonight for me to have a look at in the morning."

"The council is finally getting on the ball? That's a surprise," Stevie said. "Let me grab my things. The tools from the shed are pretty pitiful."

"Gideon actually borrowed a shovel from your mom." Lucia grinned. "Do you have the bone?"

"Yep, give me a second." She plucked a black velvet cloak from her closet and met Kit near the kitchen counter. His tall form hovered above her and her breath caught at the sight of him. "Cape off. Check. Gloves still gone. Check. Sword is fine since it might be needed. But can you make sure Inferno doesn't go so things aren't obvious?"

"I'll keep my whistles to myself," he uttered, pushing away from the counter and closer to her.

She opened her mouth to say something when the door pushed open. "I'm still out here. Waiting on the porch," Lucia called.

"Come in." Stevie fished out the bone from her purse. Lucia walked in and handed her a vial of gold dust to lightly coat across the bone. With each brush to the remain, she noticed Kit flexing his fingers, feeling her strokes. The bone flickered, then shone like real gold.

"Now add one drop of blood and tuck it away for now," Lucia said.

Stevie pricked her finger and pressed a droplet to the bone. It instantly absorbed the red bead before she slipped the remain into her backpack.

"Kudos for thinking about the shovel." Stevie patted her brother's shoulder as she slipped into the backseat of his beastly truck with Kit just behind her.

"You know I always think ahead, baby sister." Gideon smiled, pulling his brown hood over his head. When he took off down the street, he asked Kit annoying questions that Stevie had to answer. *How did it feel to have your head cut off? Why didn't you try harder to snap Clara out of her trance? Why did you ride the horse everywhere instead of walk?*

It felt like death. Because it wouldn't work and could make things worse. Why not?

Gideon eventually pulled into a grassy field where cars were starting to park since along the curb was already filled. As she stepped down from the truck, the fog glided across the grass and tickled Stevie's ankles like tiny fingers caressing her flesh.

"Don't forget the pumpkins!" Lucia shouted, standing on the back of the truck to hand one to each of them.

"Whoa! It just vanished," Gideon said, looking toward where Kit had grabbed his. "That's genius."

Cradling her pumpkin, Stevie skirted around the trees and the foliage to get to the bonfire. Smoke billowed toward the sky —the stars half gone, their light muted—from the blazing bonfire. The Crowned Witch needed to *hurry*.

Lit torches burned around clusters of people who stood near the fire drinking, snacking, and chatting. Stevie's pulse thrummed in anticipation of tossing her pumpkin into the crackling orange flames. It was a tradition that she'd done ever since she could remember. When she was younger, her mom and dad would host the celebration on a smaller scale in their back-yard with just the four of them and Roxy.

As Lucia and Gideon went to grab a few drinks, Stevie's gaze roamed around the crowd, searching for a pale white form carrying a satchel. All were empty-handed of the item. A few ghosts were scattered about, but in the distance, two white forms caught her attention. Erik and a woman who was pulling him by the wrist. His body pressed into hers against a tree as he kissed her. Good for him to get a little action that wasn't in a comic book. Maybe his residency would fade, but she would miss seeing his presence at the store.

Stevie turned to Kit and whispered while lifting her pump-kin, "Make a wish. I'll go first." *I wish for us to find Kit's head.* She then tossed the pumpkin into the fire, watching embers flick up from it.

"Do we tell one another our wish?" he drawled.

Stevie shook her head. "Nope. Just like blowing candles out on a birthday cake, it's a *secret*." But she assumed he would wish for the same thing she had. When no one was paying them any mind, he hurled his pumpkin in like a baseball.

She laughed softly and surveyed the crowd again, noticing most of the ghosts had left. Her gaze locked on a familiar form wearing a royal blue cloak—Reese. He was talking to two other guys when he glanced over his shoulder and his eyes met hers.

With a smile, he headed in her direction, raking a hand through his curly blond hair. "I didn't know you were coming, or I could've given you a ride."

"Eh, I'm not staying long. I just came to toss my pumpkin into the flames to satisfy the Horseman." Behind her Kit scoffed at her words. "I have more work to do for Lucia."

Reese cocked his head. "Oh yes, more *paranormal* things. By the way, I came across a few comic books that Gideon would die to have in his store. I can text you later about them if you want."

"Sure." Something was weird, and she couldn't put her finger on it.

"See ya, Stevie." Reese didn't return to his friends and instead left through the woods toward the cars.

"Gideon is walking this way. He could've told him about the comic books himself without asking to text you," Kit muttered under his breath.

"Sorry it took us so long," Lucia said, handing Stevie a chocolate bar. "The moon is out, so I want you to go deeper in the woods away from the bonfire. Gideon and I will keep an eye out here near the edge. If you end up needing the shovel, text me and I'll get it for you."

Stevie and Kit slipped past the bonfire and trekked farther into the woods. She looked behind her, not seeing a soul in sight. But all she could think about was what if Levi was following them, hidden in a cloaking spell?

With a shaky breath, Stevie took out the bone from her backpack. "Try holding it the best you can." She lifted the bone between them, the gold flickering beneath the moonlight. Kit's ghost hand sank right through it, but he steadied his fingers at the bone's middle. It didn't matter though—Lucia had said his energy could still ignite the spell.

"How long do we wait?" Kit asked after about sixty seconds had passed.

"Let's say five minutes," Stevie said. "It might take some time to get cranking since Lucia hasn't ever performed a spell like this." But there was the possibility it wouldn't work either.

After another minute went by, a flicker of light illuminated and the gold dust glowed brightly. Stevie stepped left and the light faded. As she walked in the opposite direction, the gold lit up once more.

"This treasure hunt might work after all." She grinned as anticipation stormed through her veins. They went forward, backward, sideways, until she made another left and a golden line, like a string of yarn, shot out, piercing through the dirt in front of a tree.

Stevie tapped her foot against the soft ground. "Have you searched here before?"

"I have, but ghosts can't truly dig in the ground."

"You're in luck, because I can. Let me text Lucia." But as she held up the bone, the line wasn't penetrating the dirt at all—it pointed toward the *tree*.

Kit knelt before the trunk, his finger brushing over the bark and trailing across a seam. "Here."

Stevie dug her fingernails into the bark and a part of the tree silently opened like a door.

"Something isn't right," Kit said, unsheathing his sword and shifting his feet in a full circle while scanning the woods. "As powerful as Levi is, it wouldn't be that easy."

"Maybe he forgot to lock it? Unless this is a different witch's treasure." She lifted the bone, its gold lighting up the small area. Within the tree rested an old black metal box and she drew it out. She easily opened the lid, finding it not quite empty. A lock of dark hair lingered inside a preserved jar. *Kit's* hair.

"That bastard," Kit growled. "He knew you would come here at some point and did it to toy with us."

"Who knows how long the head has been missing though..." she trailed off. "Even then, he can't touch bones, so someone would've had to do it. And are they still alive, or had he convinced a seer to move it long ago? It would also mean that he was most likely the one to cast the spell on your bones at the abandoned house. Maybe he got a seer to put them there after having them dug up, hoping to keep them further separated from your head?"

"I don't think we'll have an answer tonight. But I'll make damn certain we find one."

STEVIE RAN a towel through her wet hair after a hot shower. As the water pelted her skin, she kept wondering about the empty box, needing more than ever for the Crowned Witch to get into town. Even if Lucia sent her a third letter, she would get here before receiving it. Stevie had given the lock of Kit's hair to Lucia to make a spell, and if it didn't work, they would bring a few strands to Adelia.

Kit sifted through one of her coin collections on her bedroom floor. "That one's from Spain," Stevie said, studying his fingers and the way he twirled a coin between them. "Look at you and your hidden ability. You should join a magic act."

"Perhaps I'll be the man with the disappearing head," Kit purred. She continued to observe his fingers, the coin, and he chuckled. "Do you like watching my hand, Pumpkin? Do you want to feel my fingers?"

Stevie jerked her head up, trying to think of a witty retort. For one of the rare times in her life, she drew a blank. Instead she could only nod.

He caught the coin and slipped it back into her box. "My eyes are closed, in case you're curious."

"Good." She smiled, shutting hers too. "I wouldn't want to be left hanging. But don't think for a second I have a secret hand fetish." It was only because he didn't have a face she could see, so she'd come to observe other parts of him.

Slowly reaching forward, her hand brushed against his smooth, cool skin. Stevie's heart skipped a beat as he turned over her palm to draw gentle circles in the center with his fingertip.

"Sorry not everyone's skin can be as silky as yours," Stevie murmured.

"I rather like how yours feels." Even though he couldn't inhale, Stevie could've sworn she'd heard him take a shallow breath. "You're not ensnared by venom tonight. This may be forward of me, but what would you do if I kissed you?"

"*Not* imagine spelling you into an insect." Stevie's hand left his and skated up his chest to just behind his neck. "*This* might be even more forward."

Kit chuckled and his fingers entangled in her hair. Then as light as fluttering dragonfly wings, cool lips that tasted of moon-light coasted across hers. His teasing movements only made her greedier. And seeming to crave more too, his other hand drifted to her hip to pull her closer.

Stevie didn't just inch forward, she crawled right into his lap like a possessed soul willing to do his bidding.

"You know, I wouldn't mind at all if you kissed me a second time," she whispered against his lips.

"All you had to do was ask." Then Kit's mouth was on hers, his tongue slipping between her lips, deepening the kiss. She moaned, wrapping her arms around his neck and getting as close to him as possible. He hardened beneath her, and she wished she could peek at him to see his expression, but she only tightened her eyelids, not willing to risk their touches snapping apart.

"You have me at your will," Kit rasped.

"The Headless Horseman at my will? What will all the ghosts

say?" Stevie grinned. As she finally had the chance to loosen the first button of his shirt collar, a distressed whinny screeched outside in the distance. Stevie's eyes shot open and she dropped through Kit.

He was already standing and bolting through the wall. She threw back the curtains as Roxy darted from the living room into hers. No one was in the backyard except for Kit, whistling for Inferno to hear his call.

But the horse never answered.

As Stevie placed two waffles on her plate and drank her daily brew to kick Levi's magic inside her blood to the curb, a loud knock pounded on the door.

Lucia grasped a golden envelope when Stevie answered. "I have good news to help level the bad, but also some more bad."

"Would that mean someone found Levi's bones, or you felt Kit's stallion somewhere?" Stevie asked. After the council dug up Levi's bones, they'd been missing from the empty coffin, not even a strand of hair had remained. As for Inferno, Stevie and Kit had searched endlessly for him throughout Sleepy Hollow, to no avail.

"Neither, but I did bring a brew with a horse's hair for Kit to try. He just needs to drink the solution after adding a drop of your blood. There's also this." Lucia held up the envelope. "Adelia arrived early this morning and one of her servants brought it for us to meet with her this afternoon. As for the bad —I went to help spell the land this morning, as per usual, and when I pressed my hand against the earth, I not only felt warmth, but a *pulse*. The ground itself feels hollower."

Stevie's chest tightened. "It's Levi."

Lucia fidgeted with the hem of her shirt, seeming nervous for the first time since Stevie had known her. "I'm going to get ready for the meeting."

"All right." Stevie took the vial from Lucia, then forced down the waffles, but her stomach churned with nausea over what her sister-in-law had said. If the land was becoming hollower because of Levi, what exactly was he trying to do? Her heart lodged in her throat at the thought that she wouldn't have an answer before the next full moon in order to save Kit.

Stevie polished off her milk to calm her nerves.

Kit still wasn't back from searching the town, so she took a hot shower while her pulse thrummed. She needed the time to speed up so they could discuss everything with Adelia.

After toweling off and blow drying her hair, Stevie put black winged liner on top of a light gray eyeshadow. She ran a brush through her orange locks, and even though she was still weighing the possibilities, she couldn't block out how she and Kit had kissed two nights ago, the feel and coolness of him, his hands both strong and ethereal against her.

"Stop being an idiot," Stevie scolded herself as she padded into the living room. She shouldn't be reminiscing about such things when it felt like her town could crack in half.

"I suppose sometimes I can be an idiot," Kit teased.

Stevie's gaze flicked to Kit relaxing on the couch, Roxy lying beside him.

Her heart picked up that he'd made it safely back. "I wasn't talking about *you*. I meant me."

"Hmm," he said, a smile in his voice. "I would have to disagree. By the way, you look lovely."

"I thought you hated this dress." She grinned, gliding her hands down the silken skirt.

"It looks better on you."

"Well, thank you, Kit. We're finally meeting with the Crowned Witch." She sank down next to him, and Roxy hopped to the other side of the couch to sit near her. Since Inferno had been taken, she'd asked Roxy to stay inside with her or go next door to Lucia's, at least until they learned more. "Any luck finding your horse?"

"No sign of him. I know that bastard has him," he ground out.

"We can try this. Lucia made a spell." Stevie uncorked the vial that she'd left on the coffee table and pricked her finger. She squeezed out a drop of blood into the contents. "Drink it and we'll see if Inferno comes here."

Kit tossed back the liquid as Stevie rubbed the healing ointment on her finger. He released a whistle and they waited and waited, but Inferno never came.

Stevie let out a heavy breath and explained to him what Lucia had said about the earth, how it didn't feel right. "We know it's dark magic, and that he's planning something evil."

Maybe it had something to do with the ghosts not having to return to being separate from the living, but why? Stevie furrowed her brow and checked her phone. It was *time*. Forgoing her backpack, she tucked Kit's bone into a small satchel she'd used as part of her *Lord of the Rings* costume three years ago.

As they stepped outside into the light fog, Lucia was locking up her door. "Gideon said he's on standby in case we need him, which makes him feel important." She arched a brow at Stevie's feet. "Mary Janes? Really?"

Stevie placed a hand on her hip. "Would you rather I wear my Converse?" She hadn't thought about shoes when they'd been out and about, but she figured the Mary Janes would be fine since they were black.

Lucia waved a hand in the air and leather heeled boots with pointy toes and thin laces replaced her shoes. "Thank you, Fairy Godmother," Stevie cooed.

"Those will do, and I don't think Adelia will be paying enough attention to know I spelled them."

They piled into Lucia's car, and Stevie told her that the brew was a no-go for returning Kit's horse.

Lucia scowled. "Sneaky warlock. I don't like him. I promise on my life as a witch, we're going to find him, and I'm going to do worse than turn him into a cat." She looked in the rearview mirror toward Kit. "So, how was the Crowned Witch during your time? Was she bitchy? I heard that most of them before Adelia were."

"She was never there." He shrugged. "Always taking care of things outside our village, and Levi was the head of the council during those days."

Stevie repeated Kit's words to Lucia and how although the witches of the council's magic had dwindled, they were at least a step above that one. But the first thing she would do if she oversaw the town would be to have Lucia put a spell on the cemetery to make sure bones weren't so easily taken.

Lucia drove into the woods, the car jostling them. She held up a hand, making the trees part for them until they reached a dirt road leading to two iron gates. The area was hidden and protected from tourists, but even while Adelia was away, there were always servants keeping watch to make sure no one entered. Since the home was first built, every Crowned Witch had lived there, and with the help of spells, not once had it ever looked deteriorated.

A middle-aged bald man lifted his hand as they approached. Lucia rolled down her window, showing him the Crowned Witch's letter. "Hello, Julian, Adelia invited us today."

Julian's face remained neutral. "Give me a strand of your hair. You and your guest."

They both plucked their hair, then Lucia passed them to Julian. He dropped them into a liquid jar he drew out from his pocket. The strands dissipated as the color of the contents turned yellow.

"You may proceed." Julian flicked his hand and the gate opened, the creaking reverberating through the woods.

Lucia drove down the cobbled path toward the black and pink gothic home. Stevie's gaze swept from the obsidian roof with its cone-shaped towers to the large oval and rectangular windows decorating the front. Various black flowers filled the gardens, blooming to their fullest. Pansies, tulips, dahlias, petunias, irises, and roses, all peeking out from emerald bushes.

Once Lucia parked the car, she walked ahead with Stevie and Kit close behind her. A man dressed in a light gray suit straight from the 1700s opened the door for them to a maid, her hair tucked beneath a white cap.

Golden sconces were lit against the beige wall, and portraits of every past Crowned Witch hung down the hallway, not a single speck of dust anywhere. Antique pieces sprawled the tables and shelves, making Stevie's fingers itch to tuck one inside her satchel.

The maid led them down an ornate carpeted hallway into the dining area where a regal woman sat at the head of a long glass table that could easily fit twenty. A bowl of grapes and a golden goblet lingered in front of her. Adelia wore her gray hair in a curled style, her bright pink gown making her dark skin practically glow. At any angle the witch looked ageless, both young and old at the same time.

"Darling Lucia. Come here. It's been too long." Adelia held out an elegant hand and Lucia knelt at the witch's side, grasping it. "Your powers have grown much quicker than I expected. I feel the strength of your magic."

"I practice as much as I can." Lucia bowed her head, then smiled. "And I have an excellent assistant who makes it possible."

Adelia tipped up Lucia's chin. "There's another reason I wanted to meet with you. A little over a year from now, my time will come to an end, and that means I will need a replacement. I've sent word to the council today that you will be my successor."

"*Me?*" Lucia gasped. "Not Ginger?"

"Even when you were a child, your aunt always knew it would be you." She batted Lucia away. "Now, let's get on to other important matters. This is your assistant, I presume. But is the other *guest* here too?"

Stevie took a hesitant step forward after Lucia gave her the go-ahead to tell her what had been happening. "The Headless Horseman, Kit, is with us, and he isn't a demon ghost or anything close. A warlock named Levi Brom Bonham murdered him, then spread lies about him to their village. If Kit doesn't find his head before the Eyes seal shut, he'll be cursed to live eternity inside the Hollow."

Adelia tilted her head to the side, her expression neutral. "And this is important to me why?"

Stevie held her tongue from saying she wasn't finished yet. "There's more. Lucia felt that the ground in our town was hollower, warmer, and pulsing. I'm not sure if you received Lucia's second letter, but the fog has grown thicker, lingering, the darkness comes earlier each day, and the stars' lights have started to flicker out. There's no doubt in my mind that Levi is planning something for the new moon."

"We're not sure what though," Lucia added.

"You're accurate." Adelia took a sip of her drink. "The gate of the Hollow is threatening to open. I knew as soon as I returned."

"What gate?" Lucia asked, her eyes widening.

"I've never heard of any gates," Kit said, his body turning toward Stevie. And neither had she...

"Of course not. Even the Crowned Witch has rules she must obey, but because of what is occurring now, they must be broken." She set her goblet on the table. "The Hollow has seven gates around the world that were sealed long ago. However, on the night when both Eyes are open, the seal of the gate in this very town can be broken with the head of a male seer."

So the Eyes of the Hollow were literally the Eyes of the *Hollow*.

"I'm going to tear that bastard's head off myself," Kit growled.

"Levi has a seer's head. Kit's," Stevie rushed out. "The ghost part he can grasp, but we're not sure about the physical one. An empty box was left in a tree for us to find, and Kit's hair was placed there to taunt us, the head missing. If he needs it to open the gate, then someone living would have to bring it."

Adelia snapped her fingers, the sound like thunder. A book of old leather drifted into the room, straight into the witch's waiting hands. "Show me the seers living in Sleepy Hollow," she instructed the tome. The book flew open, the pages flipping until they came to a sudden stop. She clucked her tongue and spoke again, "Now take me to Levi Brom Bonham's living blood relatives." Her cool gaze lifted to Stevie after several seconds ticked by. "It seems our Levi has a living family member who is a seer. Reese Willoughby."

Stevie's eyes widened. *Reese.*

"I knew there was something off about him," Kit spat.

"That doesn't mean he has the head or consulted with Levi," Lucia said.

"He might not. There are other seers here." Adelia focused on Stevie as if she could be a suspect for assisting the warlock. "But if there is a possibility that Levi doesn't truly have the Horseman's physical head, it would mean he could find a way to use Reese's," Adelia added. "This we will keep from the council for now. I will search for Levi myself, and Stevie will bring Reese here. As for you, Lucia, it looks as though I will begin your Crowned Witch training sooner than expected. It will start tomorrow morning."

19

"That was an interesting turn of events," Stevie said to Lucia as they drove back home after their meeting. Adelia couldn't do anything to get Levi's magic out of her any faster, nor was Kit's hair any good to her. One thing was for sure though—reattaching Kit's head wouldn't bring hungry demons to Sleepy Hollow. However, Levi playing with Kit's head at the gate could. "And congrats to you, Soon-to-be Crowned Witch."

"Reese was acting strange at the bonfire since I was standing right beside you," Kit mumbled from the backseat.

"It makes sense now." Stevie recalled the bonfire, the way he'd said *paranormal*. How he'd sent her a picture of a house with pumpkins, hinting that he knew the Headless Horseman had been around her.

"What makes sense?" Lucia asked.

"When I saw Reese at the bonfire he seemed different. I thought it had something to do with you since I'd told him I was busy helping you until after the Eye. But now I know it's because he's seen the Headless Horseman with me. He was in my *house* with him. He could see him all this time. Not once did his gaze ever drift in Kit's or Roxy's direction though..."

"He could've been waiting for you to tell him?" Lucia guessed.

"Or he could've been trained," Kit said between what had to be a clenched jaw.

"As Kit just said, being trained would be a possibility since Levi could've talked to him." Stevie sighed and glanced at her phone, hoping a text was there. She'd messaged Reese from Adelia's, asking him if he could come over tomorrow to discuss the comic books. Kit had wanted to pay Reese a visit right then, but both Adelia and Lucia had agreed that he shouldn't go alone, not after Inferno went missing. All they needed was for Stevie to bring Reese to Adelia's.

Lucia turned down a narrow street, the lampposts barely providing any light at all, the fog and darkness holding the town of Sleepy Hollow in its clutches. "Nothing from him yet?"

"Zilch." After she'd practically blown him off, it was expected. But still. He was the one who'd also mentioned getting Gideon comics. She couldn't really be mad that Reese hadn't told her he was a seer because she hadn't confided in him either. While on their couple of lukewarm dates, there wasn't a reason to anyway. All she could think about was the date when Kit had talked about him right inside her house, and not once had there been a change in Reese's expression. Could he have known Kit had already been there before? He had to have.

After they went by Reese's street, finding his car gone, Lucia drove them home. She gave Stevie a tight hug on the porch. "Just stay safe, and remember, I'm only a door away."

Kit slipped into the house just as Gideon opened the other door. "I stayed on alert the whole time," he said to Lucia, waggling his brows.

"At least wait until I get inside, Gideon!" Stevie groaned just as the bolt unlocked for her. "That's my cue. Goodnight!" She shut the door behind her and gave Roxy a pet with her eyes closed in the kitchen. Stevie then sank onto a chair at the table, where Kit had poured her a glass of milk. "You're the best."

"I could hear those words for eternity from your lips."

Stevie smiled, her cheeks heating as she checked her phone again, then searched Reese's name. It was the same as before, things to do with the convention he ran. Even his social media didn't have much about him, only pictures of comic books and action figures.

They only had a week left before the second Eye opened!

Clomp. Clomp. Clomp. Kit's heavy boots thumped against the tile, and she looked up from her phone. "You're going to break a hole in the floor if you continue stomping against it."

His pacing halted in front of her. "I should go to his house tonight. I need to do more."

Stevie drank the last of her milk. "You heard Adelia. If Levi is lurking about he could do something to you. Once Reese is with the Crowned Witch, then we ask the questions we need to."

"Levi could've already done something to me if he wanted to. For centuries. As for Reese, I don't want you around that ass again."

"Aww, jealous?" she drawled.

One of his hands came down on the table, the other on the back of her chair, and she sucked in a breath at his nearness. "This is a serious matter," he said.

"And I'm serious." Stevie's gaze lifted to where Kit's head was missing. Her blood could bring him to life if he got his head back. And what after? Ride off into the Sleepy Hollow sunset? *Too far ahead, Stevie.* Because, at the moment, Kit had a real chance of not surviving past the new moon, and if the Hollow opened, the town could be run by demons that would shift into anyone's worst nightmare.

"I don't trust him," Kit growled. "We need to search his home."

Stevie inched closer to him, half forgetting what it would feel like to touch his real face. "Trust my plan. If he doesn't text back tonight, we'll go by his house first thing in the morning. If he's there, I'll drag him to Adelia's, and if he's not, then you can search the house."

Kit's fingers flexed and unflexed at his sides as he returned to pacing. But at least he didn't argue.

Stevie pulled out the chair beside her and patted the seat. "Come here."

He stopped, and she knew down to her marrow that he was giving her an incredulous look.

"I won't bite," Stevie said. "At least not like a vampire can."

Kit folded his arms and sat in the chair, his shoulders still rigid.

"Close your eyes," Stevie instructed at the same time she shut hers. Her hand brushed the hard muscle of his bicep and she stood from her chair. "Just lean forward. You need to release some stress—my floor can't take much more. You don't want me to not get my deposit back from the owner when I move, do you? All because you couldn't stand still."

Kit scoffed, and Stevie cupped her hands over both his shoulders. She dug her thumbs into his back muscles, then started to massage. A deep groan barreled up his throat as she continued to work his muscles, his body relaxing beneath her fingertips.

She bent toward his ear, while gliding her digits down to his biceps, and whispered, "Better?"

"Distract me further. If I have to be torn apart in the Hollow, I want something worthy of remembering." Kit's hand gently circled her wrist, guiding her toward him, and Roxy's paws fell against the floor as the fox left them alone.

It was a request that Stevie needed too. "Positive vibes tonight only," she said and tucked away the little horrors that could come. Stevie then trailed her fingers across his jawline. "So you want more than the massage package then?"

"Mm-hmm," Kit groaned, pulling her into his lap so that her legs straddled his thighs, his hands sliding to her hips. "Kiss me."

"I *guess* I can do that." Stevie smiled when her lips pressed to his, kissing him softly, and then like a tornado of wild bat wings, tension within her combusted once he brought her closer to him. As she deepened the kiss, his hands cupped her backside, and a heat licked between her thighs, making her gasp.

"Do you enjoy my touch?" he rasped.

"I think the massage package is about to become mine." Stevie's voice came out throaty, and Kit's forehead kissed hers. She wanted so badly to feel his hot breath mingling with hers, feel the thump of his heartbeat against her palm, the rise and fall of his chest as her head lay on top of it. But for now, their skin colliding would have to be enough.

Kit stood from the chair, holding her by the waist. A small squeak slipped out of her, but she didn't dare open her eyes.

"Keep them closed." He chuckled while cradling her. "I can't catch you if you fall, Pumpkin."

Stevie laughed, her arms around his neck. "Yes, Your Headlessness."

And then his lips were on hers again, his touch driving her crazy. His tongue flicked hers, both tender and dominant as he carried her to the couch. He rested her against the cushions, his strong body coming down on hers. Stevie's legs parted for him, and she clasped his hips, urging him to move against her.

"I'm straining to continue being a gentleman," he said gravelly.

She combed her fingers through his hair and gripped it. "You'll still be one if you make my toes curl first."

A deep laugh escaped him, and he smiled against her lips. "That I can *easily* do."

Kit lifted her dress, and she then remembered what she was wearing. "Don't open your eyes, but wait! This is a rented dress!" Stevie shouted. She unbuttoned the gown, not even wanting to think about paying full price for it. Kit leaned back as she tugged the fabric over her head and tossed it on what she hoped was the coffee table. "There! Now we resume." She lay back down in just her bra and panties while bringing Kit with her, his lips returning to hers, ravenous.

His cool hand skimmed down her stomach and slipped into her panties. She moaned as he dipped two digits inside her heat, his palm hitting and rubbing her core just right. So fantastically. His rhythmic motions continued, her breath increasing. She gripped his hair harder when she couldn't hold back, her body quaking, and came from his addicting movements.

"Now, I'll be a proper lady and return the favor," Stevie sang, her fingers fumbling for the button of his pants. Finally, she found the stupid thing and unfastened it to free his hard length. He growled when she grasped him, a deep groan rumbling up his throat as her thumb circled his tip. She pumped him in the way he seemed to like, gliding up and down his velvety skin, until a low and hypnotic sound escaped him.

Stevie hadn't meant to open her eyes so soon, but when she did, he dropped through her, both laying within one another, her catching her breath and him relaxing before he pushed himself up above her. "Pleasure and go. I see how it is," he said, a smile in his voice, and she wished there was a spell for her to see that smile.

"A massage session only lasts so long." She bit her lip, unable to contain the flying feeling soaring through her.

STEVIE TURNED her car down Reese's street since he never messaged her back. She looked toward his house, and his car was missing from action. Her eyes met the camera hanging just above the door, and she groaned. "New plan. Hang on."

She pulled farther down the street and parked along a curb. "There are cameras outside his house, and who knows what's inside, so I don't think it's best if I go with you. But I don't want you to be spotted either if he has a mystery sidekick or something worse lingering around."

"It's worth the risk," Kit said.

"All right then, here's what's going to happen," Stevie started. "If you find your head, Inferno, or something else important, come and tell me, then you can unlock the door and I'll help. Who cares about the cameras at that point. Afterward, we'll still have to find Reese though since he's a male seer. If we're wrong about our hunch, he needs to be kept away from Levi until both Eyes close."

"If for some reason I don't return, don't follow me in. Get one of the witches."

"Fine," Stevie lied. She would message Lucia, then go break inside the house, regardless if dark magic was potentially frolicking about.

Kit stepped through the car and ran toward Reese's house. She turned up the song to keep her heart from palpitating too much, crossing her fingers that he'd find his head in there, even if it meant Reese was a dirty little helper.

She texted Gideon to see if Reese had messaged her brother back. Gideon had contacted him that morning to ask about the comics for his shop.

Negative here.

With a sigh, Stevie set her phone down and kept her eyes trained on Reese's house. The night before barreled through her skull, how she and the Headless Horseman, of all people, had gotten each other off. And her greedy self wanted to do it *again* even with everything going on. "Not if he doesn't come back out first!"

As she was about to rip off her seatbelt and make way for Reese's house, Kit *finally* slipped out into the front yard.

"I couldn't find my head," he said after settling into the passenger seat, his shoulders stiffened. "Nor Inferno, or anything else of importance. It doesn't mean my head isn't there or buried elsewhere with a masking spell on it though."

She bit her lip. "There could be a third option. Let's say

Reese is helping Levi, but he doesn't know the warlock is 'evil' or whatever."

"It's possible," Kit said. "I wouldn't put anything past Levi."

Stevie started down the street, keeping her eye out for anything suspicious. "I'll have Lucia get back with Adelia and tell her Reese is missing if he isn't at his work. If we fail, there isn't a long lifeline to extend or an extra life to pluck out of the sky for you. And cauldron's teeth, I sure don't want to find out what the town will look like if the Hollow opens."

20

"So, what did Adelia say?" Stevie asked Lucia as soon as she answered the phone and put it on speaker for Kit to hear. She'd texted her sister-in-law earlier to let her know Reese still wasn't at his house and his work was locked up tight.

"No celebration news," Lucia said. "No luck with even her strongest spell at finding Levi. She's now made it a mission to contact the council and have them hunt Reese down. Then we trained for a little bit and she brushed me up on a few history secrets."

"Hopefully the council can locate him quickly."

"Something beyond fishy is going on for sure." Lucia sighed. "Reese might know the jig is up and is keeping a low profile, or Levi has him hidden somewhere with dark magic. I have a few errands to run for Adelia, but on the way, I'll collect a strand of Reese's hair from his home and try to locate him."

"Let me know what you find out."

Kit pushed away from the counter after Stevie ended the call. "Your mother's car just got here, so I'll search through Sleepy Hollow for Reese."

He could easily slip through houses and check places that she couldn't. It would be faster without her tagging along. "Be careful," Stevie said.

"For you, I will be." With that, he left toward the back of the house.

Roxy followed Stevie as she pulled out the pasta and two different sauces to start cooking for her mom. While filling the pot with hot water, the doorbell finally rang.

"White or red sauce? That's the conundrum I'm giving you." She grinned as she opened the door. "So—"

Stevie's mom grasped her chest through her blouse, beads of perspiration dotted her brow, and her skin was as pale as snow. "My heart. It just hit me," she stuttered, her breath ragged. "It's slowing."

Stevie's own heart stilled and she wrapped her arm around her mom's waist as she collapsed forward. "We have to go to Ginger's. Let me get you to my car."

"I'll be fine," her mom promised. "Your dad can take me later."

"There isn't time for that!" Stevie wouldn't wait around for the organ to slow further. It had only been inside her mom's rib cage for half the month.

Her mom didn't have the strength to argue, and so Stevie helped her into the passenger seat, then called Ginger as she drove toward the witch's house.

"Hello?" Ginger answered.

"Ginger, are you home? It's my mom. Something's going on with her heart," Stevie said hurriedly.

"I just came back from the apothecary, so you can bring her straight here. I'll meet you outside."

"See you in a couple of minutes." Stevie ended the call and was about to scroll to her dad's name when her mom's trembling hand gently pressed to Stevie's. "Don't call Jack. You're already taking me there. No need to worry him just yet."

Stevie still wanted to call her dad, but she didn't want to

stress her mom out more and make matters worse. She would wait and see how things played out.

For the first time in ages, tears stung Stevie's eyes, and she blinked them away. Her mom had always been there for her, through tears, heartbreak, holidays, nervousness, excitement. Stevie wouldn't go down the dark path of possibilities.

As promised, Ginger was waiting on the porch when Stevie arrived. The witch rushed to help Stevie's mom out of the car, and Stevie looped her arm around her mom from the other side. Her mom's body trembled, her balance wobbly. Not once when her mom's heart was due for another had she ever seen her this frail.

"You know where to take her. I'll retrieve the pig's heart," Ginger said after they crossed the threshold.

Stevie walked her mom to the basement door as Ginger fled out the back. They slowly descended the stairs and Stevie led her to a wooden chair near the cauldrons. She then grabbed a smock from a hook on the wall and draped it around her mom.

"Do you need anything else?" Stevie asked after snapping the smock at the back of her neck. "Besides a heart." She tried for humor, but her tone only came out worried as she knelt in front of her mom and held her shaking hand.

"Tell me about the meeting with the Crowned Witch like you were going to over lunch," she urged, her breath growing more ragged.

Stevie nodded and told her everything, and instead of becoming distressed, her mom only nodded. "You like him." Concern slipped out in her tone. "The Horseman."

"Are you worried because he's centuries older than the both of us?" Stevie drawled with a small smile. "Because really, he'll still look young. I've seen his head, remember?"

Her mom frowned. "I don't care about that. I just care about you getting hurt if you can't save him."

Stevie's smile faltered, but before she could reply, the basement door creaked open and Ginger's footsteps pounded down the steps. Blood smeared her hands, and a few drops spilled to the floor. "We don't have time to be nice and tidy. Grab the yellow powder just above the jar of bat eyes over there, then sprinkle it on the heart for me." Ginger pointed to the shelf in the corner.

Stevie fumbled through a few glass jars until she found the necessary one. She unscrewed the lid and sprinkled the powder on top of the bloody organ. Ginger then chanted a low incantation, the heart rising and falling as it beat in the witch's hand, before holding it out to Stevie's mom.

Shakily reaching out, her mom grasped the organ. Her lips parted, her jaw stretched, and her mouth opened wider and unnaturally wider. Every instance she'd ever seen her mom do this, it wasn't horror that coursed through Stevie but awe.

Her mom placed the beating heart inside her mouth, swallowing it whole, the squelching sound echoing throughout the basement. Stevie watched her mom's throat bulge as the organ slid down to replace the dying heart.

"I hate that you had to see me like this," her mom said, catching her breath, her blood-splotched hand on her chest. Already color returned to her pale face, her posture straightening.

As tears streaked Stevie's cheeks, she folded her arms around her mom. "I'll take you any way I can. It's part of you, and I love you."

STEVIE DROVE TO HER PARENTS' house even though her mom said she was fine to take the car home. But just in case. She called her dad and Gideon, and her brother said he would bring their mom's car later. Once her dad walked through the door, his face more worried than she'd ever seen him, he sank to his knees beside Stevie's mom. Stevie stayed a little longer before letting her parents have some alone time together.

Near the apothecary, a familiar white form, that she could easily spot anywhere, and no, not only because of his missing head, but by the way Kit sauntered down the sidewalk, assured in his movements as if he owned up to his name the Headless Horseman. She slowed the car into a parking space along the curb and rolled down the window. "Need a ride, stranger?" she called, making her accent come out deeply Southern. "I think you know these parts better than I do."

Kit's steps halted and his shoulders racked with laughter as he whirled to face her. But then he stilled, coming to her car in three long strides. "What happened? You've been crying."

Stevie knew her eyes were red-rimmed and puffy, and as the image of her mom collapsing on her porch came again, she wiped a loose tear away. "It's nothing," she lied after he sat in the passenger seat. "Cauldron's teeth, I can't keep this bottled up. It's my mom. When she came for lunch, her heart was slowing rapidly. Ginger said she'll need two a month going forward. But what if that doesn't work next time? What if nothing does?" she sobbed.

"Close your eyes," Kit said gently, inching closer, his hand falling through hers.

Taking a deep breath, she shut them, and his arms folded around her, strong and grounding as he held her. It was something she didn't know she needed, something as simple as a hug, and she relaxed against him. "Thank you," she whispered. The unease and anxiousness wouldn't grow wings and fly away completely, but the gesture lessened it.

Stevie didn't know how many minutes they sat like that, and she didn't care who crept by, gawking at her hugging air, but she finally shifted back from his cool comfort to drive home. She kept quiet on the ride, having to come to terms that her mom would just need an extra heart, and that Ginger believed it would hold her over for a while.

As soon as they walked through the door, Kit went straight to the kitchen and poured her a glass of milk. Stevie's heart fluttered at such a simple thing. Which could end in a classic heartbreak, but to Hollow with it.

"I'll gladly drink that." A small smile spread her lips as she sat on the counter and polished off the glass. She leaned back against the cabinets and sighed.

Kit stood before her, placing his hands on either side of her thighs. "Do you need anything else?"

"Lots of things." Stevie shrugged. "To find your head for one. A kiss for two."

He leaned closer and whispered like he was revealing a secret, "I do believe I don't need my head to kiss you."

"That's one good thing then, isn't it?" Stevie closed her eyes and hoped he wouldn't think she wanted his mouth for a temporary escape. She just liked the way he felt against her. But he gave her what she wanted and pressed his lips to hers, and she kissed him back, bringing him closer.

"I want my head for one very important reason," he drawled.

"And why is that?" she murmured.

Kit's hand skimmed down to her backside and he settled between her legs as he drew her against him. He sucked her bottom lip between his teeth. "I want to see your expression when you moan because of me. I want to see how you arch when I taste you to orgasm. I want to see you bare. All of you."

Heat dipped to her center, and she kissed up his jawline. "The bare part is easy peasy." She grinned, reaching for the top button of his collar. "We just have to remove each other's clothing first."

"Keep unfastening each one with those pretty little fingers of yours, then it will be my turn," he rasped.

Stevie's smile grew wider as she finished loosening the buttons to peel the shirt from his taut chest and broad shoulders. She ran her hands up his cool flesh while he tugged down her skirt. As if the Hollow would open in the next three seconds, they threw one another's clothing to the floor in between desperate kisses.

"On the count of three, we'll look," Stevie said, and he stepped backward. "One, two, three." Flicking her eyes open, she laughed when she noticed his fingers stroking his invisible face. "You cheated and looked first, didn't you?"

"I couldn't help it," Kit said innocently.

Her laughter faded as her gaze swept up his naked form, his hard length. Because of his white ethereal skin, it was like he was sculpted from marble.

"I'm no Aphrodite," she whispered, her body much softer than his, not as curvy as Clara's.

"You are more perfect than Aphrodite," he said gruffly. "Now shut your eyes for me."

Stevie couldn't argue with that, and though she anticipated his lips coming to hers, they didn't. Instead, his hands skated up her thighs to her backside, his head slipping between her legs. She gasped when his tongue tasted up her center, deftly, epically. Threading her fingers in his hair, she gripped the locks tighter while moaning. She opened her legs wider as he thoroughly tasted her to the point where she couldn't hold back another moan, her body quaking.

Then his mouth was on hers, and she could feel his satisfied smile, knowing he'd gotten her to come for him. She reached between them, gripping his cock, and she stroked him until he grazed his teeth up her neck and whispered gruffly in her ear, "Let me inside you. Let me pleasure you fully."

"Do come in then. The door is wide open." She grinned.

"I won't deny you." Kit grasped her by the waist and slid into her with one deep thrust. "You feel splendid," he growled.

"Gentleman words and animal movements. You can't get much better than that."

Kit cut off her words with a fierce kiss, his hips rolling into hers, their pants and groans filling the kitchen. "Deeper," he ground out, carrying Stevie from the counter to the kitchen table.

"If the table breaks, don't you dare stop," she chided.

"I wouldn't dare," he said, trailing kisses up her stomach, then taking a peaked nipple between his teeth. He gave it a gentle bite and soft flick of the tongue before burying himself back inside her.

They worked themselves into a frenzy, her legs tight around his waist, her fingers digging into his back. As her orgasm took root, licking its own magical spell through her, she swore it shook not only her but all of Sleepy Hollow. Kit's pace picked up, thrusting harder until he released a deep and guttural groan.

Stevie pressed her palm against Kit's chest, where his heart should be, wishing that before the end of the new moon, she would feel its wild beat.

"Keep your eyes closed," he instructed. "We have more to discover."

21

Stevie lay on her back beneath the covers. She attempted to be sly and roll to her side, ever so sneakily, while peeling open her eyes to study Kit. Her stomach dipped at what all they'd done over the past several nights after spending the long days searching for Levi and Reese with Lucia's spells. He'd brought out an animalistic part of herself that she hadn't known existed. Getting down on the kitchen table? That was new. Against the wall? Nope, hadn't done that before. Even something as simple as her riding him on the couch had been risqué to her. In the past, it had always been the bed with her ex. So these days she considered herself a bit of a sexual daredevil.

"You know I don't sleep, right?" Kit turned to face her, his hand slipping beneath his invisible head. "So I see you watching me."

"Then that would qualify as you watching me too." Stevie bit her lip.

"You look adorable in the morning."

"Wild tangled hair and raccoon mascara? I think I look more feral." Stevie grinned, her smile instantly slipping when the bubble she'd placed them in for another night popped. Tomorrow night was the new moon, and everything they'd aimed to resolve had failed. No locating Reese since there mysteriously wasn't a single strand of hair in his house. No Inferno. No less fog or darkness. No finding Kit's head. Her mom continued to remain healthy, but the next full moon could put that to an end.

"Sometimes knowing it's the end will hurt less," Kit said, his voice resigned. "I came to terms long ago that spending eternity in the Hollow could be my destiny. But it's not just about me or Inferno anymore—it's you."

Stevie tried to keep what would come next, if the gateway opened, behind a curtain to focus. "Nope, we aren't going to have that kind of attitude in this house. We still have over twenty-four hours. So positive vibes." Before Kit could respond, the doorbell rang. She shoved out of bed, grabbed a T-shirt and pajama pants from the floor, then threw them on before answering.

A familiar bald warlock, Julian, stood on her porch in the morning fog and ... darkness. The sun had never risen... In his hand rested a golden envelope. "From the Crowned Witch. See you soon." He bowed his head before leaving, and Stevie shut the door and tore open the envelope.

Stevie,

I'm summoning only you and your male guest to a meeting one hour after receiving this letter since you both were unable to fulfill the task at hand. However, I have made a wonderful discovery and we will discuss your next steps. Dress in appropriate attire once more.

The Crowned Witch,
Adelia

"Vague as ever, but it does sound like she found out something!" Stevie said, holding out the letter to Kit who was already near the door.

Kit stepped beside her, fastening the last two buttons of his shirt as he read over Adelia's words. "Perhaps she found Levi's location or the council discovered Reese."

This was most likely their last shot unless a witchy miracle occurred.

"Lucia's car is still here—let's see if she knows anything." Stevie stepped out into the fog and knocked on her sister-in-law's door. A second later Lucia answered, her hair damp with sweat.

"Good, you're here!" Lucia pulled Stevie inside. "And you too, Kit! Come to the basement—I've been working on something for the past couple of hours since Adelia dropped my errands for the day."

Stevie halted Lucia by the arm. "I think I know why. Her servant just brought me a letter, and I have to leave soon." She lifted the folded sheet of paper.

Lucia furrowed her brow as she read over the letter. "In case she doesn't have a solution, I have something to try. It'll be quick, I promise." She led them down to the basement and passed Stevie a needle, then pointed toward a vial bubbling a purple brew. "You know what to do."

Stevie pricked her finger and added a drop of blood to the liquid.

Lucia corked the vial, then shook it. "I'm attempting to tie Kit to Sleepy Hollow by using his hair, but without his head, his seer eyes might be too strong for the possibility. We'll try though. Drink it down, Kit."

"Tell Lucia I said thank you." He tossed back the contents in one shot.

After leaving Lucia's, Stevie didn't have time to fiddle around at the costume shop for a new dress, so she threw on the rented one she'd yet to return. Forgoing makeup and only brushing her hair, she flung her wallet and phone inside the satchel before they hurried out the door.

"You know what, to Hollow with this dress. We're taking the moped," Stevie said.

Kit chuckled as he climbed on behind her, and she sped toward the Crowned Witch's. The fog grew thicker, and it was hard to see even with the headlamp guiding her way through the darkness. The ghosts she passed almost blended in with the fog despite their soft glow.

As she reached the woods, Stevie zigzagged through the trees, then took the trail leading to the gate. It opened when she neared, and Julian waited outside the garden at the front of the house.

"The Crowned Witch has quite the black cat collection," Kit said, his body facing the garden.

Stevie arched a brow and found six cats near the black flower bushes. The felines meowed as she passed, but she didn't have time to pet them.

"Come on." Julian motioned them inside. "The Crowned Witch has much to do and doesn't have all day. Follow me."

"I don't like him," Kit muttered under his breath.

"Likewise. But if Adelia's found a solution to your problems, then maybe everything can be solved a day early." Stevie beamed, walking beside Kit down the hallway to hopefully change his doomed fate.

Adelia sat at the head of the dining room table, sipping from a brass goblet. A golden dress hugged her curvy form, and her hair was tucked under a white aristocratic wig, her lips a glossy red.

"Thank you for meeting me on such short notice, Stevie." Adelia smiled, setting down her goblet. "Is Kit with you? We should get started immediately since a few things have come to light."

"He's here," Stevie confirmed. "Any news on Reese or Levi?"

"The pitiful council has been as quiet as scared little rabbits."

Adelia stood from her chair and walked toward Stevie, her dress swishing. "However, I found Reese. But first I need Kit to describe what Levi looks like."

Stevie's heart practically stilled in her chest. Adelia had Reese! That meant they could get some answers if the witch hadn't already.

Kit shrugged. "He was a couple of inches shorter than me, sharp angles, thin lips, slim, blond wavy hair to his shoulders, blue eyes, used to wear a ruby amulet."

Stevie repeated Kit's description, and Adelia shook her head. "No, no, we need more than that. What was the shape of his nose? Are his teeth crooked or straight?"

"He did have a canine tooth that stuck out slightly further than the rest. And there was a bump on his nose from when it had been broken," Kit said.

Stevie's eyes widened as she put the features together, interlocking the pieces to form a deceptive little puzzle. He could've easily tied back his hair, dressed more modern, switched out the satchel for a backpack, and hid away his amulet. A simple disguise but good enough for her not to put him on a suspect list. Kit had never been around to identify him either. Besides at the bonfire where she hadn't thought to point the ghost out to him. "I think I know who Levi is."

"What do you mean *know* him?" Kit sounded alarmed.

"Go on." Adelia nodded, focusing harder on Stevie.

"The resident ghost in the comic book shop where my brother works matches that description minus the ruby amulet. He told me his name was Erik, and he always has a backpack with him." Stevie was positive she was right on the money that Erik was Levi.

And then there was Reese who also dealt with comics...

Adelia tapped a finger against her cheek. "When Kit encountered Levi before he was murdered, what was the last thing the warlock said to him?"

Before Kit spoke, another familiar voice spilled through the room. "I can tell you precisely what I said. I know the tale rather well."

Stevie whirled around to find Reese standing in the room, dressed in a similar old fashion as everyone else. A black suit with a high collar and his fingers caressing a ruby amulet hanging from a silver chain around his neck.

He hadn't said Levi, he'd said *I*.

Levi was *inside* of Reese.

The world of the living and the dead had never collided in that sense. Ghosts weren't supposed to be able to take possession of a living body the way demons from the Hollow could. But Levi had. Because of the dark magic the warlock toyed with.

"*You*," Stevie hissed. "You're so dead. You even got my fox to like you."

"*Me*. Levi, yes." The warlock smirked. "Your pathetic fox shouldn't be so trusting."

Kit barreled toward Levi, swinging his unsheathed sword, but before the blade connected with the warlock's heart, the Horseman was thrown backward, landing hard against the floor.

"In case you're wondering how it's possible, Kit." Adelia's gaze was focused on him, *seeing* the Horseman clearly as he pushed up from the floor. He reached for his weapon, but his sword slid to the other side of the room by magic. "Ghosts of a witch or warlock can take possession of the living, but only ones who gave their soul up to be tied to the Hollow."

Adelia was working with Levi. She had betrayed them all.

"You're a *seer*?" Stevie spat. "And you're working with *him*? Why?" She inched toward the Crowned Witch, then halted. Adelia was one of the most powerful witches in the world, and Stevie was nothing but a seer, a witch's assistant. She needed to book it out of there and call Lucia, not fight.

"Wrong guess." Adelia smiled wide. "I'm not a seer."

"Get away from that *lying bitch*," Kit roared. "Run, Stevie! Now!"

Stevie bolted toward the open door, but Levi was quicker,

yanking her back by the shoulders and shoving her down into one of the chairs.

"Do stay," he snarled. "We have a conversation to finish."

Stevie thought that maybe Kit had made it out until her gaze found him writhing against the floor. Translucent chains bound his ankles and wrists, and a rope was in what had to be his mouth, knotted at the back of his invisible head.

"Let him go!" Stevie shrieked, balling her hands into tight fists and twisting from Levi's firm hold. She hardly stood when a brown rope flew through the room and wound itself around her, trapping her to the chair by her chest.

"No, I believe the Horseman will stay." Adelia laughed, bending her knees in front of Stevie so they were at eye level. "My husband and I have been apart for far too long, and now, at last, we're together again."

Stevie arched a brow. "I'm sorry, *what*? You're like ninety years old! But I guess the age gap leans more toward him since, technically, he's older."

"You foolish girl." Adelia laughed again. This time though, a white glow separated from Adelia's face, displaying another head. A ghost was *inside* the Crowned Witch. Stevie should've suspected this as soon as her *husband* had revealed himself. The witch hadn't betrayed them at all—she was possessed.

Stevie gasped, unable to take her unblinking stare from the ghost's face. "Clara! How? We saw you pass on in the cemetery."

"No, you *thought* you saw me pass on." The witch's lip curled into a sneer.

Stevie rattled her chair, screaming, hoping for any other witch in Sleepy Hollow to hear her.

"No one will hear you." Levi waved a hand in the air, and her words became mute, even as she shouted louder. Terror washed over her when Levi lifted her chin. "You know, Erik wasn't really Magneto's name either. It was just an alias for the time being."

If Gideon were there, he would've told her that she should've brushed up on her comic book history. Her silent curses at Levi became more frequent as he fished out her phone from her satchel.

He cocked his head and smirked. "I do believe Lucia should know you will be remaining here and running errands for *Adelia*. We don't need that pesky witch getting involved more than she already has."

"When I'm finished with this body, her time will come soon enough," Clara cooed. "As for you, Stevie, I think it's time for you to be sent to your sleeping quarters." In Clara's grasp now rested an open glass box.

Stevie frowned, but as her muscles twitched, she peered down at her hands. Her heart skyrocketed in her chest when they shrunk to the size of a doll's, the *tiniest* of dolls. It wasn't just her hands though—her entire body was turning smaller. She screeched, still mute, but when the ropes fell from her, she ran toward the chair's edge. Before she reached it, Clara's large fingers snaked around Stevie, swiping her up.

"Did you want to die? A fall from your height to the floor would have ended in a bloody delight." Clara cackled while placing Stevie inside the glass box. "There you go. You're protected now." With a pleased smile, she studied her like a prized pet. "Don't you worry, seer, this will only be temporary until I need to tear out your eyes to open the Hollow's next six gates."

22

Clara wanted Stevie's eyes so that the witch could open the six other gates? Stevie struck the glass in horror, whistling and screaming for Roxy, but her voice remained gone. Her sidekick would never hear her.

Stevie whirled around, finding Levi and Kit no longer in the room. But then Levi sauntered out from the shadows of the hallway, a ruthless smirk on his face. "The Horseman is confined now."

With a vicious laugh, Clara placed a lid over the box and carried Stevie down the hallway, the glass prison jostling her the entire way to an antique table in the middle of the library. The table wasn't empty though—a large snake rested inside a bare terrarium atop it. The reptile's head perked up, hisses escaping its two-fanged mouth while Stevie's box was lowered into the terrarium. The snake's red gaze remained latched on Stevie, and her heart rocketed when Clara replaced the lid on the snake's home and left without so much as a glance back at her.

Stevie stood, waiting for the dizzy feeling to subside. Her hand flew to her mouth as she focused on what rested before her.

Across the room were two more glass prisons just like her own, only much larger. In the first, Kit sat on his knees, chained at the wrists, his fists banging against the clear wall. And in the second, Kit's horse stomped his hooves, his glowing eyes glazed over with fear. Stevie imagined Inferno's distressed whinnies, but no noises escaped either prison.

Shelves of books from floor to ceiling surrounded them. Nothing else.

A set of heavy boots sounded before Julian entered the room. Stevie backed into a corner as he lifted the terrarium lid, then hers, and tossed breadcrumbs at her. She cursed silent words at him while he thrust a thimble of water in the opposite corner, the liquid sloshing over the sides.

Once he left, Stevie ran up to the wall, attempting to spell out words to Kit until her fingers grew numb.

THE NEXT DAY was no different than the last—Stevie was still trapped in a stuffy glass nightmare that allowed claustrophobia to set in. Time had crept by at a snail's pace, and no matter how persistent she was to not nod off, it was unavoidable.

Stevie held her hand up to the clear wall as Kit continued to relentlessly pound his fists against his clear prison. "It's all right," she called out, but knowing he couldn't read her itty-bitty mouth. "We'll escape these death traps." They had way less than twenty-four hours to Houdini their way out of there. They knew where Levi was—she just needed to somehow get to Lucia, to warn her that Clara would try and possess her sometime after the Hollow opened. Except now Stevie's family would think she was running errands for the Crowned Witch. And then there was Reese... Or Levi... How long had the warlock been inside Reese?

The door burst open and Clara stormed toward her, lifting the lid off the terrarium. She took Stevie's box out and removed that lid too. "Where are Kit's bones, pet?" she snapped. "They are no longer in the house where Levi hid them, and I know you broke the spell with your blood."

Stevie shrugged and mimed her hands in front of her, signaling she couldn't speak.

"If you whistle for your precious fox, there will be a new wall mount in Kit's room down in the Hollow, understand?" Clara's face turned smug.

Stevie swallowed deeply and nodded. Clara snapped and Stevie opened her mouth to speak. "Levi can't hide bones himself," she chirped, her voice coming out squeakier than a mouse's.

Clara hovered above her, her smile growing wicked. "After seeing Reese tonight, I think you know how it's been possible to do things over the years." He had taken possession of people for decades, *centuries*... That was why he hadn't been found so easily.

"It doesn't matter since I don't know where any bones are." Stevie shrugged. If they also needed Kit's bones for something, she wouldn't give away the secret location, not with what would happen if she did.

"Don't forget you're the one shrunken inside the box," Clara seethed. "I can end your life and remove your eyes sooner if you wish."

Stevie folded her arms and scowled. "If you believe I know where they are, then how would you find them if I'm dead?"

"I can still torture your ghost. I see you're taken by the Headless Horseman, or is he taken by you? You were always pathetic weren't you, Kit?" Clara exchanged a glance between Kit and Stevie. "I had a lovely time getting him to fall in love with me, letting him believe I could return his affections."

"Why do you need Kit's ghost if you have his real head?" Stevie asked, attempting to collect any information she could if she managed to escape.

"Figure out the answer yourself."

"He's the sacrifice," Stevie whispered.

"Perhaps you're right. Perhaps you're not." Clara shook the box and Stevie fell hard against the floor. Her gaze met Kit's, and his bound hands slammed hard against the glass. "Now, where are the bones?"

"I never touched them, you lunatic!" Stevie shouted, staying crouched on the floor in case the witch shook the box again. Blue powder rained down on Stevie and she sneezed. "The bones are in a safe in my closet. Combination code is 13, 7, 4, 2. A protection Lucia made is also on the safe." A truth spell!

"Thank you, pet. I'll see you after the Hollow opens. Then it will be your turn. I think I'll cut out your eyes before ending your life." Clara flicked the glass with her finger, the noise like a bomb in her ears. Stevie screamed at Clara when she placed the lid over her box and lowered it back into the terrarium, but once again she was soundless.

Clara's heels clicked against the wooden floor as she left, and a second later Levi strutted in. He arched a brow at Stevie and chuckled darkly before opening the door to Kit's glass prison. Kit lunged forward and his fists went through Reese to get to Levi. The warlock lifted his hand and Kit dropped to the floor, a collar with a leash appearing around his throat.

"Come on, be a good boy," Levi said as his ghostly hands slipped out from Reese's arms and he yanked on the leash, easily dragging Kit across the floor. Kit writhed, but magic must've prevented him from rushing at Levi again. A ghost inside a living person was more dangerous than she could've imagined.

"Kit," Stevie tried to scream as she banged against the glass. Levi didn't once glance back in her direction while hauling Kit out of the room. And why would he? She was the size of a Polly Pocket. Maybe the size of a few of them put together, but still. After she got out of this box, she would shove the warlock through a paper shredder.

Inferno wilted in the corner of his prison, lying on the floor, seeming to give up. Stevie probably should've just said that she'd found the bones, then told them a fake location. But even then, Clara might've used the truth powder to confirm her answer anyway. It was too late now to go back and forth with what-ifs when she had to get out of this box ASAP. Roxy still wasn't an option with Stevie's voice gone again, regardless if the threat from Clara stood. If she had known these jackasses needed Kit's bones too, she would've had Lucia hide them better.

Stevie kicked the glass, but not even a hairline fracture cracked its surface. She again looked around the library for a clue that could help her. Books and more books.

After maybe almost an hour ticked by, a loud grunt came from outside Stevie's door and she straightened. If it was Julian coming to sprinkle more breadcrumbs inside her box, she would find a way to latch onto his arm, bite it, and thrust her way out of this glass nightmare.

The door creaked open and Stevie pointed toward her thimble, pleading for more water. And then she stilled, her lips parting. "Lucia!" she shouted.

"Stevie! I can't hear you! I just turned Julian into a cat!" Lucia ran to the terrarium and peered in with wide eyes. "Poisonous snake? Bye-bye." Holding up her hand, she chanted a few words and the snake curled up, gray fur sprouting across its skin as it shrank. Two rounded ears slipped out from its head, and the snake transformed further until a tiny mouse appeared, releasing the cutest of squeaks.

Lucia took out her box from the terrarium and opened the lid.

"You're not safe here. They want your body!" Stevie hollered.

But Lucia still couldn't hear her, and her sister-in-law chanted another spell. Stevie's tongue felt thick in her mouth as she moved it.

"Sorry, your voice will take a few seconds to come back. Your text didn't sound right, and I knew something was up when you didn't message your mom to check on her at all. Then there was the fact Adelia had asked me to stop running errands, but then replaced me with you when the Hollow could be opening. If anything, we would be stronger working together."

"It wasn't Adelia!" Stevie shouted, her voice finally escaping. "Levi has possession of Reese, and Clara didn't pass on—she's inside of Adelia! And Clara wants your body!"

"My *body*," Lucia hissed. "The second Eye will be here tonight!"

Stevie then broke down everything that had happened as fast and thoroughly as she could. How not only would Lucia be used soon, but so would Stevie.

"Adelia must not have known that the other gates could be opened," Lucia whispered.

"Did you see any other servants here besides Julian? He's on their side."

"The rest are cats in the garden. I'll make a brew for them later, but right now we're going to Ginger's to break your spell. And then from there, we'll find Levi and Clara which will be easier after this new information. For the finale, we save your Horseman."

"What about Inferno?" Stevie yelped as Lucia carried her toward the door. "He's still in the glass case and will be tagging along with Kit to the Hollow if we don't help him!"

"At the moment we need to stay focused on the things that could change this town. Helping Kit will help him." Lucia looked toward the glass, and even though she couldn't see him, she said, "We're going to save your master."

Inferno lifted his head and silently whinnied.

Lucia held up Stevie close to her face. "Let's get you out of this Thumbelina-like state now, shall we?"

23

Stevie sat on top of Lucia's shoulder, releasing one high-squealed whistle after another as her sister-in-law sped the car through the streets. If Levi and Clara had snatched Roxy, then they could easily use the fox against Stevie. Not many people or cars were out and about, the town's population most likely either getting ready to go to the cemetery tonight or staying behind warded doors. Which the second might be the best option at this point.

"Roxy will be fine. She was at your parents' after I left to come for you," Lucia soothed.

But Roxy might've still ventured home at some point, then wanted to see what all the fuss was about when the evil duo entered her home.

Lucia's phone rang, and she sighed in relief as she answered with the speaker on. "Finally! I called and thought you were kidnapped!"

"I'm at my parents. What's going on, babe? Do I need to kick some ass?" Gideon asked.

"No! Stay where you are until I say to leave. There are some dangerous shenanigans afoot and we can't afford a distraction.

Your pain tolerance is horrendous and these asshats would easily get something out of you. It's too risky," Lucia rushed out.

"What about Stevie?" Worry filled his voice.

"I have a story to tell you later, but at the moment I need to get her back to normal size after a nefarious encounter she had since Maxine could easily eat her."

"Someone is about to be dead," he ground out.

"Don't worry, they already are, but this will make time number two. Go take care of your parents, keep them safe, and I'll see you soon. I love you." Lucia ended the call just as she turned down Ginger's street, and shrill, familiar barks sounded. Stevie couldn't see through the fog, but the barks were coming right behind the car.

"Roxy's behind us!" Stevie shouted.

"She can meet us at Aunt Ginger's. There isn't time to stop for a single second."

Stevie agreed. Things were about to completely spill from the cauldron—there'd been no answer at the council, and if anything, she bet the duo had turned them into some sort of small critter. Ginger was home, working on more brews to bless the land, but Lucia had only told her to be ready for them.

As Lucia threw the car in park, Roxy met them, hopping up and down in a frenzy.

"Good girl, Foxy Roxy," Stevie squeaked.

The front door burst open and Ginger bounded toward them, her gray braid in disarray. "Charms and hexes, Lucia, what's going on?"

"So much!" Lucia took Stevie from her shoulder and held her out to Ginger.

The witch gasped. "Get to the basement and tell me everything as we work!"

"It was too risky to go to my house, so I came here," Lucia said while rushing toward the basement. She fled down the carpeted steps, and Stevie held back nausea from how the room spun around her.

Lucia placed Stevie on one of the shelves as Ginger spelled an empty glass jar into a chair that was fit for her doll size. While Lucia took a few jars from another shelf and poured their contents into the far-left cauldron, she told Ginger what had happened. Roxy lingered beside them, listening too. Levi inside of Reese, Clara taking Adelia as her own, Kit in their grasp to be used as a sacrifice, Stevie being the next, Lucia's body to become Clara's if the witch got her way.

"I'll turn them into cockroaches and crush them," Ginger seethed.

"Unfortunately, their ghosts would slither right out," Stevie said, but her voice was too meek to be heard from across the room.

Lucia dipped a teaspoon into the cauldron and poured the small amount into a silver thimble. She then rushed it to Stevie, who clasped the large thimble and drank down the liquid. A flavor of spiced cake caressed her taste buds, and she held out the polished-off thimble toward Lucia.

"Grab her from the shelf!" Ginger bellowed as Stevie's muscles twitched, her hands looking like clown hands compared to the rest of her.

"Oh right!" Lucia lifted Stevie from the shelf and placed her on the floor.

Stevie's muscles twitched again, her feet becoming larger, and she sprouted up like a weed until she was back to her normal, not-so-tall, height.

"Well, that whole situation was completely uncalled for." Stevie glanced down at her body that no longer wore the costume shop gown, the tiny ripped fabric resting near her bare foot. She would just have to pay for that. "Why am I *naked?*"

"Reversal spells can't solve everything, especially when the original spell wasn't my own. But at least you have all your fingers and toes, right? There's always the possibility not everything lines up correctly." Lucia shrugged.

Horrified, Stevie counted her toes and fingers to double-check they were all there as Ginger wrapped a knitted blanket around her. And thank the witches they were!

"We need to find Levi and Clara," Stevie said.

"I do have another trick up my sleeve." Lucia smiled. "One good thing I learned from my Crowned Witch training before it went kaput is the secret location of the gate to the Hollow. I should've told you yesterday when I saw you, but I wasn't supposed to until today."

"It's best to make sure it's out of other's hands when truth spells are a slippery tactic these days anyway. Where is it?" Stevie asked, hope bouncing in her chest.

"It's at the edge of the creek near the Headless Horseman's bridge." Lucia ran a hand over her messy bun.

Stevie furrowed her brow as she mulled something over. "Wait, you're sure it was Adelia inside of her body, or could it have been Clara giving you a false location?"

"Pretty sure it was Adelia. The training had been non-stop that day. Also, I never felt Inferno in the library, so everything must've happened with Adelia before Clara sent me the forged letter."

"So let's believe it was, but on the negative side, even if we show up there, the sketchy duo will be prepared for you to come since I'd wager both my eyes Clara knows Adelia told you about the location, which *means* she's planning on it so she can steal your body tonight!" Stevie hissed. "They didn't want to make people suspicious by taking out Adelia beforehand. It's their perfect little plot."

Lucia's forehead crinkled. "So we have Clara, who is a mediocre witch, inside of a powerful Crowned Witch that isn't quite double the power but still a lot. And then you have a warlock, who is a step below a Crowned Witch, inside of a seer. They both dabble in the dark arts, a challenging magic to fight against, but one I can easily make a barrier for that will hold if I stay concentrated on it. Clara is the one I'll have to keep my eye on the most since she has Adelia's power."

"Do you want me to call on more witches?" Ginger asked. "No one's taking my niece's body."

"Have them make sure every house in town is warded." Lucia tapped the end of her chin. "If only we had Kit's bones."

Kit's *bones*. Stevie gasped. "I still have one if they didn't find it! His finger bone is in my purse on the counter."

"Now that was an answer I needed." Lucia grinned. "So, before we retrieve Kit's bone." Lucia clapped her hands together. "The original plan I had for tonight has to be tweaked somewhat, but this might be even better. Let's start with Roxy. Go back to Stevie's parents and watch over them."

"Listen to her." Stevie nodded toward the fox when she didn't budge from her spot. Roxy nuzzled through Stevie's leg and took off up the basement stairs.

"Oh, Auntie," Lucia called. "You're next. This one will be a bit risky, a dangerous game we might not survive, but I want you to pretend you're Stevie. It won't distract them for long—however, it might catch them off guard."

"Hmm." Ginger clucked her tongue. "Look young again for an evening, feel the youth pulse within me, bones not creaking—I say it sounds like a good night. If we don't do something, then we will be a lovely dinner for demons crawling about the earth, tearing bodies in half and lapping up their blood before drinking their ghosts up as an everlasting snack."

Stevie's lips parted, clutching her blanket tighter. "I think I just pissed myself."

"I'm sure most of Sleepy Hollow will be," Lucia said, grabbing a glass from the shelf and filling it with liquid from the first cauldron. "Stevie, I need three drops of blood."

Ginger handed Stevie a needle—she pricked her finger, then squeezed the droplets into the brew. She ignored the slight sting and watched as Lucia stirred the liquid. The brew bubbled, a light red smoke curling up from the glass. Lucia blew on the contents, chanting a few words, before passing it to her aunt.

"Bottoms up," Ginger announced as she drank the brew

down. "It's a bit tangy. You'll have to show me what I did wrong with mine sometime."

As Lucia continued the chant, Stevie felt a sharp tug at her body, her skin growing wrinkled, hugging her bones, while Ginger's flesh tightened, smoothed.

Stevie knew this rodeo from when she'd first learned all of Lucia's spells, so she wasn't going to curl up and rock somewhere in the corner. Her muscles turned heavy, and in the reflection of a glass jar, her hair became limp and gray. Then, as if a balloon were filling with air inside her, Stevie's flesh plumped back up, her strength and everyday appearance returning.

Ginger stood in front of her, a perfect carbon copy of Stevie from the orange hair to her shorter legs.

"Miraculous, dear niece," Ginger exclaimed, even her voice sounding like Stevie's.

Lucia faced Stevie and scanned her over. "For you, we will start with a cloaking spell."

"And what if they performed a cloaking spell on themselves?" Stevie asked.

"That's the spell I already had prepared for if Levi showed up." Lucia smirked.

As her sister-in-law raised her hand in the air, Stevie said, "Can you make some clothes for me first? Holding up a blanket the entire time doesn't scream battle ready."

"Good catch." Lucia spun her hand in a circle and the blanket cradled Stevie's body until it formed a tube-top dress that flared out at the waist. "When we leave you can slip a pair of Ginger's shoes on and she'll fit them to your size. Now let me cloak you before we leave." She held up her hand again, and a tingle spread through Stevie's body, tickling beneath her flesh.

Stevie blinked. "Am I invisible?"

"Not to me, but to everyone else, as much as the Invisible Man, except you don't have to be naked to not be seen."

Stevie laughed softly as Lucia gathered what she needed and

passed Stevie a dagger to tuck through a belt loop that had been fashioned at her waist.

"Apologies, we're going to need more seer blood than usual tonight. Getting the ghosts out of the bodies is my main concern." Lucia sighed.

"Tonight we're going to perform our own version of an exorcism, and I think I know who can help us." Stevie grinned.

Lucia's gaze slid toward Stevie's. "Who do you have in mind?"

"Just someone we'll be borrowing from my brother," Stevie said innocently. "Her name's Maxine."

"That's perfect!" Lucia clasped her hands together. She then instructed Ginger to cloak herself until the reveal.

Before they left the house, Ginger gave Stevie a pair of flats that were two sizes too big, but as she slipped them on, they cradled her feet perfectly.

Just when she thought the fog couldn't get any thicker, it had. Not a single star lit up the sky, the darkness hiding them from all of Sleepy Hollow.

As Lucia drove toward their duplex, Stevie asked, "I know you're going to use Kit's bone for spells, but is it possible if we don't bring it, that the Hollow will stay closed?"

"The skull is what will open the gate. I believe the bones and his ghost are more for the sacrifice. If it's still at your place, you'll keep it in your dress pocket until I give you the signal."

As a backup plan, Lucia pulled up beside the curb instead of in the driveway in case for some reason she didn't come out and Stevie had to take the wheel and speed off.

It only took Lucia a couple of minutes to run into both sides of the duplex. She hopped back into the car, her chest heaving, and tossed the purse to Stevie. "Bone is inside, but the rest of Kit's skeleton is gone. Go ahead and give Maxine a drop of your blood and guard her with your life, or Gideon will never get out of bed." She carefully passed the plant to Stevie, and she held onto Maxine as the plant opened and closed her mouth.

Just as Lucia's foot hit the gas pedal, the ground shook like an earthquake and she slammed on the brakes. Stevie's heart hammered when orange smoke wafted up outside the window, swirling within the fog.

"It's beginning," Lucia breathed. "The demons are lining up at the gate, waiting for it to open."

24

Even as smoke seeped from the ground and the earth shook, lit candles illuminated the fog of the cemetery, some people not willing to give up the chance to be amongst the ghosts, wishing to speak with a loved one. If the Hollow opened, staying locked up in one's home would only be a temporary escape of what was to come anyway.

Lucia parked a short distance away from the bridge, giving them an opportunity to not be noticed so easily before cloaking herself with an invisible spell. She couldn't see Ginger or Lucia clearly, but her sister-in-law surrounded them in a lavender glow that only they could see to follow.

Stevie trailed her finger across Kit's bone one more time, hoping he could feel her, before she slipped it into her pocket. Clutching Maxine for dear life, so she wouldn't have to incur her brother's wrath, Stevie trekked beside the two witches across the shallow creek, the cool water brushing her legs.

Lucia guided them to the opposite side of the bridge, their footsteps muted, and they hid within the trees. The single red bleeding orb shone down on the trio as if the Eye were spying on them. Lucia sprinkled a vial of liquid on the ground, then softly chanted, her voice assured.

Like hands drawing back curtains to unveil a hidden mystery, the fog slowly separated where the gate should be. Stevie didn't see a sign of Levi or Clara, but then a light flickered on, revealing two kneeling robed forms. A skull and the wooden box of bones rested before them next to at least ten lit candles. Kit writhed in front of a sycamore tree mere feet away, his chains keeping him bound to the trunk, unable to pass through like he normally could've. Stevie's heart clenched at seeing Kit so incredibly close to becoming the demons' plaything.

"Someone lifted our cloaking spell," Levi purred and peered around. "Come out, come out, little witch. We've been waiting for you."

"Their protection spell is incredibly strong. This might take longer, but hopefully it won't be too late," Lucia whispered. "I need to distract them so they lose focus. You're up." She uncloaked herself and pointed to her aunt, signaling it was show-time. Ginger's own spell vanished, allowing her to mirror Stevie in every way.

"Release Kit," Ginger bellowed, stepping out from behind the tree, her voice matching Stevie's.

"How sweet, you were let out of your box early," Clara sneered, her gaze meeting Ginger's. "Where's Lucia?"

Trust me, Lucia mouthed to Stevie and gestured for her to follow behind her. She then led Stevie out from the trees, the invisibility keeping her hidden for now. "I heard you wanted my body," Lucia called while Ginger now walked with them. "It's too bad I don't share."

As they drew closer, only a small number of yards between them, neither of the duo moved from their spots until Clara thrust her hand forward. A flash of white light struck Lucia in the chest before she could dodge out of the way.

Lucia, Stevie screamed inside her skull, grasping her sister-in-law's arm, rattling Maxine in her other hand. She hadn't blown their cover, and Lucia hadn't collapsed to the ground. No harm. *Yet*.

"Aww," Clara cooed as iridescent magic from both sides pushed against one another. "You think a protection spell will save you? It's too late for that."

Kit grunted, wriggling beneath his chains. Stevie released Lucia and she trailed her fingers across his bone in her pocket and he stilled.

Clara finally stood, brushing her hands down the front of her red robe. "Now, give us Stevie and I'll perhaps let you take over *our* body here and there. Your power is great. Your body perfect. Regardless of what you choose, we'll take the seer from you though."

"Hmm. That is something to think about, isn't it?" Lucia sighed sarcastically. Stevie looked up toward the hidden new moon, its single red Eye shining like the richest of rubies. Soon, the second would crack open.

With his ghost hands, Levi lifted his backpack, making Stevie curse herself for never asking him what was in it. Her heart pounded when he unzipped it and drew out a translucent white head. This verified it. Kit's head was inside. He'd had it with him all that time in the comic book store, right under her nose.

Levi edged toward Kit and placed the pale head on his neck. It remained, not disappearing as the other one had. Kit's head. Kit's face. A face she might never get to touch for the first time.

"Stevie, hide!" Kit shouted toward Ginger. But then another cloth was between his teeth, muffling his words.

"Where will she go?" Clara taunted.

"How about this, little witch," Levi said, running a digit across his thin lower lip, "if you cease your magic, I'll make certain the demons don't touch a single hair on your foolish husband."

"And Stevie?" Lucia asked.

"We both know how that will end." Levi smirked.

As Clara and Lucia's iridescent magic battled against each other, Levi sliced his palm with a jeweled blade and spilled his blood on the ground of the gate. Reese's blood. *Seer's* blood. Another reason he needed Reese besides his body.

He emptied the box of bones near Kit. The click of them hitting one another echoed, and Kit winced. Levi lifted the skull with both hands and placed it on top of the pile of bones as if it were a crown.

The warlock whispered an incantation, then jerked his chin up after only a couple of seconds passed. "The bones aren't connecting?" he growled toward Clara.

"They are his bones, aren't they?" Clara hissed, her hand wavering.

"Without a doubt."

"What did you do?" Clara shouted toward Ginger. Magic crackled around them, a rotten odor filling the air, *darkness*. And then her magic broke through Lucia's protective barrier. Ginger floated into the air, and Lucia didn't fight back yet, even as her aunt fell to the ground in front of Clara's feet.

"You aren't Stevie—you reek of witch magic," Clara seethed, holding out her opposite hand toward Lucia's aunt. Ginger stilled, unmoving, her wide eyes frozen in a trance. "Tonight the dead will reunite with the living. Demons will walk the earth, and all the ghosts, including yours, will feed the wicked and forever be trapped below."

"And then what?" Lucia shouted, her magic visibly shoving harder against Clara's. "Rule it all? How cliché can you be?"

"Do you believe us to be so narcissistic?" Levi drawled. "We will bow down to our king and queen of the Hollow. We will be their right hands as was foretold." The people of Sleepy Hollow wouldn't just be slaughtered—their ghosts would be fed to the demons with no escape from the dark world below.

The ground trembled like it had earlier, Kit's bones rattling. The water of the creek sloshed against the dirt. Kit's skull lit up, glowing a brilliant red. They didn't have much longer. Lucia needed to break open Clara's barrier so they could get to work.

A long shadowy hand stretched from Clara and wrapped

around Ginger's throat, squeezing, the witch unable to fight back.

"Don't!" Lucia screamed, jolting forward, and the cloaking spell concealing Stevie shattered.

"Well, well, there she is," Levi said with a devious grin. "Where's the bone? One is missing from the remains."

Stevie shrugged. "How would I know? I wasn't the one who dug up Kit's bones and placed them inside a trunk."

"Don't fuck with us." Clara gritted her teeth. And then Stevie noticed a white form hovering near a tree behind Levi and Clara. Roxy. Of course she hadn't listened and gone to Stevie's parents. But as Clara returned to squeezing Ginger's throat, an idea formed. Stevie was a witch's assistant, and that was exactly what she needed to be right now.

"It's time for the exorcism," Stevie murmured to Lucia as the second Eye slowly opened and the earth shook, the sound like thunder. With the second Eye already there, Lucia wouldn't have to feel for the ghosts—she would see them now too. "I'm going to whistle. Be ready, Maxine." Setting the plant on the ground beside her, Stevie cut a thin line down her palm with the dagger and ignored its bite. She fished out Kit's bone and smeared red across the white before adding a few drops onto the ground. Lucia took the bone from her, and Stevie released a high-pitched whistle, the sound echoing across the woods. Roxy then broke from the brush as Clara whirled around, but it was too late. The fox knocked through Adelia and took Clara's ghost with her to the ground. Roxy growled violently, her maw around the witch's throat while she jerked.

"I bind you to the Hollow on this night, Clara Katrina Bonham," Lucia shouted.

As Levi smacked Roxy away from Clara with his magic, Maxine barreled forward, growing to massive size with smaller Venus flytraps snapping beside her. She clamped her rows of teeth around Levi's shoulder and rattled him like a ragdoll to exorcise the ghost from Reese's body. Clara's ghost form remained still and Lucia focused her chanting on Levi. Ginger came out of her daze, no longer looking like Stevie, and didn't hesitate to hold up her hand toward Levi too. His pale form finally spilled forward to the ground, and Roxy didn't miss a beat to pin him down.

"Release him, Maxine!" Stevie yelled, and the plant let go of Reese, his body collapsing near Levi's. Maxine drew back but didn't shrink in size just yet.

"And to you, Levi Brom Bonham," Lucia shouted louder. "I bind you to the Hollow on this night. I bind the both of you."

The earth before them split in two, a jagged fissure leading to the gate tore the ground open. Lucia continued, her voice speeding up, "The two of you will be dinner for the king and queen below. You will keep them satisfied as they feast on your magic and essence." Both ghosts roused then, clawing at the dirt as an invisible force dragged them toward the abyss, then swallowed them into its depths.

A demon's hand, decaying skin peeling back from bone, reached from the darkness and wiggled its decrepit fingers toward Stevie and Lucia. A second arm pierced through the thin opening, this one hoofed. The crack needed to be closed, but before the chant could be performed, another white form flew into the demon's grasp, the hand sinking below the surface with its treasure.

Kit.

25

"They've got Kit!" Stevie screamed and hurled herself toward the opening gate. Deep growls filled the air, but all her sense had already gone out the window after seeing Kit's ghost taken by a demon. Just as her fingers brushed the ground, Lucia yanked her back.

"We have time!" Lucia said, her chest heaving. "The Eyes are still open, and I can feel my spell trying to tie him back to the land. But we have to focus, or we won't be able to get him out."

"Fuck!" Reese gritted his teeth as he sat on his knees, gripping his bleeding shoulder.

"I'll make them suffer more than they can imagine down there," Adelia snarled.

"Go to your Horseman's remains," Lucia rushed out, placing Kit's finger bone into Stevie's palm. "Then we'll close the gate. If it cracks any further, we'll have to shut it sooner. Your blood won't be enough for Kit since his ghost is gone, so I'll have to also perform a necromancy spell to get him out of the Hollow."

Stevie sank beside Kit's remains and added his finger bone to the pile.

"I'll help with the spell," Adelia added. "You too, Ginger. A triad of strong witches is a power like no other." She turned to Reese. "And you, boy, don't you dare run."

Reese's throat bobbed as he nodded.

"Stevie, add your blood to Kit's bones and save the skull's mouth for last," Lucia instructed, handing her the dagger. "Then we'll start the necromancy spell to draw him out from the Hollow."

Stevie sliced open her hand—Lucia wasn't kidding when she'd said more blood than usual would need to be shed. Holding her palm above Kit's remains, she let the bright red liquid trickle onto his bones, and finally, inside his skull.

Adelia, Ginger, and Lucia clasped hands, forming a circle around Stevie and the bones. They chanted, the sound musical, their incantation a soft melody, one that Stevie hoped would hurry and pull Kit's soul from the Hollow. Reese stood in the same position, silently watching them, but she couldn't worry about him now.

The bones rattled, clacking together as they moved around. Stevie's lips parted when one after another slid against the next, locking in place. Her drops of blood spread across the bones, licking up each speck of white until the entire skeleton was red. Organs sprung up inside the rib cage like flowers rising from the dead. Muscle came next, followed by a spiderwebbing of veins. And then tan skin slipped out, hugging the layers of flesh beneath it. Black hair sprouted from Kit's head and grew to his shoulders. The way Kit's body was coming to life reminded her of *Hellraiser*, which was her mom's movie of choice, the way the villain's body received layers of flesh after murdering people. Minus the killing shenanigans. But Kit's chest wasn't rising, and when she pressed her hand to his chest, the heart remained still.

Stevie wasn't a witch, yet she would assist them, regardless if it didn't make the song more powerful. She enfolded her hand around Kit's, humming the song until a pale white form rose from the ground, drifting above their heads. *Kit.* But not only Kit. *Inferno.*

Tears beaded Stevie's lashes—however, she didn't stop the incantation, not even as Kit's ghost lowered into his physical body, and Inferno just outside the circle. Both their eyes were closed, though a ghost never slept. Roxy nudged the horse with her nose, but the Hollow had already begun to do something to them.

"He needs more seer blood," Adelia uttered. "Not you, Stevie. Go with Lucia and seal the gate. Kit and his horse's ghost are safe here." She looked toward Reese and snapped, "You, boy. Help fix this now. Do your part. More blood in his mouth."

Even though Stevie wanted to see if Kit and Inferno would wake, she needed to take care of the town and help close the crack. She knelt beside Lucia near the opening, where more ghoulish hands swiped at the air, beckoning them closer.

"Two more drops of blood is all we'll need," Lucia said, placing her palm against the dirt. "Repeat the words after me."

Stevie winced while squeezing her hand, the blood falling to the ground in what felt like slow motion. The demons' growls grew desperate, more ravenous for a taste of her blood. Flashes of beady yellow eyes glowed from within the darkness as the demons waiting to enter Sleepy Hollow peered up at them.

Lucia chanted, deep and otherworldly, and Stevie followed her words. The ground quaked beneath them, not pulling apart further but sealing back together. They continued repeating the spell until the line vanished as if it had never been there. Lucia smacked her hand against the dirt, giggling, actually giggling. "We did it. Me and my badass assistant."

"You mean, badass witch." Stevie smiled, her chest heaving.

"And now you and your Horseman can rekindle your romance. I do believe he's awake." Lucia grinned as Roxy trotted up to her side.

Stevie whirled around to find Kit standing, wearing Reese's robe and running a hand down Inferno's mane. Adelia, Ginger, and Reese lingered a few feet away from him.

"Hi, Your Non Headlessness," Stevie breathed, stepping

toward him, studying the face that she'd been waiting to make a comeback.

Kit's hand left Inferno and he smiled, the first bewitching smile she'd seen from him yet. "Hi, Pumpkin."

Tears stung her eyes and she ran toward him, wrapping her arms around his neck and her legs around his hips like a spider monkey. As he held her tightly, she inhaled spice and pine, something she did wish she had a candle made of. She finally stepped back to the ground and cupped his face, leaning in close. Even in the darkness, she could *finally* see the color of his irises. "Green. Your eyes are green."

"I hope that means you're pleased." He smirked.

She rolled her eyes and pressed her hand against his chest to feel the beat of his heart.

Stevie's gaze latched onto Reese and her smile dropped. He rubbed the back of his neck, seeming nervous. "What happened?" She frowned. "When did you start helping Levi?"

Reese exhaled loudly. "It's pathetic. *I'm* pathetic. I've seen Levi my whole life. He was my family. Levi told me what you were and how I had to spy on you for him because you were planning to open the Hollow with the Headless Horseman and a troop of witches. He said we needed to prevent it from happening. After I met you, I wasn't sure it was true, but then I saw the Horseman with you..."

Stevie bit her lip. "You could've asked me, Reese."

"I could've." His shoulders hunched forward. "But I didn't. Not since I didn't really know you like I thought I knew Levi. And after he possessed my body when I was leaving the bonfire, I knew you were in danger. By then, it was too late to warn you."

"It's not your fault," Kit said. "I know how they play their little games to earn your trust. I was a part of Clara's once."

Reese nodded, but shame danced in his eyes.

"So," Lucia piped in while petting Maxine's head. "Who wants to stay here for the night and make sure *that* doesn't happen again?"

The eight of them remained guarding the gate throughout the night until both Eyes finally shut, their red glow sealed away.

Lucia clasped Stevie's arm as she yawned with a smile, the fog clearing and the darkness lifting. "I'm going to take you guys home, but looks like I won't be sleeping any time soon. I have council members to find and cats to reverse spells on."

STEVIE LOCKED the door to her home behind her. With the Eyes shut, the world between the living and the dead was separated once more. "Do you want a shower before sleeping?" Eight full hours of sleep sounded like winning the lottery at the moment.

"Mm-hmm. This will be my first experience with one of those," Kit drawled.

"I think you'll be having a lot of firsts." She grinned, her gaze fixed on his green irises that were much brighter in this light. Even though, yes, his face was very much an Adonis one, at least to *her*, it wouldn't have mattered if she never set her sight on it again. Because Kit wasn't his face, nor was he the Headless Horseman anymore—he was just himself. Someone Stevie really wanted to be around. But she wouldn't lie that she hoped she wouldn't ever have to stop seeing his brilliant green eyes.

Stevie placed a fluffy towel on the counter in the bathroom and turned on the shower. She then pointed to two bottles. "You can use these to wash your hair and body. If you need me, you only have to shout my name."

"I'm certain I'll need you quite a bit." Kit's shapely lips curled up at the edges.

Stevie blinked, studying him in his robe, still *naked* beneath it, for a beat too long. "Good," she finally got out and shut the door behind her before she jumped his bones.

Roxy lay on the floor beside the kitchen sink while Kit's

horse remained in the woods until probably tonight as usual. Reese had stayed quiet for most of the night, but she'd learned that he'd yet to come across his own sidekick.

Closing her eyes, Stevie petted Roxy's head. "Don't listen to me if there's ever a Sleepy Hollow–ending event again."

The fox pawed her hand, and Stevie stood to pour herself a glass of ice-cold milk, her earlier exhaustion fading. She thought about texting her mom, but she didn't have her phone back just yet. Last night she'd checked on her with Lucia's cell, then revealed to Gideon how his plant was a lifesaver. He'd panicked about Maxine being put in danger, but his cockiness came around about his pet plant being a town hero and how he'd feed her something extra special.

"Stevie!" Kit shouted.

She almost knocked over her empty cup as she ran toward the bathroom, throwing the door wide. The patterned shower glass hid the subtle details of Kit's form, but she could still see his outline, *fine* and dandy.

"I think I exaggerated what was happening in here," Stevie croaked.

He cracked open the glass door. "You didn't leave me any clothing."

"Oh!" she chirped. "I can run next door and grab some from Gideon's closet. Not his favorites though or he'll whine."

"There's something else. Come here." Kit waggled a finger at her as he moistened his bottom lip.

She arched a brow and smiled. "Are you just trying to lure me into doing naughty things?"

"Perhaps." He smirked. "Unless you're too exhausted."

Stevie stepped closer and Kit opened the door farther, her gaze catching on taut muscle. He grasped her by the waist, making her squeal as he brought her into the shower with him.

His full lips crashed into hers, and she didn't hesitate to kiss him back, to finally feel his warmth, his taste. His flavor was still like moonlight against her tongue.

"My clothes are getting soaked." Stevie laughed, her hands grasping his wet hair.

Kit trailed kisses up her jaw to just beneath her ear, and her heart pounded at the feel of him. "Should I remove them?" he rasped.

"If you don't, I'll remove the one piece myself," she vowed.

He cut her off with a kiss, slowly unrolling the knitted tube-top dress down her body and tossing it over the shower glass. Warmth shot through Stevie at the way his fingers skimmed down her sides, in the way that she could leave her eyes open to watch him whenever she pleased. Just as she was doing at that second, her gaze holding on to his bright green eyes before drifting down his torso to the part of him that was *so* very ready for her.

"Now, let's get to work." She grinned, cradling his beautiful face.

Kit caught her mouth with his, his deft fingers stroking her center until she whimpered. He then hoisted her up against the wall, and with one spellful thrust, he was inside her and she moaned in delight. She held onto his shoulders as he moved his hips, hitting the right spot superbly.

Stevie eagerly wrapped her legs around him tighter, one of his hands cupping her backside while the other caressed her breast. He teased her with slow, meticulous movements that made her gasp. His pace picked up, becoming more reckless, harder, and she didn't think she would ever stop moaning for him. Not after an orgasm like that.

Kit thrust faster, his lips back on hers, urgent, his hand tangled in her hair, until he jerked and came with a deep groan.

As their chests heaved, they studied one another, their expressions satisfied. "I do believe you've bewitched me, Stevie," Kit murmured, his forehead pressed to hers.

Her heart swelled, and she didn't think her idiotic smile would ever go away. "Say body and soul like Mr. Darcy and we can have another round before we sleep."

"Body and soul." Kit kissed her as if the Hollow could still rip him away. "Thank you for everything. For saving Inferno."

Stevie tucked a lock of hair behind his ear and grinned. "I won't lie—it did take some convincing at first. But maybe if you hadn't been so *vague*."

"You had me the night you cursed me with your crucifix." He smirked.

"You—" Kit cut her words off with a kiss, then carried her out of the shower and into her room, where he gently lowered her to the mattress.

"We're getting the bed all wet." She laughed as he caged her in, droplets of water gliding down his neck and chest.

"More so than you?" he purred.

"Maybe? Maybe not?" Stevie shrugged, fighting a smile and staring one more time at his eyes. Because she could.

"You're the prettiest pumpkin I ever did see." Kit tugged a tendril of her wet hair and crawled down her body, trailing kisses between her breasts, to her stomach, then *lower*. He lifted her legs over his shoulders, peering up at her with hooded eyes. "I do believe I have my answer."

S tevie pulled into an empty lot and parked the car. The past month, the line between the living and the dead continued to hold. Except for seers, of course. At the moment, Sleepy Hollow was in the clear of any potential villains who wanted to tear open the gate, but that didn't mean there wasn't someone sketchy out there, be it living or ghost. The council members and Adelia's servants had all been transformed back to their previous states. Except for one. Julian. He remained a toad inside of a terrarium as Adelia's new pet, his gift for helping Levi and Clara.

After centuries of being the Headless Horseman, Kit thought this was his suckiest task to date. Well, *tedious* was the word he'd used. Stevie gripped the steering wheel while waggling her eyebrows at him. No longer did he parade town in his centuries-past attire but usually wore dark jeans and today ... a T-shirt with a graphic of the *Headless Horseman* on it. "So, are you ready for your first driving lesson?"

He glanced at her from the passenger seat, an unamused expression on his face. "I'd much rather ride my horse through town."

Stevie studied Kit's dark hair, his cheekbones, his strong jaw, the curve of his perfect lips—features that were only a bonus to him previously being the Headless Horseman. "I mean, you can still ride him with your eyes closed. *Or* you can buy a living horse."

Smirking, he lifted a brow. "I don't believe Inferno would be entertained by that notion."

Stevie bumped her arm into his. "Car it is then. Plus, it'll be easier to drive to work in this." Gideon had offered Kit a job at the comic book store in exchange for Stevie to warn him next time if she ever needed to borrow Maxine again.

"Hmph."

"If you do well, we can go into the backseat after," she sang. "There's plenty of time before we have to go to my parents' house tonight." Thankfully, her mom had remained as strong as an ox with the two hearts a month dose and now doted on Kit after they'd exchanged a couple of once-a-month stories.

"And if I do awful?" Kit trailed a seductive finger across his lower lip, making her want to throw the driving lesson out the window and take him back there that very second.

"Between you and me," she whispered. "It'll still happen."

"So I triumph either way," he noted, his eyes slitted.

Stevie ticked her finger back and forth. "One of the wins might be a bit more brazen, so I'd suggest trying harder. Now switch seats with me."

Once they traded spots, Stevie instructed Kit how to drive forward, then in reverse. The car's movements were jerky at first, resulting in her feeling like she was in a blender.

Besides a pole popping up out of nowhere and her swerving the wheel for him, the rest of the session went fairly well.

"Lesson one is dunzo for the day." Stevie brushed her hands together and nodded her approval. "I can now reveal our gift!" She unbuckled her seatbelt and reached behind her to grab the small potted plant hidden on the floor beneath a bucket.

"Maxine wasn't thrilled about the Venus flytraps that didn't go away, so they're ours now!" She held the pot up in front of him.

"They're ... charming." Kit stared at the snapping blue and white heads as if she'd just given him eight little murderers to take care of. He carefully took the pot from her hands and set it on the dashboard. "We can name all eight of them later."

Before she could start spouting out names right then, he lifted her into his lap, pulling a gasp from her.

Kit twisted a lock of her hair around his finger, his pupils dilated. "And what do I get for performing my task so brilliantly?"

Stevie rolled her eyes. "You nearly hit a pole."

"But I didn't." He tugged on one of her belt loops before roaming his hands down to her backside, drawing her closer against him.

Her breath caught, and she could barely contain herself. "Because I intervened. But I *suppose* you qualify."

"First I want to taste you here." Kit skimmed a digit across her lips and skated it down to her center. "Then here."

"Wouldn't that mean I'm getting the win instead of you?" She smiled wide.

He pressed his mouth to hers, parting her lips with his tongue. "Tasting you is a win for me."

"How about I give you double the prize when you're finished?"

"It seems we have ourselves a spoken agreement."

Stevie's heart threw confetti in the air, and she couldn't keep the bottle corked any longer, knowing it was about time to tell him how she felt. "I think I love you for that."

"Think?" He chuckled.

She tilted his chin up and coasted her lips across his. "*Do.*"

"I love you, Pumpkin." Kit's deep and hypnotic voice slipped out as alluring as ever. He leaned toward her ear, his breath hot against her neck. "Do you know what my unfinished business was?"

"What?" she asked, her voice husky.

"It wasn't to find my head. It was to be here with you." He held her gaze, a whirlwind of emotions flickering in his eyes.

Stevie cupped his face and pressed her head to his, breathing in his bewitching scent. "For those words..." She reached for the lever and reclined the seat back, his arms tightening around her waist. "Get ready for the ride."

"I think I may enjoy cars now," he said, kissing her until her toes curled.

**Did you enjoy Bewitched by the Headless Horseman?
Authors love reviews whether long or short!**

Want more of the Sleepy Hollow world? Check out the bite-sized paranormal historical romance, Charmed by a Spell, set in the same world.

Beatrice isn't the greatest witch in her village, but after her dearest friend suddenly dies, she will do anything to make certain his soul isn't trapped in the ghost realm where the Headless Horseman resides.

When Beatrice's worst fear is realized, she vows to save Heath, even if it means becoming a ghost herself.

ALSO BY CANDACE ROBINSON

Wicked Souls Duology

Vault of Glass

Bride of Glass

Marked by Magic

The Bone Valley

Merciless Stars

Cruel Curses Trilogy

Clouded By Envy

Veiled By Desire

Shadowed By Despair

Cursed Hearts Duology

Lyrics & Curses

Music & Mirrors

Untamed Darkness

Her Cruel Dahlias

And Then There Was Silence

Dearest Clementine: Dark and Romantic Monstrous Tales

These Vicious Thorns: Tales of the Lovely Grim

Savage Delights: Two Dark Tales

Between the Quiet

Hearts Are Like Balloons

Bacon Pie

Avocado Bliss

Faeries of Oz Series

Lion (Short Story Prequel)

Tin

Crow

Ozma

Tik-Tok

Vampires in Wonderland Series

Rav (Short Story Prequel)

Maddie

Chess

Knave

Once Upon A Wicked Villain

Spindle of Sin

Tower of Shadows

ACKNOWLEDGMENTS

I've always been a fan of the strange, the paranormal, and monsters. Especially the Headless Horseman! I've been aching to write a super fun book with him, and alas, Stevie's story with him was born!

I've had some wonderful people put the magical fixes into this book! Amber H. is my awesome sidekick who finds the fixes I never can! S.G.D. helped improve the things that were missing and that improved the overall story! Hayley, Jolene, Jerica, Ann, Amber D., and Gerardo, you guys are proofreading royalty!

To my husband and daughter who put up with all my talk about horror and paranormal things, you guys are the best.

Now seriously, I'm going to leave you for now and take a ride on the Headless Horseman's stallion in Sleepy Hollow!

ABOUT THE AUTHOR

Candace Robinson spends her days consumed by words and hoping to one day find her own DeLorean time machine. Her life consists of avoiding migraines, admiring Bonsai trees, watching classic movies, and living with her husband and daughter in Texas—where it can be forty degrees one day and eighty the next.